W9-AUZ-391

OUTBOUND

The Curious Secession of Latter-Day Charleston

CHARLIE GEER

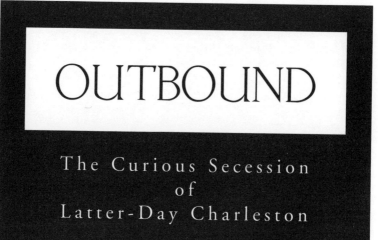

OUTBOUND

The Curious Secession
of
Latter-Day Charleston

RIVER CITY PUBLISHING
MONTGOMERY, ALABAMA

Published in the United States by River City Publishing
1719 Mulberry St.
Montgomery, AL 36106.

Designed by Lissa Monroe.

First Edition—2005
Printed in Canada
    1 3 5 7 9 10 8 6 4 2

Library of Congress Cataloging-in-Publication Data:
Geer, Charlie, 1970-
    Outbound : the curious secession of latter-day Charleston / by Charlie
Geer.-- 1st ed.
        p. cm.
    Summary: "In a satire on Charleston, South Carolina, the city's peninsula
breaks off from the mainland and floats out to sea. A mixed bag of
characters find themselves unbound from the conventions of family,
community, and geography"--Provided by publisher.
    ISBN 1-57966-062-2
    1. Charleston (S.C.)--Fiction. 2. Satire. lcsh I. Title.
    PS3607.E364O98 2005
    813'.6--dc22
                                            2004025339

for my mother and father

No hay oro sin difunto, ni mujer sin secreto.

Álvaro Mutis, *Amirbar*

·|·

WHEN FROM THE SHEER WEIGHT of humanity and its assorted accouterments the Charleston Peninsula broke off from mainland South Carolina and began floating out to sea, among the last to notice were those persons trapped on board the unlikely vessel. The rest of the state, which had always considered the old town a harbor of loose values and oddball politics, was happy enough to be rid of it. The rest of the nation, which knew the city primarily through weather reports and travel magazines, would find other, less mobile destinations to visit.

On board, the first individual to take note was eighty-eight-year-old Lawson Parker, a chronic porch sitter who, when he saw Fort Sumter sliding past the Battery, retrieved his .45 and casually opened fire on the old Yankee fort. He had dreamed of just such a close-range opportunity for years; from the former distance he had once actually cloaked a similar assault under the boom of the city's 4th of July fireworks display. But it was not the 4th of July—it was the 25th of May, and certain neighbors naturally expressed concern. They expressed their concern not to Mr. Parker but to the local authorities, who in turn expressed concern to Lawson's daughter. Elizabeth Hathaway, who did not care for the neighbors or the local authorities, was short with the two investigating officers. They were not impressed by her arguments—that the man was elderly and therefore experienced occasional difficulties with time, place, and propriety; that even had he intended to hit something, he was far too feeble to succeed; and that furthermore perhaps the two gentlemen had something better to do on another side of town. Though the officers might have liked to haul both Hathaways off to jail, they instead summoned the two to appear in Livability Court. The mayor would want it that way.

Elizabeth scowled at the summons. She had already been to Livability Court twice—the first time for having a creaky gate and the second, for hanging her linens on the line to dry. She would not go again.

"Now, you listen—" she started.

But the officers were already leaving. "Have you considered a home, ma'am?" the shorter one asked from the sidewalk. "For your father?"

"My father has a home," said Elizabeth, and she started to shut the door.

Started, because she thought she'd seen, just out the corner of her eye, a range marker slipping past the Battery. Which was, in fact, what she had seen.

Well, that's just lovely, she thought. On top of everything else, we're floating out to sea. Just lovely.

ELIZABETH HAD NOT HAD a very pleasant week, it was true. She had received three unexpected guests in as many days, and while she liked to think of herself as a hospitable and accommodating woman, she wasn't, especially when caught off guard. The first guest, Mr. T. Moffett from Phoenix, Arizona, had arrived without actually showing up. A month ago, Mr. Moffett had purchased the house beside Elizabeth's from the Daniels for an ungodly sum, and three weeks later he had commenced doing what cumyahs like him seemed to do best, which was to have the home flayed and gutted without mercy, its insides torn apart, ripped out, and hauled away. Elizabeth had spent the better part of a day watching the proceedings from her kitchen window. The old house trembling and groaning while the men worked, plaster dust billowing out the windows like smoke—it was as though the structure were being sacked from the inside by a ruthless invading army. She was certain the Daniels would not have stood for it, nor the Conrads before them, nor the McCraes before the Conrads. But of course the Daniels had taken the ungodly sum and moved to Sullivan's Island, the Conrads were piddling the end of their lives away at distant Morningside Manor, and the McCraes, being long dead, could say very little at all. In recent years Elizabeth had lost well near all her allies in the neighborhood—to beaches, retirement homes, and cemeteries. She'd had no one to turn to last year when the dignified antebellum mansion to the east of her, the Hamilton House, became the Bay House Bed and Breakfast, and she had no one to turn to now. She might have approached absent T. Moffett herself, but as of yet the man had not made an appearance, had only expressed, through the actions of his hired hands, his utter dislike for Charleston interiors. It was, Elizabeth thought, horribly arrogant of him to remain in Arizona while he so blatantly broke the rules of someone else's neighborhood. Of course, Mr. Moffett had little choice in the matter now. The current seagoing state of affairs made him a unique breed of absentee owner, the likes of which Elizabeth had never confronted—or not confronted—before. There was no telling how long he would be away. That is, how long Charleston would be away.

The second guest had arrived the day after absent T. Moffett's demolition crew, shortly before the mysterious floating off of the peninsula. He arrived midmorning, while Elizabeth was observing the progress of the destruction next door from a wingback chair beside the bay window. The crew had attached a large cylindrical chute to the second story of the house, and Elizabeth watched as the dangling apparatus spewed loads of plaster and glass into the Dumpster below, the debris rushing forth in sudden, violent heaves. When her doorbell rang, the chime seemed as sudden, as violent. It startled her as a thunderclap might. With the better part of her friends and relations long since moved away, the instrument had fallen out of use.

There was no need for her to answer the door. She had not even stood up when she heard it swing open. Then the call, all too familiar: "Oh, Maaa-meee!"

Her son, Parker. Whom she loved as a mother should, but whom she frequently wondered about. This Mommy thing, for starters. Grown men did not call their mothers Mommy. Parker was thirty-eight years old. Elizabeth herself was approaching seventy. She was nobody's "Mommy."

"Parker?" she said.

"Don't get up, sweetie." From behind, Parker kissed her on the neck, then swung an armful of gladiolas in front of her.

"Oh," Elizabeth said with as much enthusiasm as she could gather. "Lovely. They're lovely, dear."

Parker stepped away to set the flowers in a vase on the sideboard, and Elizabeth turned to have a look at him. Wearing a white linen suit, a yellow silk ascot with green polka dots, and a white boater with a blue-and-red-striped band, he was as much a fop as ever. With a new touch, even: from one of the jacket pockets dripped the gold chain of a pocket watch. Elizabeth had hoped her son might have at least taken a new hairstyle, but he hadn't. Still it was cropped at the base of the neck, still it swung about ridiculously when he moved. He might have been Prince Valiant from the funny papers, or Little Lord Fauntleroy. Or simply a jackass. Elizabeth was mildly relieved to see that Parker had at least foregone the kilt this time around. His most recent visit, two months previous, had been made for the Scottish Heritage Games and had found him trotting about in plaid skirts like a man who had been waiting all his life to. She simply could not imagine what kind of people her son was running with down in Savannah. She wasn't sure she wanted to.

"Heavens," said Parker, returning to his mother's side. "What are they doing over there?"

"What they usually do."

"Ah. A little interior desecrating, mm?"

"Something like that."

Parker chuckled mischievously. "It looks—obscene. That—thing—hanging down like a—oh, my. Spilling that—oh, my."

Missing her son's point entirely, Elizabeth said, "I do take offense to it."

"I should say so," he agreed.

"I just don't know what these people want."

"Sexy," Parker said. "They want sexy."

Embarrassed, Elizabeth glanced back at her son. "I beg your pardon?"

"People want sexy interiors," Parker explained. "Sexy black bathrooms. Sleek sexy kitchens."

"Oh, for God's sake," Elizabeth sighed. She had done her best to dismiss desire and all its complications years ago, even before Parker's father had passed—early, of drink. Such frank discussion of the matter—especially from Parker, a man who had once proposed a return to the powdered wig—unsettled her. It was uncalled for.

"Have you found anything worthwhile among the wreckage, Mommy?" Parker asked, referring to his mother's habit of picking through the junk piles of others for items she herself might yet find a use for.

"I haven't looked."

"Why not?"

"Principle."

"How adorable," said Parker.

Adorable?

Parker turned and left for the front hall, where he had, Elizabeth noticed, deposited two hang-up bags and a suitcase.

"Well, Mommy," Parker said from the hall. "I'll be staying in Liza's old room?"

"Staying?"

"Oh, yes," Parker said as he started up the steps, hang-ups and suitcase in tow. "The town is absolutely booked. Some genius has scheduled the Sportsman's Jamboree for the same week as the Bravado Festival. This week. There's not a room to be had, Mommy. Not in this town."

Bravado. Of course. The annual arts festival, which her son patronized religiously. She had once patronized the festival herself—monetarily, even. But that was years ago, at a time when she had believed in the city—and the city, she felt, in her. In those days she and others of her station had seen the festival as a kind of counterbalance to the Bubba culture that they believed posed a very real threat to the genteel character of the town. A popular novelist had claimed, quite frankly and quite publicly, that Charleston would never be any Manhattan, and the early patrons received the criticism as a kind of challenge. With Bravado, they meant to show the world that if Charleston would never be Manhattan, it was only because Charleston didn't want to be Manhattan. If it *wanted* to be Manhattan, it *could* be, which they would demonstrate with an annual festival of opera, ballet, and chamber music. Bravado was an opportunity to put the city on the cultural map, but harmlessly—the festival, after all, would last only two weeks. Unfortunately, the culture Bravado had lately come to engender—nudist ballets, outer-space operas, and bizarre puppet shows—led Elizabeth and others like her to reevaluate their former mistrust of Bubba. She had withdrawn her support several years ago and would have been just as happy if the town were removed from all maps, cultural and otherwise, entirely. This was not to be. By the time the early patrons backed off, the town had filled up with cumyahs of such extraordinary means and such extraordinary enthusiasm for all things festively cultural that Bravado had become not only a fixture but an institution, an annual gathering of kooky artists and their brazen jet set patrons. And as for Parker, Elizabeth believed the festival was little more than an excuse for him to get tremendously drunk and parade about in ridiculous clothing.

"Pawpaw looks good," Parker announced as he descended the steps. "Still on the porch, I see."

"He does favor the porch."

Parker paused to examine himself in the mirror above the sideboard. "I think he favors the Tri Delts who bounce past the porch," he said.

"He's eighty-eight years old, son."

"He's still a man, Mommy."

"I suppose."

In front of the mirror Parker fiddled with the presentation of his ascot. A ludicrous affair, Elizabeth thought. "So anyway, the festival opening is this afternoon," he said. "The unveiling of Abel Horfner's site-specific piece in Calhoun Square. Quite monumental, Mommy. He hasn't shown in six years. I've heard Carolina Gabrel is going to be there. From the *Times*."

Carolina Gabrel. Elizabeth had heard Parker mention the woman before, had in fact held out hope that Carolina Gabrel might represent some kind of conventional love interest for the boy. In the past, word of Parker's successes with Savannah's society girls had tickled her, but in recent years she'd begun to wonder if his many exploits didn't betray some kind of pathology. Perhaps he wasn't really in the market for a woman at all. So yes, there might yet be redemption in this Carolina Gabrel. But what was this business about the times?

"What times?" she said.

"THE *Times*, Mommy. THE *Times*."

"I see," said Elizabeth, though in fact she didn't.

Before turning for the door, Parker approached his mother and kissed her lightly on the back of the neck. "*Ciao*, sweets," he said. "Don't wait up, okay?" And then as suddenly as he had appeared, he was gone.

No sooner had her son shut the door than Elizabeth moved to the kitchen to collect the makings of a strong drink. It was not yet noon, but the circumstances of the morning, she decided, were unusual. Anyway, it was noon somewhere, and that would have to do.

She did not drink often, it was true. Having seen liquor kill one man and all but ruin half a dozen others, she tended to abstain. But there were certain occasions—mostly of profound confusion or profound agitation—when she indulged. And when she did, she poured the drink the deceased man and the all-but-ruined men had poured, the drink that had been poured in the house for more than a hundred years: two jiggers of bourbon splashed with water and three cubes of ice. Once she mixed the beverage she sat down at the kitchen table. Already the events of the day had exhausted her.

Elizabeth drank with a slow, measured rhythm, allowing the delicate bitterness of each swallow to pass before drawing another. Firmed up by the whiskey, she resisted the temptation to return to the window and eye the goings-on next door. She simply would not be bothered by the offenses of absent T. Moffett, not during so rare an indulgence. Mr. Moffett would not be allowed to trespass on her spirits, which, she had to confess, were rising nicely with each sip. To punctuate her resolve, she stood and drew the shades over the three bay windows when she had finished the drink. Each catch locked with a satisfying snap, and she thought she might fix another glass to commemorate the small victory.

That's when her third unexpected guest had shown up.

The knock was soft but insistent. When Elizabeth first heard it, she thought it was a rat probing a floorboard. Which would not have been unusual. The house, after all, was over one hundred years old. Elizabeth took her yardstick from beside the refrigerator and moved carefully to the front hall to investigate. Normally a slap on the floor with the stick would shut the little fiends up.

She was doing just this, slapping the hall floor with the yardstick, when the knock sounded again. Closer now, she recognized the sound—someone at the door, humbly but resolutely demanding attention. There was only one man she knew who demanded attention in such a way. There was only one man who knocked like that.

Bubby McGaw. Her son-in-law.

A realtor from upstate who years ago had infected Elizabeth's daughter with an off-brand religion and then, somehow, persuaded her to marry him.

"A glorious good morning to you, Mrs. Hathaway," he said when she cracked the door. He was smiling at her. As inane as the smile was, it had always made Elizabeth nervous. It never went away, for one thing, and for another, it pressed at two twitchy blue eyes that she had always thought were too small for the face to begin with. And too close together.

"Oh—well, hello," Elizabeth said. She glanced about for her daughter, who might yet be returned to some semblance of reality, if only given the chance. But she didn't see Liza anywhere, just a small, rather lonely-looking pile of luggage. Sorry she had answered the knock at all, she held the door to a mere crack.

"Not gonna whop me with that thing, are you?" Bubby asked, and he winked twice at her.

Winked. Appraising herself, Elizabeth saw that she was unconsciously—perhaps instinctively—holding the yardstick just off the shoulder, the way one might hold a baseball bat which one might be preparing to use, and not on a baseball. "No," she said. "I hadn't planned to." Still, she didn't exactly shift her stance.

"Well, I thank you, Mrs. Hathaway," said Bubby. "I really do." He slid a package of Big Red from his shirt pocket and extended a stick to her. "Chewing gum?"

"No, thank you," Elizabeth said. She didn't chew gum, and she didn't trust people who did. Especially people like Bubby McGaw, who chewed it with an open mouth, slowly and stupidly, like a cow working cud.

Bubby slid a stick into his mouth, then shook his head. The smile relaxed ever so slightly. "Boy, do I have a favor to ask of you, Mrs. Hathaway. Boy."

"Oh?"

"Yes, ma'am. Boy. Seems they've really filled the town up this week. I mean, really filled it up. With all kinds."

"So I hear." Elizabeth did not like where this was going. Not at all.

"Yes, ma'am. I'm here representing the Fellowship, see, and they goofed up. They put me—"

"The Fellowship?" Elizabeth interrupted.

"Right. The Fellowship of Evangelical Sportsmen, Mrs. Hathaway. Hunters for Jesus. Or Hunters _of_ Jesus, some call us."

"I see," Elizabeth said. Then, unable to resist: "And what will you do when you catch Him?"

Bubby quit chewing for a moment and cocked his head like a puzzled puppy. "Ma'am?" he said.

"Nothing."

Bubby chewed again. "Right. So they put me in a room with an opera singer, Mrs. Hathaway. Big gal. They goofed up, see. Between the Jamboree and this art thing. They goofed up."

"Yes."

"It's two beds. I said I would share. I told them I'm a Christian man and a quiet man and I wouldn't get in anybody's way. But that big gal wouldn't have it, see. Said she'd go back to Paris, France, before she'd share a room with me. What about that?"

Elizabeth could see the opera singer's point, but she didn't say so.

"I told them, I said, I've got family here. Good people. I told them about you. I said some of us know how to treat people right, and my mother-in-law, Mrs. Hathaway, is one of them."

"Well."

"So I was wondering. You know. Maybe I could stay for a few days. I would surely appreciate it, Mrs. Hathaway. You've got that old Southern hospitality. I always said it was so. I tell everybody."

Elizabeth had seen this coming. Throughout the entire conversation she'd been considering ways she might get out of it. In the end there was only the truth: she was all booked up. If he stayed, he would have to share Liza's old room with Parker. She knew that in fact there was a very real possibility that this course might work: Parker and Bubby had differences with each other. Serious differences.

It almost did work. When she told Bubby of the cohabitation option, he quit chewing entirely. His smile collapsed and his face tightened. "Oh," he said. "Parker?"

"I can't turn family away," Elizabeth said. "You know."

"Oh, I know," Bubby said. "I know." He looked off and chewed on the inside of his cheek. "Well, I—hmm. Hmm. Old Parker. How is old Parker?"

"Same as ever," Elizabeth said.

"Well. Hmm. I—well, we'll just have to work it out, Mrs. Hathaway. We'll just have to work it out."

Not what Elizabeth wanted to hear. "Oh? Oh, but—" she started, but it was too late now. Bubby McGaw had retrieved his luggage and stood at the door waiting for her to let him in. Not nearly as skilled with a yardstick as she might have liked to be, she had little choice but to do so. She watched him deposit the bags in the corner of the hall and thought thirstily about a second drink. After that, perhaps a third.

Bubby McGaw turned and checked himself in the hall mirror, smoothing his hair and working his tie into place. "I sure thank you, Mrs. Hathaway. I sure do. We'll work it out. With the Lord's help, we'll work it out."

"Are you off?" Elizabeth asked hopefully.

"Oh, yes, ma'am. They're having a pig pick down at Calhoun Square, Mrs. Hathaway. For the kick-off celebration. I'm opening it all with a blessing."

"Oh, really. This afternoon?"

"Yes, ma'am."

"Calhoun Square?"

"That's what they tell me."

"Well. That should be interesting." Quite, she thought.

"I won't stay too long. Some of those sportsmen, well, some of them do get rowdy. If you know what I mean. They aren't all the most religious of people."

"No."

Bubby turned for the door. "With a little help from Providence, Hunters for Jesus will be able to change all that," he said.

"Well, good luck," said Elizabeth, opening the door. "And good luck finding Him, too."

"Ma'am?"

"Nothing."

"Oh. Well, I thank you again, Mrs. Hathaway," Bubby McGaw said as he left across the porch. "May God bless you."

And may he damn you to Hell, Elizabeth thought. She couldn't help it. For all Bubby's smiling, all his "yes, ma'ams" and "Mrs. Hathaways," he brought out the very worst in her. Always she had believed that his relationship with her daughter had been founded unfairly, forged as it was just after the death of Liza's father, a time when anyone would be vulnerable, when even the most properly raised child might act carelessly. Surely her daughter would wake up eventually. It wasn't that Bubby McGaw didn't treat Liza well. Real estate was treating everyone well these days. It was the fact of where he came from. More important, it was the religion of where he came from. Like so many others from that part of the state, he had taken it too far. He had taken it to television, for one thing. To churches the size of coliseums. He had taken it to the theme park.

Herself, she'd been born right the first time.

Thoroughly flustered, Elizabeth returned to the kitchen for a second drink. It was after noon now—the sun past the yardarm, her mother used to say—and nobody's business anyway. She had been through a month's worth of strain in a morning, and she deserved the drink if anyone did.

The second drink, however, was not nearly so satisfying as the first. In fact it made Elizabeth more irritable and ultimately led her to return to the bay windows and release the blinds. Still the waste from the inside of the home of absent T. Moffett exploded out the chute. Elizabeth received each blast as a personal insult, an assault on her own home, which, if it was in fair need of a paint job, if not a complete restoration, was in no need of family history. What was more, 2 Bay Street had never needed a sexy kitchen or a sexy bathroom. It had never belonged to strangers, and if she could help it, it never would.

As she often did during moments of conviction, Elizabeth retrieved the brief history of her home from the lower right sideboard drawer. The one-page synopsis had been written by a representative of the Preservation Association years ago when Elizabeth, not yet thoroughly disgusted with the tourist trade, had put her home on the annual tour. She could recite the litany by heart, but always it comforted and strengthened her to see it written, to hold it in her hand.

The clapboard Queen-Anne "cottage" was commissioned by the present owner's great-grandfather, decorated Civil War veteran Colonel Thomas Parker, in the early 1880s. The yard served by generational turns as a chicken pen, a flower garden, and a playground for children and dogs. The twin wraparound porches have hosted more than a century's worth of courtships, cocktail parties, and musings. In the narrow garden to the left of the house there remains the old stone cistern into which young Thomas Parker, Jr., fell and drowned. Although the structure has long been sealed shut, notice that the present owner has encircled the cistern with a bed of irises, both in memory of the drowned ancestor and in tribute to the peculiar history his misfortune set into motion. His sole male heir deceased, Colonel Parker willed the house to his three daughters, Lea, Julia, and Mary. When Mary married a banker in Savannah, she ceded her share to Lea and Julia, the former a portraitist, the latter a concert pianist. (The den, which was used as a painting studio by Lea Parker, might now be considered a gallery for the same, dressed as it is with the deceased artist's miniatures, still lifes, and seascapes. The aging baby grand in the living room belonged to Julia and is said to have been "imported" from New York.) Having never married, the two sisters shared the house until their deaths—of the same illness, tuberculosis, on the same afternoon. With the loyalty of a bygone era, they had bequeathed the home to their sister Mary's first-born son, who promptly moved his law practice and his young family into the house. Here he brought up his only child, present owner Elizabeth Hathaway, and here, in time, Mrs. Hathaway brought up two of her own.

Elizabeth might have liked to wave the document in absent T. Moffett's face, but for the time being that was physically impossible. Too, the strength of her position was tempered somewhat by the ramifications of the last sentence. She had brought the two children up, yes, but she would hardly admit to it anymore. The one's marrying a Bible thumper and the other, well, the other's not marrying at all, for reasons she would rather not understand. What did Parker know about sexy kitchens? She hadn't taught him about sexy kitchens. Colonel Parker certainly would not have gone for sexy kitchens. If there were individuals like absent T. Moffett in the world, individuals who were so common as to require sexy kitchens, she was not one of them.

Anxious to confirm the conviction, she returned to her own unsexy kitchen. A simple, practical affair that had in the home's earliest days served as a hallway to the cook's quarters, the room contained little more than the components necessary for the preparation, storage, and serving of food. The table was modest, the cabinets unassuming. Her appliances were not terribly sleek, but they functioned well enough. A Valentine's card was posted on the icebox, but the card was months old and, having been sent by her daughter, suggested nothing inappropriate. No, there was nothing at all sexy about her kitchen. Everything in it worked. Elizabeth found the judgment profoundly satisfying and felt she deserved another drink for having reached it.

On her way to the icebox Elizabeth turned on the small transistor radio she kept on the kitchen windowsill. The selection in play was Strauss's "Blue Danube," a favorite of hers. She raised the volume, warmed by the remembrance of a debutante ball long past, the night she had first danced with handsome Park Hathaway. An exquisite dancer, he had introduced her to dips and turns that were not taught in dancing school. Later, in the lush quiet of St. Philip's cemetery, he had introduced her to other things. Elizabeth laughed lightly in spite of herself. On her way to the counter she managed a left box turn—however tenuous, however shuffling. One. Two. Three. One. Two. Three. She poured the whiskey, then dropped away with a closed change, two, three. A forward hesitation to the sink, two, three. She added water and dropped away, two, three. Another cube of ice would be right nice, two, three. She dipped her hand in the ice bowl and turned again, two, three.

It would not be the last dance of the day, nor the last drink. Elizabeth would in fact spend the better part of the afternoon indulging in both. The dances changed with the musical selections of the radio host—a fox trot, another waltz, a lindy— but the drink remained the same, through the end of one bottle and into another. It was a rare binge, to be sure—but justified, she thought. That is, for as long as she could think. After her third drink, she was done justifying; after her fourth, she was done thinking.

By the time her father made his attempt to recommence the Civil War, she might herself have believed it was 1861, or at least the 4th of July. Perhaps the small blasts were simply her father's way of calling for his lunch (it wouldn't have been the most unusual of his methods), which in the rapturous dance of memory and woozy wash of booze she had forgotten to prepare. She didn't get very far preparing it then, either, not before the doorbell rang—again. And then the police officers and then, as the police officers were leaving, the realization that whether anybody knew it or not, whether anybody cared or not, they were all floating out to sea. Meaning, among other things, that her unexpected guests might be here a while. Even worse, her chance to confront absent T. Moffett would grow more remote by the minute. With the departure of the peninsula, the man's absentee status had been all but sealed. His indecency sanctioned, it seemed, by the heavens.

It was not a pleasant turn of events, not in the least, and if Elizabeth could find a single man to blame for all of it, she would hunt him down and do so. Viciously.

·II·

HOUGH IT MIGHT BE a bit unfair to blame the peculiar events at 2 Bay, much less the splitting off of the entire peninsula, on any one individual, we might well start with Mr. Harry Biddencope, mayoral PR advisor and henchman, whose bright idea it had been to schedule two of the city's premier annual events (the internationally renowned Bravado Arts Festival and the regionally recognized Southeastern Sportsman's Jamboree) and one of its lesser ones (the Tri-County Mini-Storage Convention) all for the last two weeks in May. A former disc jockey, now the regional marketing director for Clean Air Broadcasting, Harry had been hired by the mayor for his talent in persuasion. Having jocked in almost every market, from country to candy rock to light jazz, he was a man who could talk varieties of talk to varieties of people. A man, the mayor liked to say, who could convince a turtle to give up its shell. It was a talent that had served the mayor well over the years. The more mossbacked of his constituents tended to oppose the public projects which he himself gloried in—the Wild Water Aquarium, the Olde Towne Tramway, the Office of Domestic Tranquility—and always Harry had managed, somehow, to paint these developments in an agreeable light, as projects designed not to attract even more tourists but to give the natives something contemporary to be proud of. Bald-faced lies, of course, pulled off expertly by a man the mayor had come to depend on for his political survival.

What the mayor may or may not have considered is that Harry was as much a calculating businessman as a proven PR whiz. And it was Harry the businessman, not Harry the PR man, who had come up with the plan to host the three events all at once. Privately Harry envisioned a blanket of Clean Air falling over the peninsula, an unprecedented sweeps period during which each of the syndicate's local stations would be heavily patronized, thanks to widespread site-specific marketing campaigns. The WBUB and WRAD vans would patrol the grounds of the Sportsman's Jamboree; Rock 93's Morning Mayhem and Crush 97's Noonday Knockout would divide sessions between the Jamboree and the Mini-Storage Convention; Lite 88's Jazzy Jimmy and Breathe 105's Lisa Lynn would make appearances at various Bravado events. There would be coozies, T-shirts, and live broadcasts. Clean Air would effectively sponsor the peninsula for two weeks, and in return, Harry believed, the peninsula would effectively sponsor Clean Air ever after. What was more, Clean Air's ad rates could be jacked to the sky at the end of the two-week sweep. Local advertisers were not famous for their wits, and even if they did catch on, Harry would at least have realized a particular longtime dream of his, which was to see just how many people he could fit in the city. By filling it to capacity, he might court his own personal vision of the future, a future that would be bright for all kinds of interests, not the least of which was syndicated radio. It would not be long, he knew, before the place would fill up, permanently. The city was irresistible; those who came to visit often came to stay. (He himself had done so. Having come to town a decade ago to emcee a beachside wet T-shirt contest, he had never left.) And everyone who stayed had to have a radio station. It only made sense to expose them to the options ahead of time.

Harry did not introduce any of these notions to the mayor or the members of city council. Instead he ran the old what's-one-more? argument, noting as well the vast political capital they might get out of the affair if they pulled it off—or even if they didn't. He was as surprised as anyone that the proposal went through without so much as a questioning glance, that he did not have to call on his reserves of persuasion at all. (Harry did suffer some bellyaching on the part of Reverend Anthony Lawson, councilman from the upper peninsula, who suggested that the annual Geechee Heritage Fair be held the same week. But bellyaching on the part of Reverend Anthony Lawson was nothing new and nothing for Harry to lose sleep over.) The fact was, neither the members of city council nor the mayor much cared for the events. Their respective positions on each had already earned them the votes necessary to put them in office, and each was happy enough to have all of the gatherings accomplished over the course of a few weeks. Most scheduled their annual vacations for those very weeks. The mayor, who after eighteen years in office felt so confident in the rule of his will from near and afar, departed as well—for his beach house in Hilton Head.

Which meant that the city, essentially, had been left to Harry Biddencope.

Not a bad feeling. Driving to Calhoun Square for the opening festivities, Harry reveled in the sheer numbers he had succeeded in bringing to the city. The sidewalks were swarming with visitors, the streets jammed with carriages and cars and tour buses. There were Blazers and 'Bagos, Beemers and Hummers, Rovers and Rangers. Best of all, thanks to Reverend Anthony Lawson's sour grapes—Lawson had asked the black community to boycott the entire lower peninsula for the duration of the festivals—there wasn't a troublemaker in sight. Harry winked at himself in his rearview mirror. Well, this, he thought, is a city.

Now, if only he could find a parking space.

HAD HARRY FOUND A parking space in time, he would have witnessed a remarkable affair in the opening ceremonies. Later, as much grief as that affair would bring him, he would have to confess he was sorry to have missed it.

Anticipation had been building on both sides of the square all day. On the Jamboree side, pigs had been roasting and sportsmen growing hungry. Having temporarily calmed their grumbling bellies with profound quantities of draft beer, they had been growing rowdy, too. Some of the more refined among them at first took offense to the WBUB van and its overbearing broadcast, the unabashedly red-in-the-neck influence that seemed to co-opt their genteel sporting tradition, but after a few rounds even these self-styled country gentlemen joined in the boisterous camaraderie of the occasion, touring the displays and testing the demos with their brothers in sport. They spun around the square in the camouflaged ATVs and golf carts; they blew on the Teal Teasers, Buck Busters, and Gobbler Getters; they hopped into the duck boats and climbed up the deer stands.

It was only a matter of time before a proud owner brought out his Lab for a mark-and-retrieve demonstration. Confused by the loud music, the rambunctious crowd, and the drunkenness of his owner, the dog failed miserably. Halfway back from the retrieve with the dummy still in his mouth, he abruptly stopped and squatted to take care of a more pressing personal matter. The owner blatted angrily at him with the whistle, and to the dog's credit, he did look at the man, he did keep the dummy in his mouth, but only until he had finished the personal business, at which point he dropped the dummy beside his small deposit and trotted across the square to investigate a tree trunk.

The Lab's failure prompted others to bring out their own pups, to demonstrate how this was done. What began as an impromptu field trial quickly turned into a canine carnival. Released from back seats, kennels, and truck beds, the dogs bounded in all directions across the square, glorying in the rare freedom the confused occasion offered them. Pointers ran with retrievers and setters with hounds; the lesser trained rolled with the expensively schooled; the rookies tackled the old pros; and all attempts at discipline failed. The mad ringing of whistles from the sidelines—all different frequencies, pitches, and volumes—only inflamed the chaos. Fights erupted, and spontaneous love affairs blazed. One such affair, between a diminutive English water spaniel and an enormous Chesapeake Bay retriever, both males, made a peculiar sight indeed and prompted speculations as to the sexual orientations of the respective owners. For those who did not own the dogs, and even for some who did, the entire display was enormously entertaining, more than enough to take their minds off the slowly roasting pork, at least for now.

JUST ACROSS THE SQUARE, on the Bravado side, others were growing hungry. Abel Horfner had been introducing the veiled piece before them for over an hour, and renowned art critics and general sophisticates alike were salivating to have a look. It stood directly behind and about as tall as the Calhoun monument.

Horfner's piece was no wider than five feet and was veiled with a tight-fitting purple cloak that was staked into the ground. The sculptor had been discussing, among other things, the duty of art to respond to history. He was doing his best to ignore the increasingly raucous notes from the festival across the square, the insufferable country music which, whenever the breeze shifted, settled on the Bravado gathering like nausea. The Jamboree sounded like the stands at a stock car race. Were they hosting dog fights? Abel's audience could sense his growing irritation, so much so that when a particularly bold canine trotted up behind him and casually relieved himself on one of the veil's guy ropes, no one said a thing. They did not want to further irritate the artist—who, really, had done the city a great favor to grace her with his presence at all.

In fact, as much as they were annoying him, the goings-on across the square suited Abel Horfner in a certain perverse way. Privately he wondered if perhaps he'd gone too far with the piece he was preparing to unveil, but the Cro-Magnon display at the Jamboree, he felt, more than vindicated him. Besides, he was world famous. He was often quoted and frequently sought after. He could do as he pleased.

"I've done a little research into Mr. John C. Calhoun," he continued. "And into this city which has memorialized him with a park. Let me say, I wasn't always pleased with what I found. As lovely as it is, this town was built on the backs of another race. It was built with brutality. And Mr. Calhoun favored that system. Wholeheartedly."

Much of the audience nodded in agreement with this, but some shifted uncomfortably. Parker Hathaway shifted uncomfortably. Well, here we go, he thought. They just can't resist.

"Shall we look at Mr. Calhoun?" Abel Horfner said. "He's certainly looking at us."

That much was true. The bronze figure had always looked down from his pedestal with a fierce and unforgiving eye.

"He was from a long line of Calvinists. A famously intolerant bunch. You can see the disdain in his eyes. His absolute disgust for us."

Parker looked away. It was a shame, really. He'd expected more of the occasion. A lot more wine, for starters—to loosen this group up, to get people meeting and greeting. Where were the Russian ballerinas? Were they really tied up in immigration? And the sophisto art set usually had a few glamorous women to offer up—where were they? (He might blame Anthony Lawson's boycott for that. The boycott itself was understandable—Anthony had a point—but a regrettable side effect seemed to be a significant reduction in the number of glamorous women. As a rule, glamorous women did not care to stay in understaffed quarters.) He had especially hoped to meet Carolina Gabrel, of the *Times,* whose inspired work he had been reading—devotedly, almost obsessively—for years. But nobody on this side of the square was drinking or meeting or even talking. Only Abel Horfner was talking, and he waxing historic about all the sore spots. In truth, Parker might have taken the spiel more seriously if Horfner were not so outrageously attired. The man was clothed in a black body stocking from the waist up and bright orange cargo-pant body armor from the waist down. He was sporting a bright blue scarf, in tropical May and, for toppers, a yellow porkpie hat. He looked like a space clown, Parker thought.

Parker adjusted his ascot, squared his boater, and checked his pocket watch. Interminable, this world-famous artist. Interminable. He found himself wondering about the Jamboree.

Though he might be hard-pressed to admit it, chances were he knew a fair number of the sportsmen in attendance. In all likelihood there were more childhood friends at the Jamboree than at the Bravado opening. The realization was profoundly depressing on a number of levels. He glanced over his shoulder at the rival gathering. Things seemed to be settling down over there.

THINGS WERE SETTLING DOWN. The pigs were about ready, and most of the dogs had at last been gathered and kenneled. Bubby McGaw had taken the stage and was preparing to open the banquet with a blessing. By now a good number of the guests would just as soon take naps as eat lunch, but far be it from any of them to turn away from a pig pick. Looking out over the sea of khaki and camouflage, Bubby McGaw began.

"Afternoon, gentlemen. My name is Bubby McGaw, and I'm here at the Jamboree to represent the Fellowship of Evangelical Sportsmen. We know as well as you do that the sporting life has everything to do with Jesus and vice-a-versa."

Bubby paused and smiled at the audience. Few were smiling back at him. Few were even looking at him. "Ah—anyone who would like to become a member or learn a little more, you'll find me at most all the Jamboree events. And now I'd like to open the festivities with a blessing."

Bubby paused again, then said, "Let us pray." He waited for the sportsmen to bow their heads, but only about a dozen did. Those who had been looking at him continued looking at him, though with some curiosity now, as if he were a magician preparing to perform a trick. "Let us pray," Bubby said again, a bit more insistently this time. Then he closed his eyes and lowered his head, thinking it better to not even know what his audience was doing—or not doing. "First of all, Lord, we want to thank you for giving us the earth . . ."

ACROSS THE WAY, ABEL Horfner extended his own thanks, however brief. He thanked the festival for inviting him and his many patrons for supporting him. It was not easy to be an artist with a conscience, he said. At this, Parker started to get up and leave—dramatically. But it was then that Horfner at last brought his long-winded introduction around to a climax. Taking up a pair of pruning shears and waving them, he railed, "An artist with a conscience has to take risks! He or she must stand up to the tyrants of history!" From here Horfner found an easy return to the sins of Calhoun and the city Calhoun had called home. He piled transgression upon transgression, gathering momentum with every indictment, shaking the shears violently at the audience and finally finishing with a volcanic blast:

"So I say to you, Mr. Calhoun!"

He turned and lopped one of the guy ropes with the shears.

"You intolerant wretch!"

He lopped a second guy rope.

"I say to the city of Charleston!"

He lopped a third, and then, after a dramatic pause, the fourth.

"Tolerate this!" he screamed.

Sadly, the cloak went nowhere. The breeze, which Abel had meant to whisk it away, had died for the moment, and so the cloak itself seemed to have died. It lolled limply about Abel's much-vaunted piece. "Shitmonkey!" Abel fumed. "Fuckslee!" In vain he leapt for a corner of the cloak. No one in the audience ventured to help. No one dared. Mr. Horfner's world-famous temper looked to be firing at full throttle. The entire affair was so

ludicrous that Parker couldn't stand to watch. He looked away, over his shoulder again.

"WHEN WE DROP THAT eight-pointer, dear Lord, when we land that ten-pounder, we do it with you in mind. We do it to the glory of . . ."

Seeking effect, and seeking to take account of his audience, Bubby McGaw began to lift his eyes Heavenward. He did not quite make it to Heaven, though, because it was at that moment that a gust of wind tripped across the square and whipped Abel Horfner's drape away to reveal something the likes of which Bubby had never seen or ever hoped to see.

"Well, I'll be Goddamned," he said, quite unintentionally, and quite into the microphone.

At this his congregation perked up—perked up and turned en masse to see what had so inspired the little man. There across the square, just in front of the Calhoun statue, stood what looked to be a black marble penis the size of a bridge piling.

It was at precisely that moment that the peninsula quaked.

·III·

PRECISELY THAT MOMENT, because that was the moment that six tons of assorted weight—the last six tons the peninsula could handle, evidently—descended upon the city. They descended in the form of Bo and Tater Bamber, a couple down from Alcolu for the Tri-County Mini-Storage Convention. As the founder and sole owner of the successful Daddy Bo's Attic, Bo was scheduled to address the convention the following morning. He planned to discuss the finer points of the mini-storage business and present his vision of its future. In his spare time, Bo would have a look at the Sportsman's Jamboree. As for Tater, well, Tater would shop.

The weight problem had to do not only with what Bo and Tater were driving but also with what they were hauling. They were pulling a large Daddy Bo's trailer behind their spanking new, stealth gray H2—or Mama Bess, as they called her (in honor of Bo's recently departed mother). Mama Bess and the trailer were both packed to the gills, Bess with luggage and the trailer with antiques—chairs, tables, a sideboard, and a silver service, all of which Bo had claimed from a delinquent renter at Daddy Bo's #23. As the founder, Bo retained first dibs on all delinquent properties. He employed a man, Travis Myron, whose sole responsibility it was to personally inspect the same and to report back if he found anything of value. At Daddy Bo's #23, in unit B14, Travis had definitely found something of value. Bo didn't know exactly how much value, but he did know a pricey antique chair from a K-Mart chair. After cleaning out the unit he learned the renter had passed away with no surviving kin. Well, that was sad, but that was business. He would sell the crap in Charleston, where antique dealers were thick.

If the loaded trailer and packed Hummer weren't enough, Bo and Tater themselves added considerable weight to the rig. They both liked to eat, and it showed. Friends may have called Bo "joyfully jumbo" and Tater "pleasingly plump," but the fact was that between them they carried close to half a ton.

Half a ton too much for the Charleston peninsula, it seemed. As soon as Mama Bess landed, cruising smoothly off the recently completed, much vaunted Arthur Ravenel Bridge, Bo felt a tremendous shift. Not of the Hummer—of the earth. The kind of shift you feel with your stomach. Instinctively he engaged the four-wheel drive. He looked about—no evidence of earthquake or other natural disaster—then in the side-view mirror, where he did see evidence of something. The bridge was, well, the bridge was no longer attached to the peninsula. It hung there, naked and limp as a skeleton, slowly receding as the peninsula, apparently, slowly proceeded away from it.

"Shoot, Tate!" Bo said. "That was close! We just barely made it, darlin'!"

"We'll make it," Tater said sleepily. "We'll make it." Tater scarcely knew what she was saying or even to whom she was saying it. She was lying back in her seat, nodding in and out of dreams—most of them to do with shopping.

It had been so long since she had really gone shopping. The last trip had been to Atlanta, the weekend of the Panthers-Falcons game, and that was over six months ago. She had long since quit her monthly trips to the outlets in Myrtle Beach. Now that they had money, she could spend it. What was the point in having it if you didn't spend it? If no one knew you had it? And Bo, he didn't mind. He wanted her to spend it. He was still just a simple country boy at heart. He wore his Daddy Bo's baseball cap with pride, as if he were still the young man she had married, the young man just starting out with an acre of land and a vision. The young man who had helped her with the lock at unit E39; then helped her move the old photo albums and furniture, all the leftovers from marriage number two, into unit E39; then, at their third meeting, rocked and rolled her to ecstasy in the cool dark of unit E39. It had become a weekly affair and eventually a marriage. She had married him for his jolly nature and his wild loving. And who would have guessed it would not be long before the money started rolling in, franchises sprouting around the county and then the state? Mini-storage! Who would have guessed it? It was not long before they were very much in the money and she could quit her monthly trips to the outlets in Myrtle Beach in favor of high-style junkets to Charlotte and Nashville. And the glossy catalogues arrived as soon as the money did, as if the whole world knew that her Bo had made it. And he had. With fair rates and reasonable terms, he had.

Tater stretched and rubbed the sleep from her eyes. She leaned over and goosed Bo on the belly. "Almost there, honey-bun?" she asked, smiling suggestively at him.

"Almost there, Tater Tot."

"Mmm. I can't wait."

Tater couldn't wait. That was true. They were staying at the fancy Bay House Bed and Breakfast, and she had imagined all sorts of naughty christenings for each of their suite's rooms. There was something about distant locales that energized Bo beyond even his usual appetites. Take unit E39. Sixteen years after their first rendezvous there at the first Daddy Bo's, they still visited the unit once or twice a month, to copulate on husband number two's easy chair. She could only guess what the high-class Bay House would inspire in him. She had packed accordingly—for anything, for everything. To the miniskirts, halter tops, and pumps; the sequined tube dresses, lace stockings, and heels; the half-dozen pounds of cosmetics and the dozen pounds of jewelry; to all this she added the purple merry widow, the tiger-print silk thong, her Scarlett O'Hara costume, her new G.R.I.T.S. (Girls Raised in the South) panties, and a variety of favorite toys. There was much to be done here in old Charleston by the sea, and no, Tater couldn't wait to get started.

For the moment, though, Tater would have to wait. The traffic on King Street was outrageous. Total gridlock. She grew impatient.

"What in Heaven's name?" she said.

"I know," Bo said. He lowered his window, leaned out to get a better look. "Something's happening in the park up there."

Something was happening in the park up there, and as Bo and Tater approached it, inch by maddening inch, the magnitude of the commotion, if not the source of it, became clear. They could see swarms of people running out of the square, urgently, and others running toward it, just as urgently. There were fire engines and police cars with lights flashing. All of the activity seemed centered on the one section of the square they could not see, obscured as it was by the high-rise king cab of the jacked-up Ford beside them.

"What—get that redneck to move, Bo," Tater said. "I can't see!"

"He can't move, Tay-tay. Not any more than we can."

"Well—what in the devil's going on?" Tater asked. She searched the scene before them for clues.

A moment later both lanes budged forward a foot. The high-rise truck beside them lunged forward to take it, but Bo stayed put—much to the disdain of the driver behind him, who immediately commenced honking. But neither Bo nor Tater heard the angry blasts. With the truck out of the way, the source of the disturbance had been revealed: a giant, well, a giant black cock, there in the middle of the park. A cock so big as to make even Tater blush.

"My lord!" she cried. "Would you look at that!"

"That is one gimungous tallywhacker," said Bo. "Jesus Knieval."

Yes, it was one gimungous tallywhacker, and not surprisingly the sight of it made Tater horny. "Ooh," she said. "My lord, Bobo. Would you—my lord. Would you just look at that."

"I don't see how you couldn't. It's damn near big as a—as a— as a space rocket! A church steeple!"

Bo stared at the bizarre object, transfixed. Tater pulled off her tank top.

She nuzzled up to her husband and slid her hand down his pants. "Right here, big Bobo," she cooed. "Mmm. Right now. We didn't get tinted windows for nothing."

IN THE SQUARE, THERE WAS more order to things than the flashing lights might have suggested. The art critics and reporters had for the most part fled to their hotel rooms, where laptops awaited. A good number of the Bravado patrons—representing banks, HMOs, and brokerage firms—had run away as well, eager to put as much distance as possible between their sponsorship and the scandal. Of the original audience there remained only Abel Horfner's most dedicated fans, who nodded approvingly at the structure, speaking of it with hushed, serious voices, and a few dozen miscellaneous others, some who felt compelled to stick around and express their complete disapproval and others of the sort who find humor in such things. Among these latter was Parker Hathaway, who found great humor in the unveiling. Who in fact had laughed raucously when the drape first blew away. He had always had a thing for the ridiculous, and if this was nothing else, it was utterly ridiculous.

Horfner himself was nowhere to be found. The insulting laughter was one thing, the reaction of the camouflaged brutes across the way quite another. He had watched as they collectively rose from their seats, then slowly amassed. A stormy ocean of ignorance and malice now moving his way. When they began walking across the square toward the sculpture, Abel Horfner, fearing no less than a public lynching, turned and ran. He had not been seen since.

In fact, Horfner had little to fear from the sportsmen as a whole. Most of them were drunk enough or fun-loving enough to find the display enormously funny and were simply crossing the square for a closer look. Horfner might have concerned himself with Bubby McGaw, though. Bubby McGaw wasn't the least bit drunk, and even if he liked to think of himself as fun-loving, he wasn't, not really. At that moment, he was outraged and might very well have lynched Horfner or at least dreamed it.

It was Bubby who had called the police. The police weren't exactly sure what to do with or about the thing, though they did issue two Livability Court summonses—one for public vagrancy and one to a group of scrappy teenagers for public skateboarding. Then the police called the fire department. But the fire department didn't know what to do with or about the thing either.

Bubby McGaw knew what to do. Fed up, he took Horfner's former place on the podium before the sculpture and began a tirade.

"This is an outrage! A perverted, elitist outrage! The liberal media! Public radio! You people! You will be punished for this! You don't even know! The wrath! You people! You have gone and—"

Bubby stopped. Somebody was laughing at him. Loudly. Wildly. Abruptly it broke.

"You go, Bubby!" the voice called. "You go, brother!"

Laughter again. Horrible laughter. Bubby recognized that laughter. He recognized that voice. Searching his audience hard for the source, he found it soon enough—three rows back, with a schoolgirl's hairdo and a homo's get-up, stood Parker Hathaway, his brother-in-law.

Bubby shivered twice. "You!" he cried, pointing at Parker. "You!"

Still Parker laughed.

"You—" Bubby couldn't find anything else. Nothing. "You!"

At last he left the podium—flustered, humiliated, and bent on revenge.

REVENGE. PRECISELY WHAT Abel Horfner was running from. Precisely what he had meant to accomplish with his sculpture, and now precisely what he was running from. Bubba's revenge.

He fled down Calhoun Street and then cut down Beaufain. At the end of Beaufain he hooked a left on Pinckney, a narrow side street which was, for the moment, empty. Abel took the opportunity to catch his breath—regrettably, as it turned out: the air on Pinckney stank like damp, sour underwear. And for good reason, too. Pinckney, Abel discovered, was home to the carriage tour trade. The entire right side of the street presented recesses, some housing carriages and others, stables. Signs above the alcoves designated ownership—the Livin' Past Tour Company, Palmetto Royale Expeditions, General Lee's Livery Service. Abel pinched his nose against the stink and began to walk on. He had not gotten very far when a big Bronco turned onto Pinckney from Battery Street with a squeal of burning rubber. A redneck tank, fast approaching. Panicked, Abel jumped to the nearest alcove and into an empty stable. From relative safety, he listened to the Bronco storm past.

They were after him. That much was certain. Abel took quick stock of his surroundings. All the stables were empty, with no one about. A stable might have made an ideal hideout if only it didn't stink so. If only the floor were not littered with squashed manure cakes. Safe as the place appeared, Abel would not stay. Could not. He left the stable and stepped quietly toward the back door of the garage. Along his way Abel happened to notice, hanging between a tangled collection of bridles and a pair of horse diapers, an old-fashioned military uniform, gray, of the sort worn by some of the local tour guides. Without a second thought, he shed his clothes and changed into the costume—jacket, kepi, strap-on beard, and all—then resumed his flight.

He left through the back door of the garage and crossed the street to a shaded cobblestone alley. Alone in the alley for as far as he could see, and afforded a certain sense of security by the uniform, he walked at a more relaxed pace. He could breathe now. Indeed, he found great pleasure in breathing now: the scent of the wisteria dripping from the limbs of the oaks was intoxicating. It laced the light afternoon breeze with a luxurious sweetness. Without at all intending to, Abel found himself strolling. Yes, Abel Horfner was, for the first time in his life, out for what people might call a stroll. If the sweet, lazy motion was completely unfamiliar to him, it was truly, to use a word Abel himself rarely found use for, delightful.

Abel should have known better than to grow complacent. It was only a matter of time before he found his transcendence shattered by a clamoring commotion from up the alley. A horse and carriage, he saw. Of all things. A horse and carriage being driven down the alley, toward him, by a man wearing the very same costume as he. The horse was running at full gallop and the man was hollering, whipping the beast on, the carriage bouncing and tipping along behind like a small boat caught in a gale. Abel's options were limited: he could either turn and run or he could scale the alley wall. He thought he would turn and run. Unfortunately, the short time it took for him to choose the option to turn and run cost him the option of turning and running. The hell-bent get-up was bearing down, fast. Abel had no choice but to scale the alley wall.

He landed, rather painfully, in a patch of manicured boxwood. The carriage rattled past and on down the alley.

"Shitslee!" Abel said as he began to gather himself.

"There's no need for that."

Abel jumped at the voice and turned. A sharp-featured, white-haired man in a seersucker suit, drink in hand, was sitting at a patio table, looking off with the vague, longing eyes of a man drinking.

"Cussing," said the man, now looking at Abel and shaking his head. "It's one thing to just drop in, so to speak. Uninvited. But the cussing. Really."

"I—"

"Mary!" the man called over his shoulder, toward the house behind him. "Bring another drink! We got company!"

"I—"

"Have a seat, son. Won't you?"

Before Abel could respond, an elderly woman appeared at the door to the house. She looked at Abel the way he would expect someone to look at a costumed stranger who had just dropped out of the sky and into the boxwood: with confusion and horror. Mary, apparently, had not had as much to drink as her husband.

Abel ran.

A short hop over a fallen-down iron fence into the next garden, an easy push through a stand of hollies into the next. And so he traveled, through garden, driveway, and patio— hollered at, barked at, chased at one point by a wretched little dog he first mistook for a discarded mop—to finally reach a dead end at the rear of a house that was under construction.

Or destruction, really: windowless and doorless, with a clumsy plywood chute dropping from the second story into a waste bin. There were workers moving about the place, but they seemed to be packing up—with great excitement and haste, at that. He heard talk of going down to Calhoun Square. They were going down to Calhoun Square. Now.

Abel wasn't. As soon as the last of the work trucks had pulled away, he slid into the house through a side entrance. Inside, he found the place entirely vacant save assorted piles of lumber, insulation, and plaster dust. Coming to the stairwell, he walked up to the second floor, in case anyone should return.

Frightened, unraveled, and thoroughly exhausted, Abel Horfner settled in a corner of the empty house and waited for night.

·IV·

HEN BO AND TATER Bamber at last arrived at the Bay House Bed and Breakfast, the concierge, one Mr. Brimkey, was more than a little thrown off. Matching oversized baseball caps advertising sports teams—of which Mr. Brimkey guessed the Carolina Panthers to be an example—were not customary attire at the Bay House. The Bay House had not been called "superb" by *Travel and Leisure* for oversized baseball caps advertising sports teams. Mr. Brimkey assumed—or rather, Mr. Brimkey hoped— that the couple was simply lost, as less experienced visitors to the old city tended to become after a day of lurching carriage tours and yawing harbor cruises. Occasionally the more brazen would lumber in uninvited, seeking directions and more often than not a restroom, of which Mr. Brimkey would coolly dispense the former and firmly refuse the latter, so as to be done with the intruders as quickly as possible. So yes, Mr. Brimkey guessed the two before him to be, sartorially and geographically, terribly lost.

Mr. Brimkey was mistaken.

"Got a boy can get the lady's bags for her?" the gentleman, if Mr. Brimkey could call him that, asked.

"I beg your pardon?" said Mr. Brimkey. He glanced at the woman, who grinned at him and winked once. He thought the stretch-fabric blouse entirely too liberal with her enormous breasts and found her red leather miniskirt less than flattering of her roundish waist. The makeup would have put Joan Rivers to shame, and the bangles and hoop earrings had likely mined half a mountain. Still she grinned at him and winked again.

"Mister? The lady's bags?"

"I'm sorry, I—" Mr. Brimkey said, flustered.

"Bo and Tater Bamber?" the man said. "Friday through Friday?"

Bo and Tater? Mr Brimkey walked to his desk and checked the registry, where he found written, startlingly enough, *B. Bamber: May 25-June 1.* "Mr. Bamber?" he said.

"That's me!" the man said, and then, in perfect imitation of his wife, he grinned a large, overfed grin and winked.

"Well, I—" Mr. Brimkey started, bowing in spite of himself. "We welcome you to the Bay House, Mr. and Mrs. Bamber. I'll— I'll ring for Beto."

A young Hispanic man appeared in the foyer. He held the door for Bo and Tater, then followed them out to Mama Bess, where, under the direction of Bo, he began unloading the suitcases and carryalls onto a wheeled luggage cart. Tater took a moment to glance about Bay Street. It looked to her like something out of a movie—the regal antebellum mansions and well-groomed gardens, the evenly spaced street lamps. Call me Scarlett, she thought with immense satisfaction.

Turning back, she observed that one house did intrude on the mood: adjacent to the B&B stood a relatively modest wooden home that might have suited the neighborhood well enough if only its owner would take some care with it. The paint was flaked and peeling in spots, giving the structure the look of some blistery disease, and the wrought-iron fence was so grown over with vines that it leaned heavily forward and looked as though it might fall to the sidewalk at any moment. Two of the railings on the first-story porch were gone entirely, and Tater could only conclude (or hope, for the owner's sake) that the house had been abandoned. Next door to the ruin, a similarly modest home was undergoing some kind of work—a trash chute ran from a second-story window down into a scrap bin. Without bothering to explain to herself exactly how or why, Tater presumed that the work crew would in time move on to the neighboring home, which was in far greater need of attention.

"Ready, Tay?" Bo asked. He pinched her lightly on the behind. "Look like you're dreaming, darlin'."

"Only of you!" Tater said. She goosed him back, and the two of them followed Beto inside.

The second floor of the Bay House B&B was expansive and exquisite, the three rooms (bed, bath, living) outfitted with enough mod cons to keep things comfortable but not so many that guests would forget where they were. Luxuries and extravagances of old complemented luxuries and extravagances of the day. In front of the broad four-poster rice bed stood an antique sideboard that opened to reveal a wide-screen television, an Onkyo surround-sound system, and a well-stocked bar; beside the porcelain bath, which was as big as a car, Tater found a wide marble shower and Jacuzzi. The embroidered silk drapes could be opened by remote control, and, upon discovering this, Tater opened them all by remote control. Bathed in afternoon sunlight, the suite glowed, and really there was no need to draw the drapes closed, even considering her lascivious plans: next door was the abandoned, rundown house, and out front, through the bedroom bays, only ocean. Mighty stormy ocean, but ocean. No people, anyway.

"Why's it so rough?" Tater said, gazing out.

"Oh," said Bo. He joined Tater at the window. "Beto says we're floating off. Out to sea."

"Hmm." Tater considered. "Really?"

"Yep. Says we're about thirty miles off."

"Huh," said Tater. "Thirty miles." She considered the notion for a moment longer, then turned and nuzzled up to her husband. She flashed him a mischievous grin, and for the second time in as many hours she slid her hand down his pants. "Oh, Bobo," she said. "Did you see the size of that tub?"

NEXT DOOR, AT 2 BAY, in a house that was not abandoned at all—and if Elizabeth Hathaway had anything to say about it, never would be—the matriarch danced on, fueled as much by the half-gallon of whiskey as by a most intriguing recent development. Not a half hour earlier, absent T. Moffett's demolition crew had piled into their trucks and torn off, hooting and hollering like banshees. For all their sudden commotion, they might have been off to put out a fire or start one. Something was up somewhere else, and that, really, suited Elizabeth just fine. The sudden flight in fact presented her with an unusual opportunity: a chance to investigate the transgressions of absent T. Moffett personally. To find out exactly what he was up to over there. Perhaps even find something useful within his trash pile. She had resisted the temptation for too long.

Never mind that her house was fast filling up. There was a reason Bubby and Parker were to share her daughter's former quarters, and it was that there simply wasn't room anywhere else in the house. Over the years Elizabeth had filled the home with varied trash collections and heirlooms. Parker's old room was stuffed to the doorjamb with everything from stereo speakers to dish racks to old snow skis, none of it of any use to Elizabeth, but none of which she could stand to see thrown away, either. For the better half of her life she had walked the neighborhood early Tuesday mornings—the day when local sanitation services picked up sidewalk trash—in search of goodies. She had never been alone in her curious habit. Always she would meet friends and neighbors scouring the selfsame discard piles, and frequently the women would trade the services of husbands, sons, and grandsons in hauling the stuff to their respective homes, said sons and grandsons at once irritated and confused by the chore. Invariably the goods went to the back of the house or to the shed, never to see the light of day again. The point, it seemed, was not to use the various finds but simply to keep them from being thrown away.

The back of Elizabeth's home, which had once housed servants and a kitchen and had since fallen to dust and disrepair, was packed with discards of another sort—generations of heirlooms, some of extraordinary value, others all but worthless to anyone save a student of family history. Holding on, it seemed, was in the blood: some of the objects dated three centuries. There was little organization whatsoever to the room, unless one counted the loosely assembled shrine to the home's founding father and Elizabeth's personal hero, Colonel Thomas Parker. A collection of daguerreotypes, documents, uniforms, medals, and arms that had once belonged to or at least had something to do with the man was stacked and folded neatly in a nearby, accessible corner, in case Elizabeth should feel the need to sit and spend time with the memory of the man, which she often did. Otherwise the old furnishings, objets d'art, curios, and keepsakes were all jammed together, as if the goods had not gradually accumulated over time but, rather, had been stashed all at once in

a moment of great urgency. There were sideboards and silver chests, steamer trunks and rocking chairs. A Bible the size of a cinderblock and a ship's log detailing a voyage from Barbados to Charleston. A crate full of tarnished swords, bayonets, and spurs; a cardboard box with daguerreotypes and tintypes shuffled among yellowed Polaroids and wrinkled black-and-whites. Boxes and boxes of books and a wardrobe with antiquated, moth-eaten ball gowns yet hanging. All of it finding its way here over the years, as holders-on passed on. The back of 2 Bay, a receptacle for all the prides of Hathaway yesterdays, now gathering rust and dust.

But not discarded. Never discarded.

To be sure, it was a kind of local disease, this holding on to things. Reconstruction- and Depression-era frugality had been passed down obsessively for generations in the town; it was not at all uncommon to find descendants of the most prosperous planters, many of whom had since drawn wealth from other, more contemporary enterprises, picking through the moving trash of neighbors or driving ancient Buicks and Pontiacs until the wheels quite literally fell off. In such a way outward neediness became a sign of great wealth, current or onetime. And if the membership policies of local social clubs did not so much anymore, the system clearly distinguished the old blood from the new. New blood was flashy, trashy, and wasteful; old blood was discreet, frugal, and tasteful. Old blood did not throw away anything. New blood threw out with gusto.

Lately, of course, most of the old blood had moved out. Elizabeth had thought it somewhat curious that the exodus had begotten a wealth of trash piles. It was as though, in finally saying farewell to the old town, the natives had said farewell to their deeply rooted principles. On more than one occasion she had actually found objects that she remembered from former trash piles—objects she herself had perhaps conceded to a fellow trash-picker some Tuesday morning years ago. She found the phenomenon deeply disturbing on one level but fairly satisfying on another: now, the bounty was all hers. It was true that she was older now and had not a man to call on for assistance, but still she could manage small things like curtains, toasters, clock radios, and the like. In the past year, she had filled two entire rooms with small things.

There was always, Elizabeth believed, room for more.

It was this conviction that led her now to wander off her porch and into the lot of absent T. Moffett. With the flood of booze and the excitement of the afternoon she found herself abandoning a personal principle of her own—that she would never so much as consider the discards of her newest neighbor, whose crass attack on the neighborhood exceeded all precedent and warranted no less than a complete and utter shunning of everything that had anything to do with the man. But with the workers gone and the afternoon lingering, with the heady pulse of booze beating in her blood, she simply could not resist taking a peek. First in the Dumpster beside the house, below the chute, where she found, to her great disappointment, nothing more than heaps of old insulation and scattered scraps of lumber. The lumber might have been redeemable were there a craftsman about the house at 2 Bay, but there wasn't. Never had been. Determined not to leave the bin empty-handed, she pulled out a short two-by-four scrap anyway, thinking it might find use as a—well, it might find use as a something or other.

Elizabeth moved on, up the brick steps and through the doorjamb. There was no door, of course: that had been one of the first features to go, likely to be replaced by some mirrored

Phoenix-style horror down the road. Who could say what. She didn't want to even think what.

Inside, the place looked little different than she expected, only worse. The walls had been ripped out, and aside from a dense layer of saw- and plaster-dust on the floor, the room was entirely, frightfully vacant. All the charm of a warehouse. Recalling dinner parties with the Daniels and Christmas visits with the Conrads, she became disoriented and dizzy. The plain emptiness, the hollowness, the space—it was overwhelming. Indeed, she would have fallen to the floor if it weren't for the two-by-four, which she used as a kind of cane to steady and prop herself.

Righted, Elizabeth took on the stairs and came, in time, to the second-story drawing room, which she found as hollow as the first floor, as vacant, but for one exception.

A man stood in the corner.

A man in a Confederate uniform. With a thick, dark beard. The resemblance to her great-grandfather Colonel Thomas Parker, legendary war hero and statesman, whose portrait hung above her sideboard, who yet lived in memory, was staggering. She felt sure she had come upon his ghost.

"Colonel Parker?" she asked.

At this the man looked left, then right, then behind him. He might have seen a ghost himself. Now, apparently, he wanted a way out.

"Great-gran?" Elizabeth asked. Carefully she stepped forward. As soon as she did, the figure leapt, it appeared, into the wall—no, through it. Through the wall. A short hiss was followed by a loud and painful-sounding PLANG! Elizabeth hurried to the point of the figure's departure. The chute. Her great-grandfather had jumped down the chute.

Outside, she found him breathing, but little more. Certainly not responding when she took his face in her hands and shook it. His head, it appeared, had slammed against the edge of the bin. He had been knocked unconscious. His gray cap had fallen to the ground.

Elizabeth called 911, but all authorities, she was told, were tending to more important matters midtown.

"What could be more important than a dying colonel?" Elizabeth asked.

"A giant Negro penis, that's what," said the operator.

"I beg your pardon?" Elizabeth said. Surely she hadn't heard the woman right.

"You heard me," the operator said.

"I hope I didn't," said Elizabeth.

"Not to mention that the whole fucking city is halfway to China."

"I'm well aware of that, miss. There's no need for cursing. Do you understand me?"

"Piss off," the operator laughed.

Laughed. Elizabeth dropped the phone as she might the handle of a hot skillet, then fumbled through the house to gather a towel, two trays of ice, and, last, the old time-honored cure: a fresh bottle of whiskey.

WAKING, ABEL HORFNER COULD not say where he was, or when he was, or even who. He could say only that his head felt split open with a hammer and that an elderly woman whose breath stank of booze was padding the pain with a cold towel, dribbling liquor on his lips, and urging him to rise. Which, eventually, he did. He nudged the bottle away, collected himself, and climbed, slowly, carefully, out of the bin. The woman placed a small gray cap on his head, took him gently by the arm, and led him into the house next door. She showed him to a table and clumsily pulled out a chair for him. After he had settled, she offered him a drink. He accepted. She called him Colonel Parker. He said thank you. She said it was just awful what they were doing to his former hometown. Sinful. Could he believe it? He shook his head. And did he know that the entire peninsula had broken off? Was that, maybe, what had brought him back? To save them?

"Perhaps so," he said. For all he knew, yes, he was Colonel Parker, come to save them. Whoever they were.

"I knew somebody would come," the woman said. "I just knew it."

For a long while she gazed at him, her expression by turns adoring, amazed, enchanted. Embarrassed and confused, he drank with a quick, clipped rhythm, pausing only so often to look down at his glass and trace curves in the condensation. When he had finished the drink, the woman asked if he didn't want to rest. He said that he did, and she led him up the stairs to a four-poster rice bed the size of a small ship. Sinking into it, he felt he was exquisitely melting, a pat of butter in a bowl of oatmeal.

The woman removed his cap and kissed him lightly on the forehead. On her way out, she stopped at the bay window and looked out to the sea.

"I'd say we're fifty miles off," she said.

"Mmm," he said. Melting, melting. Surrendering to sleep and no pain.

"You came just in time, Colonel. Just in time."

"Just in time," he repeated drowsily. She turned, smiled at him, and then left the room. He was out before she'd reached the stairs.

· V ·

I N FACT THEY WERE not fifty miles off but two hundred. Propelled by its own land breeze, the peninsula was sailing along at twenty knots or so, a good clip by any measure. Thus far the strange craft had been spared the violent squalls and thunderstorms normally associated with the ocean in late spring, thanks in large part to the massive gusts of hot air issuing from Calhoun Square. Between the inebriated sportsmen, the theorizing art patrons, and the always-eager-to-advise local authorities, talk in the square had generated a substantial low-pressure system, which in turn formed a frontal boundary sturdy enough to keep foul weather at bay. If local events had been more than a little turbulent, the weather could not have been nicer. It was springtime in Charleston: clear, bright, mid-seventies.

In the course of the afternoon, the mood in the square came to complement the weather. The sportsmen, all but wiped out from a day of eating, drinking, and guffawing, pulled out lawn chairs and so as to continue their good time, set them up around the new statue. Though many of the onlookers were repulsed and scandalized by the very sight of the thing, few wanted to leave it for fear they might miss something even more scandalous if it were removed. They left briefly to retrieve picnic baskets and blankets, children, and recreation. Before long, footballs and Frisbees sailed across the square and dogs and youngsters chased each other about. By sunset, the square again had the look of a festival, and as dark fell the spirit of the occasion lifted still another notch. Rested now, refreshed, the sportsmen were ready to begin anew. That is, to fall into the drink anew. As for the others, most soon discovered a thing the natives had long known—that there is nothing so right as a gin and tonic or three at sunset in Charleston. Liquor was fetched, and beer and wine, and as the street lamps flickered to life the square fell into a kind of merry roar. At a distance, the affair might have been some pagan rite of spring centered on the phallic sculpture. A celebration honoring virility, say, or endurance.

Closer inspection always turns up something, of course. There was nothing merry about Bubby McGaw just now. There hadn't been since the unveiling. He had not succeeded in catching his brother-in-law after the pervert ruined the testimony before the statue—Parker had skipped off into the crowd just as dandily and fancifully as could be—nor was he able to regain the attention of the audience thereafter. When he had returned to the podium, he had been quickly forced down from it. Adding insult to injury, the man who removed him was an officer of the law. Bubby was not accustomed to being accosted by officers of the law. Normally they were on his side. Normally they were moral people.

Indeed, Bubby was hard pressed to find a moral person anywhere. Those who didn't laugh or squint him away, those who seemed just as outraged as he was, seemed outraged for a different reason. "Bad art," they said. Or, "Not becoming of the old town at all." When Bubby brought up the matter of sin, these individuals, as a rule, looked him over once and turned away.

So he fumed. He returned to the Jamboree side of the park, all but empty now, and he sat down and he fumed.

Bubby had not been fuming long before he was approached by a stout, thirtyish man in golf-style clothing. The man carried a bundle of T-shirts in one hand and several foam can-coolers in the other. Bubby did not know the man, but the man, apparently, knew him.

"Mr. McGaw," the man said. "You're not looking too happy."

"I'm not too happy," Bubby said. "And who are you?"

The man nodded. "I'm Harry Biddencope."

The name sounded familiar.

"Festival organizer. I'm the one who brought you here. Remember?"

"Biddencope. Right." Bubby looked up at Harry Biddencope and narrowed his eyes. "You responsible for all this? It's an outrage, Mr. Biddencope. A perverted elitist outrage."

Harry looked over his shoulder, across the green. "I know it, Mr. McGaw," he said. "Had no idea what these artists were capable of."

"They're capable of going to Hell, I'll tell you that."

Harry nodded slowly, then turned back to Bubby. "Would a free T-shirt cheer you up, Mr. McGaw? Or maybe a coozie?"

"You know what would cheer me up, Mr. Biddencope?" Bubby said. "That statue coming down. That's what."

Again Harry looked over his shoulder. "I know it. I saw your speech, there. Have to say, Mr. McGaw, I agree. Especially the public-radio part. You got that exactly right. It's public radio that leads people to do these kind of things."

"Well? Can't you do something about it? You're in charge, aren't you?"

Harry told Bubby that he was just on his way to do something about the sculpture, but in fact he wasn't. He had no intention of doing anything at all about the piece, not yet. It's true that when he had first come upon it, he had quickly backed away, keeping his distance lest anyone present recognize him and, in recognizing him, blame him. Behind the hedgerow he had quietly raged at Abel Horfner for such an atrocity, such an embarrassment. That was the danger with this art thing and public radio, too. You never knew what you were going to get. With commercial radio, you knew. With commercial radio, there was control.

So yes, Harry had first hidden away and quietly raged. Gradually, though, as the mood in the square shifted from stunned to festive, Harry's own outlook transformed. What had first seemed a disaster of epic proportions soon presented itself as an opportunity. For every one person leaving, three more showed up. Several wedding receptions had relocated to the square. Picnics were blooming. All, it seemed, because of the sculpture. Harry wasn't about to have it moved—not yet. The only thing he would have moved was the WBUB broadcast van, from the vacated Jamboree section of the square out to the middle. He had instructed all on-site DJs to steer clear of the subject of the sculpture entirely and talk up the afternoon in the square as simply the biggest bash of the year. So far, the strategy seemed to be working. They had given away several hundred T-shirts and almost all of the coozies.

That statue wasn't coming down anytime soon.

Of course, Harry didn't tell Bubby McGaw all this. He told Bubby he was off to see what he could do, and then he left the angry little man to his fuming.

BUBBY SAT UNTIL SUNSET, and then, as the park took on a second wind and geared up into a festive occasion—celebrating the statue?—he headed down to Bay Street, where he hoped to find some solace in family. Decent people, with the notable exception of Parker. Perhaps the only decent people left on the peninsula. Bubby looked forward to telling Mrs. Hathaway all, to finding in her an ally in the struggle against perversion. Telling her would be tricky, of course. He would have to find a way to explain what had happened without offending the upright woman. As he walked, he shuffled through his options. "They've erected—" No, that wasn't the right word. "They've put a giant—" No. He would tell her simply that something horribly obscene, not to mention immoral, had occurred during the opening ceremonies. That, he was sure, would be enough.

As it turned out, it didn't much matter what Bubby came up with, because Mrs. Hathaway was in no position to hear him. After knocking twice, Bubby quietly entered the house to find Elizabeth Hathaway slumped over the dining room table, her right hand feebly wrapped around a tall glass.

At first he thought the worst: the old woman was dead. But rushing to the collapsed body, he found breathing. Heavy, rhythmic breathing, the breathing of deep sleep. The breaths themselves were putrid. They stank of—alcohol. Bubby recoiled. The woman was not dead. She was passed-out drunk.

Well.

He shook his mother-in-law gently, speaking her name. The woman woke only briefly. Raising her head, she said blearily, "Dance taken. This dance already taken," then collapsed again.

It was a shame. A horrible shame. Bubby said a quick prayer for the woman, then began a search through the house for his last hope, old Lawson. A man who, if he was prone to the drink himself, not to mention sudden fits of cursing, was old enough to know the difference between a moral value and an immoral one.

He found Lawson where he expected to find him, in a rocker on the upstairs porch. This he expected. He did not expect the old man to be studying the neighboring mansion with what looked to be a small, ancient, handheld telescope. What might have been a pirate's spyglass.

"Mr. Parker!" Bubby said in a raised voice, the only kind that would get through. He walked to the railing, stood in front of the old man to get his attention. But the old man quickly waved him off with a furious sweep of his free arm.

"Goddammit!" Lawson said. He did not lower the spyglass. "Get out the goddamn way, you!"

Bubby jumped to the side. He might have just been shot. The urgency of the command, the blasphemy of it, completely shocked him, even coming from Lawson. He turned to see what could possibly be holding the man so rapt. He wasn't long in finding it. Just across from the porch, through the second-story bay window of the neighboring mansion, pressed up against the second-story bay window of the neighboring mansion, was the rump of a large woman. And pressing this large rump to the window, a blubbery man wearing nothing but a football helmet. With each forward thrust from the man, the woman's rump flattened and squished against the window, a rhythmic, fluid splishing that suggested the death throes of some strange deep-sea creature. What was more, the woman appeared to be wearing— half-wearing, anyway—an old-fashioned ball gown and a wig.

Bubby quite nearly collapsed and fell off the porch. Catching himself, he walked quickly inside without another word to the old man.

He'd had it.

For his part, Lawson Parker was glad to be rid of the intruder. He felt he had been waiting a long time for an opportunity such as this. The College of Charleston co-eds who hopped down the Battery every afternoon, firm young bosoms bouncing wonderfully, they were one thing. But this, this was something else entirely. The guests next door had been entertaining him off and on for several hours with feats he did not know the human body was even capable of.

They had begun in the living room—at least, Lawson had begun in the living room. Nightly he scanned the windows of the near neighborhood with a telescope that had belonged to his grandfather, Captain Richard Cooper, but aside from a few undressings here and stray kisses there, he had for the most part been disappointed. Visitors and residents alike had been, to date, notably discreet.

Not so this evening. Lawson's heart had skipped a beat when he first discovered the second-floor drapes at the Bay House B&B drawn open. It had skipped two when, on further inspection, he discovered a pair of feet dangling off the edge of a chaise longue in the most distant room. Fat feet, but naked feet. Wriggling.

Pay dirt.

Lawson sat up straight and leaned into the view. The feet wriggled once more, the toes clenched tight for a long moment, and then the feet disappeared. Another moment and a large rump presented itself in profile. A large rump sashaying and jiggling in place. Then the rump, too, disappeared. A garment of some sort flew out of the darkness and landed on the floor. Something silky.

Eagerly Lawson had searched for more, but for a time the activities subsided, or at any rate took place out of range. Very well, then. He could wait.

The wait, it turned out, was well worth it. A half hour later a woman emerged from the darkness. A woman in an old-fashioned ball gown of the sort worn by Scarlett O'Hara. The woman looked—well, she looked to Lawson like Scarlett O'Hara. A chunky Scarlett O'Hara, maybe, but even so, she was as wonderful a sight as he had seen in years. He recalled a debutante ball long past, a dance with young Virginia DuChamp. The woman before him began dancing, after a fashion. Her hands on her hips, bending over at the waist just slightly, she began swaying her rump widely in the direction of the darkness from which she had emerged.

Great goodness.

Before Lawson could catch his breath, another figure appeared out of the darkness. This one a man. A big, naked man carrying a large instrument of some sort. He was grinning wide, and as he emerged into the light he said something. The woman looked over her shoulder. When she turned back around she was laughing. She quit swaying her rump. The man approached, still grinning. He raised the instrument to rump level.

Lawson fainted.

When he woke, he could not say how much time had passed. If events at the neighboring B&B were any gauge, some had. He could not say what had happened in between, but when he woke he found the woman straddling an ottoman in the near room. Her gown had been pulled down from her chest and up over her thighs. Her enormous breasts hung and swung droopily, the flesh of her large rump spread over the ottoman like a store of Glad-bagged vanilla pudding.

She was indeed chunky, but she was a woman and she was naked, and looking on her Lawson said a quiet prayer of thanks. He felt a sting of jealousy when the man returned to the room, but only briefly, because the man engaged the woman in another intriguing act, and that, after all, was what Lawson was after.

More intriguing acts followed, one after the other—across, under, and on various furnishings in various rooms, each act bringing the couple closer to Lawson, that is, closer to the window, until at last the woman was pressed up against the window, the man doing the pressing. It was then, of course, that Lawson was so rudely interrupted, but he rid himself of the intruder with efficiency and cast his scope back to the randy couple.

His blood was beating hard with all the excitement—harder than it had beat in decades. It pounded his skull and chest as surely as the man was pounding the woman against the window, matching beat for beat, the frequency picking up, rising, beat for beat. Likely his heart wouldn't be able to keep up with this for much longer, but no way in Hell could he look away. No way in Hell.

INSIDE, BUBBY MCGAW SULKED his way down the stairs. So far, the trip had been a disaster. All his worst notions about Charleston had been confirmed—a place of extreme decadence and moral depravity, where not even the oldest, most traditional citizens could be counted on for direction—and he had not yet brought a single individual into the Fellowship of Evangelical Sportsmen. What was more, unless he took some measure, he would be sleeping with Parker Hathaway tonight. Flustered, Bubby retrieved his cell phone from his suitcase in the front hall and phoned Liza. He had much to tell her.

And she, it turned out, had much to tell him. He had not gotten past "Hey, baby doll" when she interrupted to tell him of some urgent business.

"I just saw it on the news, honey. Y'all are floating out to sea!"

"Floating out to sea," Bubby said. "What?"

"The whole peninsula! Is mother all right?"

"She's—" On his way to the bay window Bubby glanced at the slumped-over woman. At the window, he pulled the shade aside. Nothing but darkness off the Battery, and next door, at the bed and breakfast, well—he let the shade fall back over the window.

"Bu_____! My___ she_____right? Is everybody all _____?"

"You're breaking up, babe," Bubby said. "We're fine. Your mother's . . . sleeping. What's this floating off?"

"The news! The peninsula! ____off! You're on your_____France! I've_____to call!"

"Calm down, Lize. Calm down."

"You're_____right?"

"I can hardly hear you. But I'm fine. France?"

Silence.

"Liza? You there?"

She wasn't. He'd lost her.

Bubby headed out the door and down to the Battery, to see what he could see. Which was that, yes, the entire peninsula was clipping right along through the ocean, ten-foot swells breaking over the Battery wall. What was more, they seemed to be headed into a massive thunderstorm. Lightning wrangled through the darkness ahead in sprawling veinish patterns. Something massive was happening. Something disastrous. Wrathful.

The revelation did not evoke fear in Bubby. It did not bring panic. Instead it filled him with a certain satisfaction. Indeed, nothing in the world could have pleased Bubby McGaw more. It was as if everything he had ever stood for, everything he had ever spoken to, had at last found fruition. The people had brought it on themselves, and here it was. The end was not near, it was here. Back inside, he tried Liza again, but the connection was completely dead. No matter. He had more important things to think about now.

He had work to do.

·VI·

OR THE NEXT FEW HOURS, the storm held off, buffeted as it was by the sturdy gusts of hot air that continued to blast forth from the grounds of Calhoun Square. Indeed, the scene in the square had approached total abandon. When news of the peninsula's detachment spread through the gathering, a few responsible souls may have been inspired to head home and check on loved ones, but the vast majority of the revelers were inspired simply to turn up the party's volume. It was only a matter of time before the Jamboreeans built a bonfire in the middle of the square. The temperate spring weather notwithstanding, a crowd quickly gathered around the blaze and sprang into a clumsy line dance.

From the sidelines Harry Biddencope grew increasingly nervous. He watched as the short woman at the end of the dance line lost her balance and nearly fell into the fire, then stood up laughing. Harry turned away. What had first presented itself as a golden marketing opportunity had most decidedly degenerated into an uncontrollable orgy of debauchery. If it was true that the peninsula was presently floating out to sea, then Harry, now more than ever, held sole responsibility for the activities of the city. He would need the police, then. Without their help, his authority would amount to nothing.

He approached Chief Bevenly, only to be offered a can of beer.

"Harry!" the Chief said, bracing himself against the side of his patrol car to keep from falling over completely. "Less drinssome beer! We've succeeded!"

"Succeeded in what?"

"Succeeded from the Union, Harry! It's gonna work this time, by damn! We've succeeded! Come on! Drinssome beer!"

"I'd rather we cleaned the place up, Chief," Harry said, well aware of just how futile the request was. "Don't you think?"

But Chief Bevenly wasn't listening. He leaned—fell, really—into his squad car, took up his CB, flipped on the hailer, and proceeded to sing along with the WBUB broadcast: Jimmy Winyah's "Leavin' with a Smile."

There was some satisfaction in this, but not much. WBUB ruled the revelry, and the Chief did in fact have a marvelous, lilting voice that danced across the square, but the drunken mass of people he inspired to join in sounded like a flock of dying geese and quickly called Harry back to the disaster before him. The middle of the square was ablaze, the tremendous cock surrounded by dancing drunks. Thoroughly flustered, Harry nabbed the megaphone from the WBUB van, but once he had the thing to his lips, he had no idea what he might say or to whom he might say it.

All Harry Biddencope really knew was that if ever he saw the mayor again, he simply would not know where to begin.

BESIDE THE SCULPTURE, Parker Hathaway was trying, through the din, to hold a conversation with a childhood friend and distant cousin, Phillip Lawson, who had flown in from LA for Bravado. When Parker first ran into Phillip—quite literally, in a rowdy, gin-inspired dance around the giant phallus—he hardly recognized him. In middle school, Phillip had been skinny and pallid, shy, a bit of a loner. Still, because Phillip was a Lawson, one of the few natives left at the school, Parker had always felt a certain connection there. They had played Little League and gone to the same church, St. Michael's, before Phillip had quit sports and most other social activities altogether. Now Phillip seemed perfectly well adjusted. A production assistant for New World Films, he carried himself with bright confidence and with about fifty solid pounds of new muscle, which he showcased by way of an awfully tight jet black crewneck and snug chinos. With a sailor's tan and shining eyes, he looked successful and happy, and Parker told him so.

"LA's done you well, huh?" he said. Shouted, really.

"It's not Charleston," Phillip laughed. "Thank God."

"I hear you," Parker said.

"What's that?"

"I said, 'I hear you.' "

It was at this point that Parker caught sight of a good-looking, long-legged woman heading their way through the crowd. The woman had a notepad tucked under her arm, and she looked remarkably self-assured given the circumstances. When she reached them, she asked, quite matter-of-factly, if they were locals.

"That depends," Phillip said. "Who wants to know?"

The woman didn't miss a beat. "The *New York Times*," she said.

Phillip took her hand and started to introduce himself, but Parker cut him off. "Carolina Gabrel?" he said.

The woman seemed taken aback, but only for a moment. "Okay," she said, and she grinned impishly at Parker.

"Sorry?" said Parker.

"It's CaroLEEna," she said, smiling big. Her teeth were magnificent. "CaroLEEna GahBREL. Not CaroLYEna GAYbrul so much."

"Ah," Parker said. "But Miss—"

"You say CaroLYEna, she says CaroLEEna," Phillip interrupted. "Hi. I'm Phillip."

"Hi, Phillip," Carolina said, and she offered Phillip her slender hand. Phillip kissed it. This seemed to delight the young woman. She laughed, turned to Parker, and offered him her hand. "And you, sir?" she said.

And then Parker Hathaway scarcely knew what to do.

Because although he had never met Carolina Gabrel before, Parker had been infatuated with her for years, from afar. He had dutifully read her ever since the publication of her first book, *Miss DeVeaux's Savannah*, a poignant history of his adopted town as told to Miss Gabrel by the quirky, opinionated Savannah native, Margaret DeVeaux, who was known as much for her expansive knowledge of local history as for her expansive reserve of local gossip. The weight of personal and regional history was offset delightfully (and brilliantly, Parker thought) with gardening tips and family recipes. The book had in fact inspired Parker to move to Savannah, a town which, if the story were to be trusted, had protected its quirks and charms even as Charleston sold itself off to the highest bidders. Through a Charleston connection, Parker had been introduced to Miss DeVeaux, and over time he established a kind of friendship with her. Each Wednesday afternoon he joined her for drinks in her garden, exchanging tales and theories of old days and new days, old money and new money, old blood and new blood. Mostly, Parker would listen. Whenever possible he would steer the conversation to Carolina Gabrel, who, he believed, had told Miss DeVeaux's story masterfully, balancing her obvious affection for the woman with precisely the proper amount of distance required of a reporter.

It had shocked Parker to learn from Miss DeVeaux that Carolina Gabrel was not a Savannah native at all, nor even a Southerner.

Rather, a New York-based culture and travel writer. When he asked how on earth Miss DeVeaux could have placed the responsibility for her story in the hands of an outsider, Miss DeVeaux replied that she, Margaret Delilah Porcher Hamilton DeVeaux, was related to everyone in the South and therefore, as a matter of course, could not trust a single one of them. (That is, a single Southerner.) If Miss DeVeaux's story was to be told, it would be told by Miss DeVeaux, and not by a party she recognized or, more important, by a party who recognized her and might have some reason, however ludicrous, however ill-conceived, to distort her tale. Besides, she had found Carolina Gabrel charming, bright, and driven, three qualities Miss DeVeaux had always looked for in others and cultivated in herself. Without charm, she said, a body was unlikable; without wits, unknowable; without drive, simply useless. Parker had wondered aloud if the two still kept in touch, and when Miss DeVeaux replied that of course they did—with an expression that suggested it utterly inane to speculate otherwise—he asked if Carolina Gabrel ever returned for a visit. Miss DeVeaux responded that the young woman certainly would if she could, but as the surprising nationwide success of the book had earned her a number of assignments from _Travel and Leisure_, the _New York Times_, and _Outside_, she was forever out of town, every other week zipping off to this exotic locale or that one. So no, as of yet the two of them had not met up again. A shame, Parker had said. I'm not dead yet, Miss DeVeaux had replied petulantly. Parker had asked her to be sure and let him know when and if any such meeting with Carolina Gabrel were arranged, and that evening he ordered subscriptions to _Travel and Leisure_, the _Times,_ and _Outside._

If he never had the opportunity to meet her, to talk with her, he would know her through her work. In the year or so since he had started taking the publications, Parker had been all over the world with Carolina Gabrel: from the steamy, battle-ridden hills of Chiapas to the elegant gardens of the Loire Valley, from the cavernous interiors of Cambodia to the emerald waters of Eleuthera. Particular anecdotes and references in her pieces led him to believe that she was fluent in both French and Spanish, had a reasonable grasp of German, and knew enough Burmese to at least get by in far Rangoon. What was more, to be taking the kinds of risks she took on her travels, she could not be so very old. At the end of each article, Parker hoped against hope to find a business e-mail address, but of course writers for *Travel and Leisure* and *Outside* were too sophisticated for that, too busy. They were not writing for the Charleston *Current* or the Savannah *Herald*. They were not hard up for ideas; they were not looking for suggestions. Parker might have gone to the publications' websites and pursued Carolina Gabrel's address there, but that, he knew, bordered on the creepy. Besides, he was not obsessed. Fascinated, maybe, but not obsessed. Mostly, he was interested. If only he were given the chance to talk to her— hell, just to meet her.

And now here she was, before him. Already he'd blundered things with this pronunciation bit; already she'd ribbed him. He might have explained that he was only pronouncing the name the way he'd heard it pronounced by Miss DeVeaux, but face to face with Carolina Gabrel, he stumbled over his own words. His awkwardness was compounded by her incomparable beauty. The young woman was far more striking than he might even have imagined, which in fact he had not. He had not once imagined what she might look like—the photo on the dust jacket of *Miss DeVeaux's Savannah* was of Miss DeVeaux herself. He had only imagined what she might say, the questions she might ask, the speculations she might offer. But the woman was, indeed, irresistibly gorgeous. She looked at once the young girl—her nose freckled, her teeth bright, her eyes lively—and the determined woman—easily five-eleven, with the long, strong legs of a colt, her raven hair pulled back in a high ponytail. She was dressed not in the stiffly elegant garb of a sophisticated New Yorker but in well-worn blue jeans, a snug baby-blue tank top, and, he noticed, running shoes.

"Parker," she said after he at last introduced himself. "Is that a family name?"

She wrote as she talked. Taking notes, Parker presumed. "Well—sure—sure it is," he stumbled.

"Silly question?" she said, grinning again, but at Phillip.

"Well—Miss DeVeaux—I've befriended Miss DeVeaux and—would you like some gin?"

Before she could answer, Phillip interrupted the exchange. "We must scale this fabulous cock!" he said. "We simply *must*! What do you say, Park? Come show Miss Gabrel how Charleston boys do it!"

And Parker said of course, yes, that is what they would do, and he took the lead even, a great venting of the nerves, this, a reaching to the sky. With the bonfire blazing and the line dance shuffling, the three of them scaled the sculpture and then slid down it, tumbling to the ground together, a cozy trio. Standing up, Parker briefly considered the goose pinch Phillip had planted on his ass as they rolled from their fall to the ground. He had guessed this about Phillip, but he wished Phillip—and however many others, for that matter—wouldn't assume the same about him. Parker was a dandy, nothing more. If anyone should understand what that meant, Phillip should. But perhaps Phillip didn't. Perhaps nobody did. Perhaps the dandy's day really had come and gone. An awfully depressing thought. At any rate, Parker considered the grope only briefly, because really his attention was focused on Carolina Gabrel. She had fallen, essentially, in Parker's lap and didn't seem overly concerned one way or the other. Without pulling away from him, she took up her notepad and resumed taking notes.

"I didn't dream anything like this," Phillip said, rolling his eyes and smirking at Parker. "Giving pleasure to such a—grand specimen. I have to take it home with me."

"You'll need a mighty big plane," Parker said. Carolina's hair, he noted, smelled like strawberries.

NOT A BLOCK FROM THE sculpture, in the crook of an oak that bordered the park, Bubby McGaw sat quietly steeping over the gross display. Parker and one of his fun boys, with a woman thrown in for an extra kink. Parker, clinging to the head of the thing, dropping his freak-haired head back and laughing raucously. Sliding slowly down, his fanny bumping the head of the pervert below, whose fanny then bumped the head of the woman before all three slid to the ground in a close, laughing bundle that rolled together on the ground for much longer than Bubby thought necessary.

Bubby had to control himself. He had to be patient. Easy as it would be to nab his brother-in-law now, he would have to resist the temptation. Because he wanted something bigger. Extreme hours, after all, call for extreme measures.

He'd been eyeing the WBUB broadcast van across the park for some time. Shaped like an enormous boom box, antenna pole raised skyward, the vehicle seemed as suitable as any for the task of announcing the Apocalypse. What was more, the van's operator, a tubby bald man in a too-tight WBUB tank top, could scarcely stand up, for reasons the knee-high pile of beer cans behind the van might explain. The tubby bald man kept staggering off after passing women, only to stagger on back, rejected. If Bubby timed it right, between the staggering off and the staggering back, well . . .

"WHOO!" SAID PHILLIP. Then, "Encore, anybody? I say we do it—" Phillip stopped. His eyes, fixed on something across the park, widened. "Oh, my," he said. "Would you look at that." Parker and Carolina turned to see the WBUB boom-box van cutting doughnuts just the other side of the bonfire, the van's antenna pole waving wildly with the turns. A spoken message sounded from the speakers, tuning in and out eerily with the turns of the van so that only disconnected fragments of the message made it across the park: HERE . . . IS . . . THE END . . . THE END . . . HERE . . . THE END IS . . . Hounds barked madly and chased after the van, and the crowd barked madly and ran away from it. People were scattering in all directions but mostly toward the sculpture, as if some sanctuary might be found there.

Carolina and Parker stood up.

They watched as the van, after some dozen more circles, took pause to gauge the situation. Aimed at the sculpture, the high beams cut twin cones of light through the square. Now they flashed insistently. The engine revved with menace, the van roaring in place for a long moment before dropping into gear at high rev, at which point the rear wheels tore twin ruts in the earth. The van skidded—left, right, left again, right again—then commenced a deliberate, if swerving, advance through the park. Again the crowd barked and scattered.

From across Calhoun Street, Parker watched as the gigantic boom box approached the gigantic cock and began cutting doughnuts around it. With each revolution, the van increased speed and tightened the circle. Tighter and tighter, faster and faster, until at last the top-heavy vehicle could hold itself no longer. Antenna pole dipping, the boom box tipped onto two wheels for half a turn, then fell flat on its side and stopped moving. As if kicked to life, the speakers sounded music again, however weakly: Susie Hayrow's "I Just Wanna Be Mad," broadcast to the heavens.

Once it had caught its collective breath, the crowd approached the wreck, as crowds will. A small group of Jamboreeans took it upon themselves to investigate. Because the van's cab was not nearly so wide as its boom-box body, it hung in a sort of suspended state, affording access to the driver's door from the ground. Parker watched as the men crept around the capsized truck. They were crouching low, stalking the perp like a SWAT team. When the front man reached the driver's door, he stretched from a crouched position to pull the handle. The door fell open, then off. Hanging there in the seat belt, looking perfectly intact—if frightened out of his wits—was a man Parker recognized.

"Bubby McGaw," he said. He was not ashamed so much as bewildered. "My brother-in-law."

"Brother-in-law?" Phillip said.

"Brother-in-law."

"That's the one Liza—that's the holy roller?"

"That's him," Parker said.

"Your sister married a holy roller?" Carolina Gabrel said. She was scribbling furiously, now.

"I'm afraid so."

"Oh. I'm sorry," Carolina said absently.

"Me, too," Parker said.

If Parker recognized the crazed driver, the Jamboreeans who yanked him out of the cab likely did not, except to say that the man had ruined a perfectly good party and would now, naturally, have to be tied to a tree. A length of rope was collected from a nearby truck, and Bubby McGaw was escorted across the square to the trunk of an oak he would get to know well over the course of the night. Anyone with a mind to rescue him thought better of it as the three vigilantes proceeded to set up drink-camp before the prisoner. They were not interested in interrogating or torturing him—they did not even ask his name—so much as in looking at him tied to a tree. Always great fun.

BACK AT THE SCULPTURE, the mood gradually mellowed from nervy horror to stunned fascination. The good spirits engendered by spirits had been tempered by the wreck, and if the party was not over, it had certainly slipped into remission.

"Fun while it lasted," Parker said. He straightened his ascot, then his watch chain.

Phillip asked if Parker wouldn't like to come up to the hotel for a late-night toddy. Parker politely refused, saying he had better check on Bubby.

"Oh, Lawsy me," Phillip said. "Miss Gabrel?"

"I think I'd like to see this," Carolina Gabrel said. She was looking off toward Bubby and his captors departing, her eyes searching the space they had abandoned, her mouth cutting an oddly mischievous grin, as if there were some secret she kept about her own curiosity, more to her interest than she would ever tell.

"Trust me, honey," Phillip said. "It's nothing you haven't already seen on the Discovery channel. You know, Primate Week?"

"Still," Carolina said. She was not looking at Phillip or Parker but off still, in the direction of Bubby and company. She looked ready to get moving, to go after them.

"Oh, all right," Phillip said, with what seemed to be feigned reluctance. Then, as the three of them started across the park to the site of Bubby's incarceration, "If we must."

When at last the three located Parker's brother-in-law, they found him tied to a tree in a seated position. His captors sat in lawn chairs around the tree, drinking and laughing. Bubby seemed relatively calm about the whole affair—until, that is, he recognized the man come to see him, at which point he scowled bitterly at Parker and struggled against the rope without success. "Easy, son," the largest of the sportsmen said. He weighed two 250 pounds, easy. "Ain't goin' nowhere. I told you."

Laughing, Bubby's wardens turned to Parker's crew. Mainly they turned to Carolina Gabrel.

"Bubby," Parker said. "What's this all about?"

Bubby refused to acknowledge him.

"He ain't feeling real talky at the moment," said the big sportsman. Another round of laughter and the big one turned to Parker. "His name's Bubby, huh?"

"Bubby McGaw. My brother-in-law."

The big one studied Parker for a long, rather uncomfortable moment. "Parker?" he said.

"Yeah?"

"Parker Hathaway?"

"Yeah?"

"Well, goddamn, I reckon," said the big one, and he stood up and extended his hand. "Kirk. Kirk Ashley."

"Kirk Ashley." Of course. He took the hand but quickly regretted doing so: Kirk tugged him close for a bear hug and a slap on the back that nearly knocked the wind out of him.

"Ain't seen you in a coon's age, son!" said Kirk.

He hadn't, it was true. Several years, at least. Enough time for Kirk to take on a hundred pounds, a third chin, and, strangest of all, this Geechee shrimper accent. Kirk was not a Geechee shrimper. He was an Ashley. Heir not only to Bounty, one of the oldest plantations on the continent, but to one of the newest fortunes in the state—the Livin' Past Enterprises, which had owned several tour companies (bus, van, carriage, walking, and harbor) and half a dozen local hotels and restaurants before Kirk's grandfather sold the whole affair to a Saudi Arabian investment group. The group had kept the younger generation of Ashleys on as "domestic cultural advisors," liaisons between historical Charleston and global finance. So no, Kirk Ashley was not a Geechee shrimper. Kirk Ashley was a multimillionaire. A multimillionaire who said *ain't*.

"The hell you been up to, son? Still in Hotlanta?"

"Savannah."

"Savannah," Kirk said. Even as he addressed Parker, he kept shifting a hungry eye toward Carolina Gabrel. Understandable, Parker thought, but gross even so. "Goddamn, I reckon. We's just talkin' about doin' business in Savannah. How 'bout that?"

How about it, indeed. "Well," Parker said. Then, eager to leave the subject, "You remember Phillip Lawson."

Kirk turned to Phillip. "Little Philly!" he said. He extended his hand, grinned. But the grin seemed oddly rigid. Forced.

Phillip was not so enthusiastic himself, and for good reason: Kirk had not been terribly kind to Phillip growing up. Quite cruel, in fact. Suffice it to say Bubby McGaw was not the first man Kirk Ashley had tied to a tree.

As though recognizing the memory in Phillip's expression, Kirk backed off a step before Phillip could introduce Carolina. He then surveyed the three of them, nodding rapid little I-see-how-it-is nods, his expression stuck somewhere between a hard grin and a hard squint. Finally he turned back to Bubby, who had not looked at any of them once during the entire conversation.

"So, this the rascal married Liza?" Kirk asked.

"It is."

"Well, why didn't he say so? Lize Hathway's old man. Crazier than a damn coot! Goddamn, I reckon. No offense, Park."

Still Bubby looked away.

"You want us to let the crazy rascal go? Huh, Park?"

Parker said that he would appreciate it, and despite the objections of his fellow sportsmen, Kirk moved to untie the rope. But as he approached, Bubby McGaw fixed a stern look on him and shook his head no.

"What, you crazy sumbitch?" Kirk said.

"Leave me tied," said Bubby. He scowled at Parker's crew, then at Kirk again.

"Beg pardon?" Kirk said.

"I won't be saved by that man."

"What man?"

"That one."

"Park?"

"Leave me tied. I won't be saved by him."

"You hear this, Park?" Kirk said.

"Come on, Bubby," said Parker. "Let's get you home to bed."

"Wouldn't you like to," Bubby said.

"What? Come on. There's trouble about."

"Trouble," said Bubby, and then he laughed a short, haunting laugh. "You don't even know."

"What don't I know?"

Bubby shook his head, looked off. "Leave me tied. I won't be saved by him."

"Well, Park?" Kirk said, turning to Parker.

"The hell with it," Parker said. "Leave him tied."

"All right, then. You folks want a beer?"

Parker said thanks, but no.

"You sure?" Kirk said.

"Yeah. You won't hurt him, will you?"

"Naw, we ain' gon' hurt him," Kirk chuckled. "We just gon' watch him."

Parker looked at Bubby again and said, "I'll leave the door unlocked."

Bubby would not look at him. "I'm sure you will," he said.

Parker didn't know what to make of this—any of it—and it was with some hesitation that he said his good-byes to Kirk and Kirk's associates. He did not like to leave things undone. But things were undone all over the place tonight. He would have to accept things undone.

"Fruitcake," Phillip said as the three of them left the strange scene.

"Which one?" Carolina asked.

"All of them!"

Carolina made a note in her book, then wondered aloud if they shouldn't check into the rumor that was going around, which had the entire peninsula adrift at sea. Parker and Phillip agreed, they most definitely should check into this, and so when they came to King Street, they turned left, south, toward the water.

As it turned out, they were some time in reaching Bay Street, because King presented a swarm of humanity so thick they could not have escaped it even had they wanted to. The festival was not over at all. It had simply moved to the clubs and bars, which quickly filled to capacity and spilled gangs of revelers back into the street. The cobblestones thumped with Moby, swirled with Gotan, churned with Marilyn Manson. Young entrepreneurs sold cold beer from their lemonade stands; boiled-peanut hawkers and hot-dog vendors ran through stock.

"Fucking A!" said Carolina Gabrel, pointing at the flats above. From the windows, college kids were waving enormous Budweiser and NASCAR flags, hooting and hollering.

"Tow us your shits!" a student screamed—then vomited. A cascade of bile and what looked to be half-digested pizza splashed onto the sidewalk and sent the crowd scattering. Despite the collective boo-and-hiss from below, the young man proceeded to gather himself, rub his mouth with his wrist, and revise his request. "Show us yer tits!" he hollered hoarsely.

Carolina Gabrel scowled at this, but Phillip beamed. He peeled his shirt up to reveal a perfectly hairless, thoroughly ripped chest and then commenced a rather provocative dance in the street, the sight of which seemed to stun the drunken student. The young man glared at Phillip's display for a long moment, then squinted hard and extended his keg cup, as if preparing to pronounce some profound judgment from on high. "You goddamn—" he started and then seized up and vomited again. He produced more a rivulet than a cascade this time around, but not for lack of tortured effort.

"Lovely!" Phillip cheered. "You beautiful boy!"

At this, Carolina clutched Phillip by the arm, then Parker. For protection, Parker thought. The lady wanted protection. But he could not have been more mistaken: Carolina Gabrel took complete charge and, as if she had been assigned to lead the two men in some dark pagan ritual, began swinging and twirling them through the boisterous crowd. For Parker, the dance became a swirling montage of faces, some distorted and ghoulish, others clownish and delightful. The three of them twirled and swung, Carolina and Phillip laughing the entire way, Parker doing his best to simply hold on—to his ascot, to his hat, to his mind—until at last she swung them off the chaotic street and into the relative order of a nightclub.

Relative indeed. Because whether she had meant to or not, Carolina had chosen King Street's premier gay club, the Outhouse, as their escape. Parker knew of the place, but he had never actually patronized it. Not his scene.

Definitely Phillip's, though. If there were any lingering doubts as to Phillip's new lifestyle, Parker's short time in the Outhouse cleared them up. No sooner were they inside the club than Phillip gleefully took to the dance floor. Up came his shirt again—up and off. In deference, Parker supposed, to the rest of the dancers, few of whom were wearing shirts, and nearly all of whom were bronzed, cut, and male. When Carolina joined them, they seemed to welcome her as an amusing curiosity, little more.

Parker looked about awkwardly. It was fine and well for Phillip to have come out. Good for him. But did he have to come so far out? Straight out the closet, off the porch, and into—well, into the Outhouse. Aptly named, the club. Every move on the dance floor suggesting some bodily function. And Phillip and Carolina literally in the middle of it, forming the center of a lascivious hurricane. Parker edged to the bar and ordered a gin and tonic.

"Stiff?" the bartender asked between his own tornadic gyrations, which incorporated martini shakers, minibottles, and various fruits.

"Beg your pardon?" Parker said.

"Wanna stiff one?"

"I'd like a drink, if you don't mind."

"A stiff drink? It's free-pour tonight. All out at the Outhouse."

The bartender gestured to a promotional poster behind him. Under the headline ALL OUT AT THE OUTHOUSE, a list of drink specials included free-pour gins and bourbons, "Pole Positions," "Wet Woodies," "Slippery Slopes." Below this, a finely detailed watercolor pictured two men in Rebel uniforms sitting on a horse. They were facing the wrong direction, sitting crotch-to-fanny, and grinning mischievously. Beside the horse's mouth someone had drawn a word bubble: "Confederates Gone Wild!"

"He*llo*?" the bartender said.

"Oh, why, yes," Parker said. "Yes. I'd like a stiff one."

The bartender winked. "I get off at two," he said. "You?"

Before Parker could respond, the bartender danced off to the other end of the bar, and whether Parker had successfully ordered a drink or not, he couldn't say.

No matter. He was done with the Outhouse. He glanced in the direction of the dance floor. Carolina was now heading a conga line, with Phillip bringing up the rear—or rears, as it were. Parker would wait for them outside.

He stepped away from the bar, but a hand gripped his arm and pulled him back.

"Hathaway!"

The grip was firm, the voice tough. Parker turned to find himself facing his high-school PE teacher, Coach Remley. Remley was totally bald now and even plumper. If the man hadn't been wearing his coach clothes—tight polyester bike shorts and matching shirt, track cleats, even a whistle and a stopwatch—Parker might not have recognized him at all. Especially not here.

"Coach Remley?"

"Hathaway!" Coach Remley said, and then he pulled Parker close for a big bear hug.

Recalling the weekly "jockstrap checks" in high school, Parker obliged uneasily.

"Hathaway!" Coach Remley said again. "What was the first name?"

"Parker," said a voice from beside Coach Remley. "Parker Hathaway."

Parker turned. Seated at the bar, clutching a cocktail, was— Tobron Haynely? Sixteen-Bay-Street Tobron Haynely? Husband-of-Melinda Tobron Haynely? Father of Robert and Louise? Impassioned crusader, in editorial after vicious editorial, for Family Values?

"Mr. Haynely?" said Parker, and instinctively he offered his hand.

Mr. Haynely did not offer his. Apparently the man's sense of propriety had gone the way of his public op-ed persona tonight. "Don't look so surprised," he said, somewhat bitterly. In fact Mr. Haynely hadn't checked to see how Parker looked at all. He was studying the business on the dance floor—by turns grinning at it and scowling.

"Parker Hathaway!" Coach Remley said. He gripped Parker by the shoulder. "At the Outhouse! Didn't know you—you know."

"I don't—" Parker stammered. "I mean, I'm not—"

"Whatcha drinking, stud?"

When Coach Remley turned to flag the bartender, Parker made for the door.

OUTSIDE, PARKER ADJUSTED his boater, straightened his ascot, and considered the scene before him. Dear Charleston, awash in a river of booze. Things were not letting up at all. He observed a rickshaw trying to make its way through the madcap throng, the two enormous passengers griping loudly. They looked to be sisters, twinned in rancor and heft. Parker's heart went out to the driver. Over the years the rickshaw boys—college kids, mostly—had seemed to get thinner and thinner, while their passengers got chubbier and chubbier. If thermodynamics could explain the trend easily enough, that was small consolation for the kid at the pedals. Farther up the street, a horse carriage, too, struggled with the usual load, the tour guide no doubt taking the customary liberties with history.

It was as disturbing a scene as Parker had witnessed in a very long time, and had not Carolina soon joined him on the sidewalk, he might have gone so far as to step back into the Outhouse. But Carolina did walk out the door—or burst out, really, with two well-tanned men in tow. She was speaking rapid Spanish and laughing loudly with the men; after half a dozen kisses and *ciao*s, she saw them off. Then she pulled her notepad from her pocket and began to write. When she asked Parker what he was doing, the question seemed an afterthought.

"Thought we were going to Bay Street," Parker said. "For a porch sit."

"Oh, right," said Carolina without looking up from her work.

Was it really possible to take notes and make conversation at the same time? Or was she perhaps taking notes on the conversation itself?

"Shall we?" Parker said.

"Phillip ran into somebody," said Carolina. "Some coach?"

"Yeah. Some coach."

"He's wondering where you went."

"Who is?"

"Phillip, silly."

"He'll figure it out," said Parker. "I thought we were going down to the water."

"All right. Don't get your panties in a wad," said Carolina. She slipped her notepad back into her pocket and kissed Parker on the cheek. "I'll go get him."

Panties in a wad? Parker had half a mind to leave both of them. Then again, there was that peck on the cheek. That counted for something. Didn't it?

THIS TIME PARKER TOOK THE LEAD, so as to prevent any further diversions. Behind him, Phillip and Carolina walked arm in arm. Phillip wouldn't shut up about Coach Remley. How much friendlier he was to Phillip now. How hilarious the evolution was, from tormenter to suitor. How the man had, yes, come on to him. Strongly.

"As if!" Phillip cackled. "What a goon! He stank! Like—jock itch!"

Carolina laughed. Parker did not. He thought it best not to inquire how it was that Phillip had come to be wearing Tobron Haynely's linen jacket, which was obscenely tight on him. There were some things—at this point, quite a few things—best left unknown.

At last they made their way out the other end of the occasion, onto lower King. The shopping district, in stark contrast to upper King, was utterly dark and still. They passed the Omni and its various storefronts—Gap and Baby Gap, Banana Republic, the Sunglass Hut, Pottery Barn, HOME. The window dressings in each store offered a thematic nod to the Bravado Festival or the Jamboree, some to both. Approaching Victoria's Secret, Parker fully expected to find a display of camouflaged thongs and garter belts. But no. Lingerie didn't need to nod.

At the corner of King and Market, Phillip paused to gaze at the Saks Fifth Avenue. "The new Saks!" he said.

"Disgusting," said Parker.

"Beautiful!" said Phillip.

Parker grimaced. "Should call it Saks King Street. Or just kick it out altogether."

Phillip pinched Parker on the ear. "So adorable when he's mossbacked and bitter!" he said. "Anyway, I think it's fabulous. Just fabulous. Bring this backass old town into the world."

Parker stepped away from Phillip's attentions. "Hardly matters now. I mean, we may be in the middle of the damn ocean."

"So they say," Phillip said. "I'll see that when I believe it. I mean, no—believe it when I see it."

The three were in agreement: they needed to look into this floating-out-to-sea rumor. They cut left on Broad Street, east toward the Battery, the water. The law office district was darker and quieter still than the shopping district. No one was about.

There were, however, flags about. Up and down the street, from railings, thresholds, and gates, an assortment of flags whipped and rapped eerily in the gusts.

"What in God's name?" Parker said.

"Would you look at them all," Carolina Gabrel said. She was jotting feverishly now.

"Is that—the Tricolor?" Phillip said.

It was. Strung from the second-story porch of the French Huguenot Society, the national standard of France.

"The Huguenots were expelled from France," Carolina said. "Weren't they?"

"Never seen them fly the flag, that's for sure," said Parker.

Indeed he hadn't; by city ordinance, flags were prohibited on Broad Street. The rule had been passed in the wake of a particularly heated dispute involving the Daughters of the American Revolution at 3 Broad and Bill McCutchenson, proprietor of the Confederate Museum at 4 Broad. When the DAR had first moved into number 3, they hung an old colonial American flag from the second story. McCutchenson, at once offended and inspired, responded with a flag of his own: the Confederate battle flag. McCutchenson's display naturally created a great deal of commotion. A year's worth, to be exact. For months the editorial pages of the *Current* had burned with debate. Some demanded removal and burning of the flag; some demanded a sculpture to honor McCutchenson; and an occasional few demanded that attention be paid to more pressing issues, such as equine sanitation. The NAACP threatened to boycott the city if the flag didn't come down; the Sons of Confederate Veterans threatened to sue the city if it did. McCutchenson, who was from Indiana, could never have imagined, when he moved to the city two years earlier, the celebrity he would earn for himself. Through protest and rant he let the flag fly, arguing First Amendment rights and pointing, in interview after interview, to the old colonial flag across the street. At last, after more than a dozen fruitless emergency sessions, city council ruled that no flags would be flown over Broad Street, period. If this was not the most constitutional way to settle the dispute, it did seem the most effective way to settle it. And the dispute did have to be settled. It was, statistics had begun to show, costing the city visitors.

So no, as many times as he had strolled down Broad, as many debutante balls and cocktail parties as he had attended at the Huguenot Society, Parker had never seen the French flag flown from the porch. He had never seen the Stars and Bars strung from the third story of the old Confederate Home, either, but yonder the colors flew. And from the steps of Ashley-Cooper Hall, a Union Jack. From the thresholds of the law offices, a whole variety of smaller-sized standards—a few American, a dozen South Carolina, a half dozen Scottish, several Irish, three Gadsden Don't Tread On Me's, an Italian, even one German. Down toward the end of Broad, Bill McCutchenson's Confederate battle flag, opposed across the street by the DAR's old colonial. Which Parker had seen done, but not in a very long time.

"What was the slogan?" Carolina said. "Heritage, not Hate?"

"That was it," Phillip said. "Heritage, not Hate."

"All kinds of heritage going on tonight, huh?"

"I'll say," Phillip said.

"So much for unity," said Carolina, still writing. "Coming together in times of need. All that."

"Somebody's getting right serious about all this," Parker said. "Right serious."

At Battery Street the trio stopped for a last look at the congress of flags before turning right, toward the water. The colors jerking and whipping in the stout breeze filled each of them with a strangely nervous awe.

·VII·

OT TWO BLOCKS AWAY, down at the Atlantic Club, somebody was in fact getting right serious about all this. A meeting of the minds had been assembled on the club's harborside veranda. They were elderly minds, curmudgeonly minds set in hard heads, but determined minds. Commodore Harold Crumfield had called the club's vice-presidents—Murray DuChamp, Hathaway "Hat" Lawson, and Captain Sam Haynely—for an emergency session. In earlier centuries the city's fate had been decided on this same porch, in these same rocking chairs, over bourbon drinks sipped from these same tumblers; the decisions that most affected the peninsula were made not by publicly elected officials but by privately tapped club members. In more recent years the influence of the club's board had waned dramatically, but its members, if they were no longer able to command the course the town would take, were always eager to map and discuss the course it had. That is, generally, to map and denounce the course it had taken. That course, after all, had left this, the oldest, most exclusive yacht club on the continent, all but powerless. Times had most certainly changed in the last century, and not for the better.

Now it seemed the times were changing again. Whether they were changing for the better or worse, none of those gathered could yet say. What could be said, what was certain, is that the peninsula's current tack was beyond the control of those powers which had over the years robbed the club of its own. If the board members weren't at all sure what they might do about the current situation, they took no small pleasure in the fact that their usual adversaries were equally powerless. The mayor couldn't do a thing, nor could city council: they weren't even on board. The South Carolina State House, always overprotective of upstate interests, lay some five hundred miles distant, and Washington, D.C., the federals, historically the most resented power of all, over a thousand miles distant. If none of those seated here had ever much cared for democratization—of education, of wealth, of influence—none could argue that for once the phenomenon seemed to be serving them. This sudden equalization of power— or powerlessness, really—this democratization of impotency, meant if nothing else a blank slate, a fair playing field. And a fair playing field, a fair start, that meant a chance—no, a responsibility—for the well-blooded to once again rise to the top, seize the reins, and establish their rightful, God-beknighted place at the helm.

If, that is, they could find a helm.

They would be well advised to find one; that much was certain. Captain Sam Haynely, who sat on the board of both the Atlantic Club and the Harbor Pilots' Association, had been plotting the course of the peninsula throughout the evening by way of a jury-rigged card table navstation. (His stack included weather radar, a chartplotter GPS, and a VHF, all salvaged from the pilots' supply shed next door. He'd mounted a whip antenna, a GPS receiver ball, and a radome on the railing, giving the veranda the aspect of a ship's bridge.) Captain Sam's readings were anything but consistent: no sooner had a heading been determined than it shifted again. One moment the old port city was steaming hard for San Juan; the next moment it was floundering toward Monrovia. Captain Sam's most recent reading suggested a heading that would land the peninsula in Bermuda.

"Bermuda," said Murray DuChamp, rocking backwards to toss down what was left of his fifth bourbon. "Nev' been to Bermuda."

At the rail, looking hard out to the dark, stirring sea and gathering squalls, Commodore Crumfield tightened his jaw. "I'm guessing you aren't going to Bermuda now," he said. "The way this thing is going."

"Well, it's a damn shame, Harold," DuChamp said. "Cynthia always wanted to go to Bermuda." Yes, Cynthia had always wanted to go to Bermuda, but in fact Murray DuChamp, right buzzed, was hoping for a turn due east, for France. He had Huguenot blood and was certain he would find warm welcome in France, perhaps even an estate-in-waiting. The liquor on his brain, of course, provided him a great deal more faith in the dream than he had a right to.

"I don't think you get it, Murray," said Commodore Crumfield. He glanced over his shoulder at his three vice-presidents: Murray DuChamp, drunk; Hat Lawson, near-drunk; and Captain Sam Haynely, obsessing with the instruments that could only map a course, not determine one. "We could end up in goddamn Africa," Crumfield said. "Do you understand me? Africa! Ring any bells? Huh? Gentlemen?"

"Not pleasant bells, Harold, no," said Hat Lawson. "But I'm not at all sure we need to get in a fuss over this. If we keep our heads about us—"

"Keep our heads about us!" Commodore Crumfield spat. He shook his own head furiously but did not turn. "Jolly good job we're doing of keeping our heads about us! Murray is well nigh potted!"

"Now, Harold," said Hat. "I'm sure this is going to work out. Really."

Commodore Crumfield turned and looked hard at Hat Lawson. "How in the hell? Huh, Hat?"

"Well. Let's just not get in a fuss. That's no way to go about it."

"How can you sit there like that, Hat? So sure of yourself. Huh? At a time like this?"

"Must be in my blood."

"Pff. Your blood. I'll show you your goddamn blood."

"A duel!" Murray DuChamp hollered. "Fetch the sidearms!"

"Your blood isn't any bluer than mine," Commodore Crumfield said to Hat, and then he turned away again.

"Come on, Harold," said Hat. "I wasn't saying that."

In fact, if he wasn't saying that, Hat Lawson was thinking it. That his blood, really, had a better shot in the Old World than anybody else's. He could trace it through some two dozen plantations and on back across the pond to Essex County, England, from which land his earliest stateside ancestors had not been banished but, rather, properly blessed. The early Lawson plantations—Brick Point, the Bank, Appletree—had all been established through royal land grants, while the early Haynely holdings and yes, dare he say, even the early Crumfield holdings, had been seized from the wilderness outlaw style, by ingrate orphan Haynelys and Crumfields who had been kicked out of England for all manner of crimes. As for the DuChamps, well, they had not even hailed from the proper side of the Channel.

Yes, Hat Lawson knew his history and everyone else's. And it was what he knew that afforded him his relative calm in this, the most unusual and uncertain of situations. Hat was not uncertain at all. In time, with the will of God and the push of history behind it, the peninsula would shape itself up and make a proper course back to the motherland that had hatched it so many centuries ago. Awaiting Hat there, landed cousins whom he knew, in fact, quite well. With whom he had been pheasant shooting in Scotland only a few months ago. No, Hat Lawson was not overly concerned about the current course. Offended by Commodore Crumfield's rather rude display, maybe, but not overly concerned about the current course.

At the railing, Commodore Crumfield stood very much concerned. They were getting nowhere. Moving right along through the Atlantic at some twenty knots and getting nowhere. "Murray," he said, hoping against hope that the one-time ace defense attorney hadn't yet stewed what was left of his wits and that he might offer some semblance of direction before losing himself entirely to the drink. "What are you thinking about all this?"

"I'm thinking about another bourbon, goddammit!" Murray DuChamp said.

"I bet you are," said Commodore Crumfield, resigned.

"Then you win! Where's our boy? CJ! CJ Lawson!"

Murray DuChamp rocked back and pulled the bar bell, and CJ Lawson, who was not a boy at all but a seventy-four-year-old man who had been working for the club since the age of twelve, appeared with a bourbon drink in hand and offered it to Mr. DuChamp. The chore finished, he began to turn away, but DuChamp stopped him.

"CJ," said DuChamp. "Where you think we're headed? Huh, son?"

"I couldn't say, Mr. DuChamp."

"You couldn't? Well, why not?"

"Because I don't know, Mr. DuChamp."

"Hah. Good one." Murray DuChamp knocked back a long pull and looked over to Hat Lawson. "Cousin pulled a funny, Hat. How about it?"

"Now, Murray. Let's take care," Hat Lawson said. He was not protesting the "cousin" jab so much—he did not have to protest the cousin jab so much. There was an old joke about that, and it had been told countless times in this very same company: CJ might be a cousin of Hat's, but Hat was in no way a cousin of CJ's. Mostly Hat was protesting Murray DuChamp's public cruelty. No place for that kind of behavior in polite, civilized society. Honestly.

"Where you want to go, CJ?" DuChamp jabbed on.

"I don't know, Mr. DuChamp."

"Might be headed to Africa, CJ. What about that? Would you like that?"

"I couldn't say, Mr. DuChamp."

"Because you've never been," DuChamp laughed. "Now I played a funny on you, CJ. But really. You might like Africa. Hmm? Don't you think? What do you say?"

"I couldn't say, Mr. DuChamp."

"Because you've—"

"That'll be all, CJ," Commodore Crumfield interrupted. He'd had it. As soon as CJ was through the door the Commodore crossed to DuChamp's rocker, leaned in, and took it by the armrests with a severe grip. He stood inches from DuChamp's face. "For God's sake, you Froguenut son of a bitch," he said. "Can you keep your goddamn mouth shut?"

"Whoaaa, Cap'n," Murray DuChamp said. He did not look away, eager as he seemed to want to.

"You want to get them riled up? Huh?"

"Who?"

"The goddamn darkies, fool," said Commodore Crumfield.

"CJ's harmless, Cap. Really. He won't cause trouble. He's harmless."

"He is, but his kids aren't." Commodore Crumfield pushed himself back from the rocker and began to pace gruffly in front of his three vice-presidents. DuChamp and Hat watched him uneasily; Captain Sam, headphoned, completely oblivious of the goings on around him, continued his work with the GPS and the charts.

"CJ's boy? Anthony?" Commodore Crumfield asked. "You want to get him all riled up? Huh? This is just the excuse he goddamn needs!"

"To do what, Harold?" Hat asked.

"To—goddamn—rise up! To take the streets! What about that big, black johnson in Calhoun Square? Huh? What do you think that means?"

"The what?" DuChamp asked.

"Just an overindulged artist getting his jollies," Hat said, and he grinned at Crumfield.

"I guess I don't find it quite so 'jolly' as you do, Hat," Crumfield said. "For Christ's sake. There's no law, boys! There's no nothing! We're adrift! Do you read me?'

It seems they did. Or the two who were paying attention did, anyway. DuChamp and Hat sat staring at Commodore Crumfield—DuChamp, slack jawed, and Hat, stern eyed.

That is, concerned.

At last Hat snapped the spell. He shook his head and looked off. "I think we're okay with them, Harold," he said. "Really. Anthony's boycott, for one thing. That worked out well. And we haven't heard anything from him, have we? He's been right quiet so far. Through all this. Hasn't he?"

Commodore Crumfield turned to the railing again and gazed out at the gathering squall. "That's what scares me, gentlemen. That's what scares me." He paused, then, "Captain Sam! Where we headed now?"

Captain Sam, completely engrossed in his charts and monitoring a ragged transmission from an oil tanker some forty miles off, did not look up. So Commodore Crumfield approached the jury-rigged navigation bay, pulled the left headphone out from Captain Sam's ear, and hollered, "Anything new for us, Sam?"

Captain Sam pulled the headphones to his neck and looked up at Crumfield, then over at DuChamp and Hat. "I'm thinking maybe a sail." he said. "A big sail."

"A sale?" Commodore Crumfield asked.

"Of what?" said DuChamp.

"Waterfront property?" said Hat.

Captain Sam said, "A *sail.* Canvas. Or whatever we could engineer. Run it from St. Michael's steeple, down to the port authority cranes. Or from St. Michael's to St. Philip's. Depending on which tack we want to take. Where we want to go."

"You can't be serious, Sam," said the Commodore.

In fact, Captain Sam was serious. With no means of steering the vessel, with only the means to read where the vessel was steering itself, he had, essentially, been reduced from the rank of harbormaster to navigator. Lower than navigator, really—at this point, he could not plot a course and relay it to the helmsman. There was no helmsman. Captain Sam was tiring of the subordinate, all but useless role, fast.

"I am serious," he said. "A big sail."

"A big sail," Commodore Crumfield said. "Ludicrous. Where the hell we headed, is what I was asking."

"For the moment, Barbados."

"Barbados?"

"Barbados. Roger that," Captain Sam said.

"Oh, for God's sake," Commodore Crumfield said. "Bar-goddamn-bados. Isn't that delightful!" Out of patience and faith—in his crew, in his club, in his peninsula—he threw back what was left of his drink and pulled the bar bell for another. Commodore Crumfield was not a man to surrender easily, but the times were proving especially stubborn, and drink did lend some legitimacy, some sense of empowerment, to impotence. If you were drinking, you had not resigned yourself to the fates so much as embraced them, however roundaboutly, however stumblingly. Let the wind and water do as they will, you'll be singing fucking sea chanteys.

CJ Lawson appeared with Commodore Crumfield's drink. With the weight of Crumfield's Black Power talk still lingering, the white men grew quiet—no laughter with the old man, however patronizing, no jokes, no thank-yous, no nothing. Instead they eyed the man with suspicion. Particularly Murray DuChamp. Commodore Crumfield's talk had not only sobered him but unnerved him. He had never asked for the black problem. He felt sure there was no black problem in France. If they could get to France before the black problem here became a problem, there would be no problem. He felt sure.

Of course, they were headed to Barbados.

In a subdued voice, leaning in toward Hat and the Commodore, DuChamp said, "What will we do with them in Barbados?"

"What?" asked Commodore Crumfield. "With who?"

"The nigras."

Commodore Crumfield took a long pull. "What the hell are we going to do in Barbados, Murray? Huh? I don't know what we're going to do with them. I'm wondering what they're going to do with us. You understand me?"

"I think I'm starting to," DuChamp said.

"To hell with it," said Commodore Crumfield. "Let's drink." He raised his glass to the wind. "To not knowing where in the good hell we're going and not giving a flyin' wharf rat's ass about it!"

DuChamp grinned at Commodore Crumfield, then raised his glass and did what he could to second the toast: "To knowing where not in the flying hell we're giving and not going a good rat's wharf ass about it! Come on, Hat!"

He tried to engage Hat Lawson in the toast, but Hat only sipped once from his drink and looked off. He had been considering the situation—Barbados and colored people—from a historical perspective. In fact, the historical perspective lent the situation some cause for optimism, if his cohorts here would only think into it a little.

Hat began, "If you gentlemen knew your history, or remembered it, you'd understand that, really, Barbados might suit us right nicely."

"What?" DuChamp asked.

"Sure. You've heard of the old Atlantic Trading Triangle?"

"The do-what?" said Commodore Crumfield.

"Well, then you haven't." Hat resisted the urge to criticize Commodore Crumfield for his ignorance of things historical. Not everyone was fortunate enough to have been raised in a historically minded household; Hat knew that, but there were some things a proper Charlestonian should know. Particularly, historical facts pertaining to proper Charlestonians. Of course, the Crumfields had not always been proper Charlestonians. (And as for DuChamp, wanting to go back to France as a proud Huguenot— one could only hope, for his sake, that the French did not know their history any better than he did.) At any rate, Hat resisted the urge to criticize and instead took the opportunity to teach.

"In the old days, Barbados served as a kind of stopover point," he said. "Slave merchants followed the trade winds from Africa to the island and sold the slaves to traders from the colonies. The slaves that fell ill during the crossing or caused trouble, they were simply abandoned in Barbados. The rest, the strong ones, they came here. To us."

"Well goody for them," Commodore Crumfield said. "What does that do for us now? Huh, Hat? Those days are over. If you haven't noticed."

"I've noticed!" said DuChamp.

Hat continued, "If they want to cause trouble, as you're saying they might, why not drop them off in Barbados? The way we used to, only going the other way. It could even be seen as an act of kindness. After all, most of them have got family there, whether they know it or not. I've got family there, Harold."

"You and CJ," Commodore Crumfield said. He was not buying.

"Well. So to speak. Yes. CJ would have relations there, and so would I."

"Well isn't that just jimdiddlydandy, Hat!" DuChamp jumped in. "You and all the happy Lawson Negroes sittin' on a beach sipping blue drinks from coconut shells! That's just by-God jimdiddlydandy!"

"I wouldn't be so quick to dismiss, Murray," said Hat. "There's a Huguenot presence on the island. Not a big one, but even so."

"Honestly?"

"Sure. And the island's right lovely in the winter months, I've been told. We wouldn't be drinking from coconut shells, either. I dare say my relations are living in some exquisite old colonials and still speak the Queen's English."

"You would stay, then?" Commodore Crumfield said.

"Well, I would look into it. If necessary. Maybe a long vacation in an old relative's house. Why not?"

Commodore Crumfield shook his head and looked back out to the sea. "A vacation. In times like this. That's just like a goddamn Lawson."

"Well, what do you propose, Harold?"

"All I'm saying is it must be nice to have relations in foreign ports," Commodore Crumfield said, with no small bitterness. "Must be damn nice."

"It's nice to know I do. Sure. But you might, too. You just don't know it. You haven't studied your history. You'd be surprised, Harold. You'd be surprised where you find your people."

"Don't you tell me what I've studied. Don't you tell me about my—" Commodore Crumfield stopped, his attention turned by some activity in the parking lot below them. It looked to be three individuals headed, rather shamelessly, for the club pier. "For God's sake, would you look at that," Commodore Crumfield said. "It's started. Anybody recognize them?"

"Not from here," Hat said.

"I don't recognize them," said Commodore Crumfield. "It's anarchy. Like I was saying."

"That's a long-legged woman, I recognize that," Murray DuChamp said.

"It is," said Hat. It was. Long-legged and well crafted, with a walk like a panther. "But what's that other one? A man or a woman?"

"Awful thin in the hips for a woman," Commodore Crumfield noted.

"Awful long in the hair for a man," said Murray DuChamp. "And look at the other now! Skipping along! That is a man. Isn't it? Twirling around like a little girl!"

"You see? This is what I'm talking about! They're taking over! Like they always wanted! Time was, we could call the police! Not anymore!"

"Don't need the police for them," Murray DuChamp said. "We could take them. I know we could."

"We might drop them in Barbados," Hat suggested. "As I was saying. If they cause trouble, we'll simply leave them in Barbados. But they don't seem up to trouble, really."

"Could be insurgents! Enemy combatants!" Crumfield said. "Hey!" he hollered. "You freak-nuts want to get dropped off in Barbados?"

But with all the wind and roar of the swells, the three below could not hear him hailing. Or if they could, they were flat-out ignoring him because they continued their way to the club pier.

"We'll get them," said Commodore Crumfield. "We can take those old swords from the display case downstairs. We'll get them and hold them hostage, and then we'll leave them in Barbados, by God. Come on."

But before anyone could make a move, Captain Sam spoke up. "We're not headed to Barbados anymore," he said.

The three turned to him. His headphones were hung down around his neck, and he looked, well, worried.

"Well?" Crumfield asked. "Where we headed?"

"Cape Verde."

AT THE END OF THE CLUB PIER, Parker, Phillip, and Carolina came face to face with the swelling storm. Breakers were crashing against the pilings, frothy plumes blasting skyward before cascading over the pier's edge. Parker watched as his two companions embraced the surge. Carolina, after placing her notepad in Parker's care, ran into the falling water with the glee of a child, and Phillip stepped up with the cocky sidle of a matador meeting his bull. Carolina twirled under the spray, a delightful spinning dance, while Phillip met it with his chest. Parker watched the two at a safe, dry distance. In no time, his companions were drenched and quite happy about it.

"Wheeeee-hooooo!" Carolina squealed. Still she spun, her long dark hair waving.

"I'm so fabulously alive! Alive!" Phillip hollered to the night. Without turning he said, "Come on, Park! Join us!"

Parker was thinking about it; he really might join them, ascot and pocket watch and notepad be damned. He might very well have joined them, but it was then, while he stood thinking about it and was just about to join them, that he was suddenly seized from behind, taken by the shoulders, and a long blade pressed to his jugular. A sword blade, if he wasn't mistaken.

"Private property, you people!" the voice of his captor boomed. Just as Carolina and Phillip turned, and before Parker could squeak, two figures appeared from behind him. Drunk figures, or perhaps elderly, or both. At any rate, they were not walking very straight lines. They were carrying coils of sheetline and poking what looked to be Confederate field swords at Carolina and Phillip in a threatening fashion. Perplexed, Phillip raised his hands in surrender. Carolina did not.

"What the hell is this?" she said. "A reenactment?"

At this, the man approaching her stopped. "That's no way for a lady to talk."

"Who said I was a lady?"

"You're damn sure shaped like one."

"That's enough, Murray," said Parker's captor. "Now, Hat—"

"Sorry?" said Parker.

"What?" Parker's captor said. "Lawson, you—"

"Yes?" said Phillip.

Confusion all around, then Phillip grinned. "Is that Hat?" he asked the man before him. "Hat Lawson?"

Hat Lawson? It could be. It could very well be. Confusion fell over the gathering and then a tremendous wave of water. All were soaked but none shifted.

"Who are you?" Hat Lawson, if that was Hat Lawson, asked.

"Why, I'm Phillip!" said Phillip. "Phillip Lawson!"

The man began to lower his sword, but before he could, Parker's captor barked, "Don't you dare, Hat! Doesn't look a thing like Phillip Lawson! Phillip Lawson was a—he was—"

"Queer!" said the man before Carolina. "I remember! Left town! Went queer! That's no Phillip Lawson! He's too—big!"

"Puh-leese, girls," said Phillip. "Get with it! I may be buff, and I may be tough, but I don't care a lick for the big bad muff! I'm Phillip!"

Parker thought Phillip might better tone down the gayness, for preservation's sake. Unabashed pride, he knew, was a sure way to lose any mileage they might gain through blood, through kinship. It was as though Phillip expected the old men to—what? Respect his pride? Internalize it? Embrace him?

Abruptly shed centuries of prejudice, thanks to a witty turn of phrase? Or perhaps Phillip was simply being Phillip. Perhaps he had spent too many years of his life hiding himself to ever do that again.

"I'm Phillip!" he repeated. "Ask my buddy, there! That's Parker Hathaway! Another cousin!"

All turned to look at Parker. Hat Lawson, indeed. And Murray DuChamp, if Parker wasn't mistaken.

"Another freak!" Murray DuChamp said. "Now I'll believe that! I'll believe that's Parker Hathaway! Look at him!"

They all most certainly were looking at him. Parker's captor shifted but did not loosen his hold or withdraw the sword. "That true?" the captor said.

"What true?" Parker squeaked.

"You Parker Hathaway?"

Parker nodded as best he could.

"Tell me how Hat's mother died, then," said the man. "You're Parker Hathaway, you'll know."

Phillip answered for him. "Bless her dear little heart," he said. "Fell off her third-story porch while yelling at a tourist carriage."

The sword fell away from Parker's throat; the grip slackened. Hat Lawson lowered his sword. Murray DuChamp did not. Wild-eyed as a rabid raccoon, he continued to poke his sword toward Carolina. "So who's she?"

"Carolina Gabrel," said Carolina.

"Gabrel," DuChamp said. "I don't know any Gabrel. What is it—German?"

Carolina grimaced at Murray DuChamp with a look of absolute disgust. "Spanish," she said.

"Wonderful, huh, Harold?" Murray DuChamp said. "Two freaks and a Spaniard!"

"I'm an American," Carolina protested.

"Sure you are, hon. Sure you are." DuChamp laughed bitterly. "What will we do with them? Huh, Harold?"

A good question, it seemed. Parker's captor, whom he guessed to be Commodore Crumfield, considered for a long moment before answering. At last he said, "Don't want any trouble with the Hathaway family or the Lawsons. We need the Hathaways and the Lawsons. But these two—I don't know. They aren't exactly representative. The question is, what are you people doing out here?"

"Walked out to look at this fabulous storm!" said Phillip.

As if he had not heard him, Murray DuChamp said, "And is it true that your kind is planning to take over the city?"

"Our *kind*?" Carolina said.

"Yes, your kind," said Murray DuChamp. "The queers and the Yanks and the nigras. You've just been waiting to, haven't you? All these years."

Apparently this was too much for Carolina. No sooner had DuChamp finished his little spiel than she spun a roundhouse one-eighty, kicking the sword from his hand and tripping him backwards onto his rear in one fluid motion. To the astonishment of all, she had the man cowering, sword tip pressed to his crotch, in a matter of seconds.

"Oh, my!" said Phillip.

"Drop your swords, gentlemen, or this man is a man no more," Carolina said. To make her resolve perfectly clear, she pressed the sword tip deeper into DuChamp's crotch.

There was no need for the display. As if they had been waiting all their lives for a beautiful woman to tell them what to do, Commodore Crumfield and Hat Lawson let their swords fall to the decking.

"Parker, Phillip," Carolina directed. "Take up your weapons."

Parker and Phillip took up the fallen swords and awkwardly turned them on their former captors.

"Now," said Carolina, "I want you two over here, with your big-mouthed little buddy."

Encouraged by Parker and Phillip—or rather, by Parker and Phillip's weapons—Commodore Crumfield and Hat Lawson joined Murray DuChamp on the decking. Carolina arranged the three older men in a small back-to-back circle, then called for Phillip to fetch the sheetline that had been dropped by Hat.

"Easy, son," Commodore Crumfield said to Parker. "It's the Commodore you're dealing with, here. This club's been right good to the Hathaways."

It was true. These were Charleston people. This was old Charleston he was getting ready to tie up. Commodore Crumfield, for God's sake. "Really, Carolina," he said. "There's no need to—"

"You're going to sit by and let these old bastards talk to you that way?" Carolina said.

"It's just how they are," said Parker. "They can't help it."

"We can't help it," Murray DuChamp said.

"Quiet!" Carolina said.

It was not easy to refuse her. Parker had not seen, or even imagined, this side of the woman. Ruthless, almost. But anyone who had accomplished as much as she had already, in so brief a life—maybe that took ruthlessness.

"Look at what you're doing, boys," Hat Lawson said as Parker and Phillip ran the rope around. Hat—and everyone else, for that matter—kept a watchful, nervous eye on Carolina. "Look who you're bullying," Hat said. "We're your people, boys. We're on your side. This is no time to be—"

"You are not on their side," Carolina said without changing her position. "And we are taking over the city. Remember?"

"Told you," Murray DuChamp grumbled. Then, to Parker and Phillip, "We're your people. It's shameful."

Parker could not go through with it, not even for Carolina. "I can't do this," he said. "Come on, Phillip. We don't need to do this."

"No?" said Carolina. "So what do you propose instead?"

"I don't know. Maybe a ceasefire? We'll go on our way and let them go on theirs. We'll all leave each other alone. What do you say?"

"Phillip?" asked Carolina. "You're willing to let them get away with this?"

"It is rather exciting," Phillip said. "Tying men up. I never knew. So much I could do with them! But alas . . ." He paused for a dramatic sigh. "I suppose I'm with Parker. Let's all just leave each other alone."

"Impressive loyalty," Carolina said. "If misguided." She shook her head. "All right, then. A ceasefire it is." She poked each of the sitting men with her sword. "A ceasefire, you understand? You are not to so much as breathe before we reach the end of that driveway."

"Yes, ma'am," said Hat Lawson.

Just before Parker turned he noticed two things: one, Murray DuChamp's giving Hat Lawson a wicked squint and two, Commodore Crumfield's going suddenly wide-eyed at something behind Parker and his companions.

"Well, if it isn't Captain Sam Haynely," the Commodore said.

And yes, when Parker and his companions turned they found themselves face to face with Captain Sam Haynely—and

Captain Sam Haynely's handgun. "Weapons down, kids," said Captain Sam Haynely. "Hands up."

Parker and Carolina did as they'd been told. Phillip did not.

"Captain Haynely!" he said, tugging at the lapel of his sport-jacket. "Your brother's jacket! Tobron! We just saw him! At—"

"Shut your mouth, boy," Captain Haynely spat, and to show he meant it, he fired a shot just to the side of Phillip.

Phillip shut his mouth and put his hands up.

"A ceasefire!" Murray DuChamp laughed behind them, and in short order their hands were being bound behind their backs.

"Assholes," Carolina said.

"What a mouth, hey, Sam?" DuChamp said.

"We're not trying to take over the city," Parker said.

"Sure you're not," Commodore Crumfield said, cinching the rope tight around Parker's wrist. "You people are a disgrace. To your blood and to your town. Let's go."

At gunpoint the three were led back up the drive and into the club, up the stairs and through the kitchen door. They were then bound together and made to sit in the middle of the kitchen floor, where they would remain for the rest of the night. It was a side of the club Parker had never seen before, a side he would now get to know quite well.

WHEN THE PRISONERS HAD BEEN secured in the makeshift brig, Commodore Crumfield and his vice-presidents dried off, moved to the veranda, and called up CJ for another round of drinks. Once they had settled in, the Commodore brought them directly back to the business at hand. "I'm wondering how we're going to take care of this little problem, gentlemen," he said. "This insurrection."

"We've got a good start, I'll say that," DuChamp said. "Thanks to Captain Sam, here."

Captain Sam made no reply. He had already taken his position and pulled his headphones on.

"It's bigger than those three goofballs," the Commodore said. "I'm sure of that. I wouldn't be at all surprised if the whole north side of the peninsula is in on it."

"It's possible," Hat said.

"So I want to hear some ideas. What are we going to do about this thing?"

They thought on it. And thought on it. And thought on it. At last DuChamp came up with a suggestion. "Well, why don't we do it the old-fashioned way?" he said.

"The old-fashioned way," the Commodore said.

"Secede, by damn!" DuChamp said. "We'll secede!"

They all agreed it was a fine idea. In theory, anyway. The problem was, how to go about it. And not just how to go about it, but how to make it work for the long haul. Because if history had taught them anything, it was that the act of secession itself was not enough. Secession had to stick. This time around, it would have to stick.

The board members considered again. In time, Hat posed a question. "Lehigh still around?" he said.

Reggie Lehigh, of Lehigh Marine Contracting, had been trying to get into the club for years, but being an *arriviste* from Myrtle Beach had found himself blackballed at each attempt, despite the fact—or perhaps because of the fact—that the booming marine construction business had made his family a substantial local power in recent years.

"I imagine he's around," Commodore Crumfield said. "So?"

"Well, a big dredge might come in handy," Hat said. "If we want to really secede. I mean, for good."

It took a moment, but then the Commodore and DuChamp could see what Hat was getting at: properly managed, a big dredge could cut the peninsula in two.

The Commodore's eyes brightened. "He does it right, we can split ourselves straight off," he said.

DuChamp cackled. "Never have to worry about the dark side of town again! And if we got that sail Captain Sam was talking about—hell, we'll be sitting pretty. Go wherever we want to go. Be our town again, boys! Hell!"

"Precisely," said Hat. "I'm guessing that if we offer him a membership, he'll hardly be in a position to refuse."

It wasn't a bad idea, and the Commodore said so. He did have a question, though: "How much would we take with us?"

"Do what?" DuChamp said.

"Where would we split off?"

Hat and DuChamp considered. "Queen Street might work," DuChamp said. "Nobody I want around lives above it, that's for sure."

"We'd lose a few churches that way," Hat noted. "St. Philip's, for one."

"Churches," said DuChamp. "I guess we could live without churches. If they aren't there, you aren't obliged to go. Sleep late on Sundays, come straight to the club! For brunch! Hey, Hat?"

"Oh, I don't know. A church is good to have. In case you need it."

"Well, we'd have St. Michael's, and First Scots, and the French Congregational. That covers Episcopalians and

Huguenots and Presbies, and I don't know any other kind that lives south of Queen. I'm voting we split at Queen."

"There are plenty of Catholics south of Queen, Murray," Hat said. "And Jews, and even a few Lutherans."

"Cumyah carpetbaggers," DuChamp said. "I can live without the damn cumyah carpetbaggers. You, Harold?"

"I'm sure we could all live without the cumyah carpetbaggers," said the Commodore. "They can be 'most as dangerous as the others. Don't you think, Hat?"

"I suppose," Hat said.

"We might be able to move them out," said the Commodore. "Somehow."

"Now you're talking!" said DuChamp. He chuckled. "You know, this whole disaster might just be a blessing in disguise, Harold. We might just get our town back, once and for all. You with us, Hat? Or against us?"

"I'm with you," said Hat. "Of course I'm with you. Where else would I be?"

"I'll drink to that," said the Commodore. "CJ!"

"We'll all drink to that!" DuChamp cheered, and he leaned back and yanked the bar bell.

Yes, they would all drink to that. And then they would all drink to the good old days, and then to yachting, and then to women, and then to drinking itself—to just about any half-processed notion that synapsed through their swelling heads. By the time the savage heart of the storm at last slammed into the wayward peninsula, they were each of them passed out in their rockers. Mouths agape and bodies slack, they looked innocent and vulnerable as babes.

·VIII·

ORNING FOUND THE greater part of the peninsula locked in the clutches of a blistering hangover—not exactly a new sensation for the town, but paralyzing nonetheless. Calhoun Square, in particular, looked like war: display booths and demo deer stands lay toppled and mangled; in the deeper puddles, upturned duck boats floated like coffins. Collapsed sportsmen were strewn everywhere, fallen soldiers who were not dead but, for the time being, certainly lifeless. The only thing stirring in the square at all was Bubby McGaw.

Still lashed to the far oak tree, he was not stirring very vigorously. He had not slept all night and had weathered the thunderstorm with the iron will of the righteous and without fear. He had no reason to hide from the end of things, to close his eyes. If the time had come, then the time had come. In the midst of the storm, with lightning blasting across the park and rain thrashing his face like a thousand tiny whips, Bubby had been certain that, yes, the time had come. At any moment now the earth would collapse in on itself to swallow up the Parker Hathaways and Abel Horfners of the world—all the artists and queers, all the drunkards and druggies, all the perverts and parasites. All spiraling down into the flames of Hell, never to soil the God-fearing world again. At any moment now, down they would fall. And at any moment now, Bubby had been sure, up he would rise. He would find himself delivered from the maelstrom completely, lifted up on the wings of angels to a land of eternal light and happiness. As he ascended, he would look down on the horrors below without pity, without so much as a batted eye.

Bring it on, Lord, Bubby had thought. Bring it on.

But then the storm had ended. It ended the way oceangoing thunderstorms do—abruptly and completely, without a tapering off or winding down, as if the system itself had changed its mind. The end of the storm, in a sense, was as ruthless as the heart of it had been. In a matter of minutes, this howling chaos, this near Apocalypse, had given way to deadest calm, the park utterly quiet save the occasional far-off hoots and hollers of the drunkards who'd embraced the foment as the natural climax of the night's revelry. They had not been swallowed up by a fiery vengeance, and Bubby had not ascended to light on the wings of angels. They were still drunk and prideful and obnoxious, and he was still Bubby McGaw, tied to a tree.

Which he remained—Bubby McGaw tied to a tree—until morning. Confused and not a little disappointed, not a little let down, he did not sleep but worked desperately to reconcile all the tenets of his theology with the facts of the matter, the situation at hand. He could not. All the signs had been there, all the foundations laid. The obscene sculpture and its perverse celebrants, the detached peninsula, the rising storm: each and every event of the past twenty-four hours had pointed to the end of things. But things had not ended. He would just have to accept that for now. He could not lose faith. What this was, he finally decided, was a test. A test of his faith. Yes, it had all been a test of his faith, and he would not allow himself to fail that test. He would stand strong.

Sit strong, anyway.

It was not so easy. In the wake of the storm, revelers of especial endurance descended upon the park in four-wheelers and jacked-up pickup trucks to cut doughnuts and fishtails in the fresh mud. Between the hollering rednecks and roaring engines, the spinning wheels and flying mud, Bubby might have been witnessing a monster truck rally. There were minor collisions and near capsizes, but nothing so disastrous as to curb the drivers' wild time. In a near corner of the park, not fifty yards from Bubby, a handful of college kids gathered to slip and slide in the mud—now wrestling, now sliding and laughing, now grabbing and fondling each other like apes. If anyone noticed Bubby, they did not approach him. Nor did he ask them to. Absolutely certain, now, that he was being tested, a veritable Job, he sat patiently and waited for the mayhem to end. By first light, finally, it had.

In the light of day the wholesale calamity that had marked the previous night became clear. Shredded and sodden, littered with beer cans and liquor bottles—some attached to spraddle-legged, passed-out bodies—the grounds of the park looked like a hog pen. Through all of it, to Bubby's great disgust, the gigantic peter had stood tall, the toppled radio van beside it a testament to his own failure to undo the thing. The entire scene was a picture of sickness and perversion, and had he the energy, Bubby might have screamed out against it all at the top of his lungs. But he did not have that energy. He had been worn thin by a night of hard weather and heavy thought, and in time, lulled by the soothing warmth of the morning sun and the gentle rock of the wayward peninsula, Bubby dozed off. The park quiet now, Bubby slept soundly, undisturbed for the better part of the morning.

He was awakened midmorning by the rattle and stamp of an approaching horse carriage. Not the approach, as it turned out (as he first imagined, even hoped), of a horseman of the Apocalypse, but rather the approach of one of the men who had tied him up. Sitting beside this man in the carriage was Harry Biddencope, the very man who had organized the doomed festivals. For some reason, Biddencope held a WBUB megaphone. Bubby was not delighted to see either of the men, but he could not very well walk away.

"Damn, son," the driver said. "You been here all night?"

"Doesn't look like he had much choice," said Harry Biddencope, and he stepped out of the carriage and proceeded to untie Bubby. "You're welcome," Harry said after giving Bubby a moment to say thank you.

Bubby didn't say thank you, just scowled at each man alternately.

"The man wants to know why you had to go and wreck his van, son," the carriage driver said.

Son? Who was this kid, to call him son? "It was my duty," Bubby said.

"Your duty," the driver said.

Bubby pointed at the obscene sculpture. "To try and take that—thing—down. To stand up for moral values. I did what was right with the tools available."

Harry looked over the grounds and said absently, "Place is a disaster area."

"You can't blame that on me," Bubby said.

"Who we gon' blame it on?" the driver wondered.

"Whoever brought that thing here!" said Bubby. He was losing patience. "He can pay for your damn van! He can clean this place up, too! Don't you see? The very presence of that thing—it brought all this on! It's heathens worshipping idols! The man who brought that thing, he could be the devil himself! That's the man you want!"

Harry looked up at the driver. The driver shrugged. "Well, what we gon' do?" he asked.

"Mr. McGaw's got a point," Harry said, thinking anything to keep the blame off himself would do. Anyway, Horfner had failed him. He owed the man nothing.

"I say we hunt the man down," Bubby said. "Teach him a lesson."

"Could we do that, Kirk?" Harry asked the driver. "Could we hunt him down?"

The driver nodded. "We could do that," he said. "We sure could."

Indeed they could. Kirk, who knew Harry through their mutual interest in the tourist industry, was never one to pass up a hunt. Naturally he would take the role of master huntsman (a role his father, despite Kirk's pleadings, had not yet allowed him out at Bounty). He would organize the hunt in the manner of an old-fashioned plantation deer drive. There were plenty of hounds in town for the Jamboree, and of course plenty of hunters. With Bubby's help, the hunters could be recruited to form a posse, which would follow behind the hounds as they worked to flush out the fugitive artist. They would need an item of the artist's clothing for scenting purposes; using his connections, Harry would find a way into the artist's hotel room. At noon they would all meet in the park, and at the sound of the bugle, the hunt would begin.

And so, having entered into an uneasy but, he felt, holy alliance with Harry and Kirk, Bubby set about the task of recruiting hunters and hounds. He located them easily enough—

passed out in the mud and in the trucks and SUVs parked around the grounds—and recruited them without difficulty, the hungover and ashamed needing only to be told that there was a man they could blame for their condition, and that if they liked they could join the hunt for this man. By midday, Bubby and Kirk had assembled a formidable gang of several dozen men and as many hounds.

For his part, Harry hoped against hope to find Abel Horfner in his hotel room, that he might give the man some warning, a head start, and by the same stroke distance himself from the men who were hellbent on tracking Abel down. Biddencope, after all, had invited Horfner to town, arranged the room for him, everything. Sadly, he did not find the artist, and after some deliberation he headed back to Calhoun Square with a pair of the artist's silk briefs, purple.

Approaching the park, Harry stopped in his tracks at the sight of the sizable posse. He was stunned not by what the men were doing, which was not much more than standing around like a herd of cattle, but by what they were holding: guns. The only men not armed, it seemed, were Kirk Ashley and Bubby McGaw, in the carriage. Kirk did have a bugle, but nothing to match the arsenal that surrounded him.

"Guns, Kirk?" Harry said.

Before Kirk could answer, a short, tubby sportsman wearing a Mercruiser cap approached and swiped the briefs from Harry's hand, then began scenting the dogs.

"Can't very well have a hunt without guns, can we?" Kirk said.

"But we're hunting a man," said Harry.

"That's a matter of opinion," Bubby called.

"What? Honestly, Kirk—this isn't a war."

"Another matter of opinion," Bubby said.

"Easy, now," Kirk said. "Nobody plans to use 'em. Just want to have 'em."

"Nobody *plans* to use them?"

"Come on, son," Kirk said. "You not really gon' tell these fine gentlemen to put down their weapons, are you?"

Harry surveyed the gang. A rough-looking bunch. No, he wasn't going to tell them to put down their weapons. He wasn't going to tell them anything.

"You with us?" asked Kirk. "Or against us."

Harry knew that if he ducked out, the mob might find a way to blame him for something. A lot of things. And they wouldn't be far off the mark, either. He knew that. "With you, I guess," he said, and reluctantly he climbed into the carriage. He picked his megaphone up off the floor of the carriage and set it in his lap. It wasn't a gun, but it was something.

"All right, then," Kirk said. Then, to the man who'd swiped the briefs, "You all set, Georgie?"

"Sho' 'nuff," Georgie said.

Kirk raised the old infantry bugle to his lips and gave a long, mournful blow that seemed to cling to the air before settling over the town. The hounds gave a yelp, the men gave a whoop, and with that, the hunt was on.

ACROSS THE PENINSULA, ON the porch of the Atlantic Club, Commodore Crumfield started at the call of the distant bugle, just as he'd started at the call of the distant bugle however many fall mornings on however many Lowcountry plantations, when, after one too many pulls of shooting sherry, he'd dozed off on the stand. Only, this morning he wasn't sitting on a stand on the plantation. He was sitting in a rocker on the porch of the Atlantic

Club. And he hadn't just dozed off for a minute or two. He'd plumb passed out for the night. So had Murray DuChamp and Hat Lawson and Sam Haynely, each of them stirring, now at the call of the bugle.

"You hear that?" Crumfield said.

Hat Lawson rubbed the sleep from his eyes. "I do," he said.

"What in hell?" Murray DuChamp said. He squinted hard at the morning. "Where the hell are—what in the hell?"

"Wasn't a dream, Murray," Crumfield said. "Unfortunately."

"Well, hell," DuChamp said. "Somebody deer hunting out there?"

"Somebody's up to something," Hat said.

At once confused and wistful, the Commodore and Hat and DuChamp gazed off in the direction of the bugle call. For his part, Captain Sam Haynely took up his charts and navigation instruments. He was eager to see what kind of progress, or retrogress, had been made during the night. The peninsula, he determined, had traveled a total of seven hundred forty-eight nautical miles northeast of its point of departure from mainland South Carolina. It was still clipping along at a frenzied twenty-two knots but had, at some time during the night, made a hard tack to the north, so that it was no longer steaming toward Cape Verde but, rather, Reykjavik.

"Captain Sam," Crumfield said. "Where we—"

"Iceland," Sam Haynely said.

"Iceland," said Hat with some disgust. "For God's sake."

"Beats Cape Fairy," DuChamp said.

"Verde," Hat corrected. "And I'm not sure it does. I'm thinking we're going to need that sail, Harold. We're flying out of control, here."

"And the dredge," Murray DuChamp said. "Don't forget the dredge."

"It's time to call a meeting, Harold. Really."

"I'm with both of you," Commodore Crumfield said. "The first—" he stopped, cocked his head. A look of intense study gripped his face. "You hear that?"

His companions sat up and listened, and yes, in another moment they did hear it: hounds yelping and baying, men hooting and whooping. All in the far distance yet, but definitely drawing closer.

"Sounds like they're headed this way," Hat said. "Time to sound that horn, Harold. I'm serious."

"All right, then," said Commodore Crumfield, turning for the door. "I'll sound it."

"The horn" was an old air raid siren that had been mounted on the roof of the club during the early 1960s, when the fear of a black uprising had had the club's members in a state of constant worry and preparedness. Most had been well schooled in the story of the slave revolt of 1822, in which the white population, caught off guard, lost a number of its own. Upon induction, each member was educated in the club's "horn rule": at the sound of the siren, members and their families were to make speed to the clubhouse, where the nature of the emergency would be explained and further instructions provided. If a member or a member's wife was within earshot of the siren when it was sounded and did not heed it, then he or she was in danger of losing the membership. Since its installment, the siren had only been sounded twice—once when a Catholic won the mayoral election, and a second time when a Baptist won the governorship. Commodore Crumfield couldn't be sure whom this morning's call would bring. The circumstances of the day were beyond unusual, and so exclusive was the club that its membership had dwindled considerably in the last decade. There just weren't that many Charlestonians left in Charleston, and Commodore Crumfield knew that better than anyone. Still, there were some, and these he knew to be, for the most part, stubborn and tough as nails, if a little on the eccentric side. If they were still on board, they could be counted on. And so Commodore Crumfield, confident in his role as civic guardian, unlocked the breaker box and switched on the emergency siren for its third, and what would prove to be its penultimate, wail.

ELIZABETH HATHAWAY WAS IN her kitchen nibbling tentatively on an English muffin when the siren rang. She was not feeling terribly chipper; in fact she felt rather nauseated, but she would scarcely think of neglecting her duty as a "Clubhouse Gal," as the wives of club members were known. She could guess the nature of the emergency easily enough—something to do with the breaking off of the peninsula—and she felt she had just the solution, or at least what might prove to be a very big part of a solution: Colonel Parker, who yet lay resting in the bedroom upstairs. She had checked on him twice already, to make sure she had not dreamed the entire affair—that Colonel Parker, or some incarnation of him, anyway, had indeed returned to save the town—and to make sure that the man was resting comfortably. At the sound of the siren, she stood and made her way up the stairs. If he was not awake, she would have to wake him. Because he was coming to the meeting with her.

She found him just beginning to stir—startled awake, perhaps, by the sound of the siren. There was no time for formalities.

"Let's go, Colonel," she said, throwing the sheet off of him. "The club is waiting."

"The club?" the man asked. He looked completely confused. "No time to explain," Elizabeth said. She took him by the arm. "Put on your hat and let's go. Chop-chop."

It was not until they reached the Battery that Abel Horfner's memory engaged and he began to comprehend what was happening. He knew that, despite his getup, he was not the colonel this woman thought he was. He knew that he was Abel Horfner, world-famous sculptor. But he also knew that Abel Horfner, world-famous sculptor, was in a bit of trouble with the town of Charleston. That much he could remember. He could not remember how it was he had come to be dressed this way or how it was he had ended up in this woman's care. But he determined that, for the time being, he would do best to remain in this woman's care. If she was tugging him along a little insistently, she was lavishing him (or lavishing the man she thought he was, anyway) with high praise. She had respect for him as Colonel Parker; she cared for him as Colonel Parker. For now, Abel Horfner decided, he would be well advised to be Colonel Parker.

The woman paused at the drive that ran alongside the club. "Would you listen to that?" she said. "Dogs?"

Yes, Abel could hear dogs howling in the distance, feverishly. And men hollering. He didn't like the sound of it. Not at all.

"Old town is falling to ruin," the woman said. She shook her head. "Absolute ruin."

With that she started along again and Abel followed, down the drive and into the side entrance of the club.

Inside, Elizabeth led her man up the stairs and into the ballroom, where club members were already beginning to assemble. They took a seat among what was left of old Charleston—a few dozen men and women from Elizabeth's generation and a dozen from Parker's. Guessing Abel Horfner to be one of Elizabeth's many afflicted cousins, few looked twice. Elizabeth herself had decided not to make a point of him until the meeting required it.

In time Commodore Crumfield, flanked by Murray DuChamp and Hat Lawson, called the meeting to order. He said that he guessed all in attendance could surmise the nature of the emergency but perhaps not the full extent of it. A number of disturbing details had, over the course of the past twenty-four hours, come to their attention. First, there was simply no way to predict exactly where the peninsula would land. Headings had included such varied destinations as Bermuda, Barbados, and Iceland. At the mercy of wind and water, the town's tack shifted almost hourly. There was the unfortunate possibility that when all was said and done, they might find themselves on the shores of Africa.

At this, the assembled members gasped.

"Just a possibility," Commodore Crumfield said. "But given the sheer size of the Dark Continent, a very real possibility. In light of this very real possibility, my vice-presidents and I have developed a plan, subject to your approval and, of course, requiring your participation. We are thinking of raising a large sail over the city, the better to navigate with. As for an agreeable destination, that will be decided democratically by a vote of club members. The sail itself will be constructed of linens requisitioned from your own linen presses, then patched together with needle and thread. We have in mind turning the ballroom here into a sort of ladies' auxiliary. By the end of the day, the room should be singing with the hum of sewing machines."

"Who's going to do all this sewing?" a member asked.

"Whoever knows how. And whoever doesn't will have to learn. Those of you who've kept your maids on in these difficult times may of course employ them."

"It's going to have to be a mighty big sail to turn the whole peninsula, isn't it?" said another member.

"Which brings me to the second issue at hand. It has come to our attention that a conspiracy to overthrow the old order of the town is currently being staged. As if recent years had not dealt us enough blows already, we have it on pretty good authority that certain elements intend to take advantage of the present unfortunate situation."

"What sort of elements?"

"The usual elements," Crumfield said. "Colored people, cumyahs, and carpertbaggers."

Again the assemblage gasped.

"You all know as well as I do that they've been awaiting their chance for years. Ever since the sixties. The *eighteen*-sixties. The vice-presidents and I are afraid that if we don't take measures, this could finally be it for our venerable town. Last call, if you will. If something isn't done, we may very well lose her forever."

Nervous murmurs flared from the audience, and Commodore Crumfield raised his hand to quiet them.

"All is not lost, good people!" he continued, his voice rising to match and further provoke the emotional stir of the audience. "As it has been for time immemorial, intelligence is on our side! Reason is on our side! Good sense is on our side!"

At this, the Commodore's audience began to nod and grunt in approval.

"We will not be defeated by ruthless savages! We will stand up and use the situation to our own advantage! We will take measures! We will take back what is ours! We will take back our town!"

Fired up, the audience cheered. Eighty-four-year-old Lofton Wheeler, who had once proposed an import tax on all tourists, levered himself up with his cane and raised his fist—then, dizzied by his own sudden movement, he fell back into his seat.

"How will we do it? I'll tell you how we'll do it! The old-fashioned way! We will secede, ladies and gentlemen! Secede!"

"Secede!" the audience chimed in unison.

Commodore Crumfield pounded a fist against an open palm. "How will we secede? I'll tell you how we'll secede! In a word, ladies and gentlemen—with a dredge!"

They hollered, scarcely aware what they were saying, "A dredge!"

At that moment the ballroom doors burst open. The hunt for Abel Horfner, after a number of false leads, wrong turns, and general fallings-apart (not the least of which at the sound of the air-raid siren, which had completely disoriented the dogs), had at last descended upon its man. As the members of the oldest yacht club on the continent looked on—with horror—a pack of baying, slobbering hounds launched itself across the ballroom floor to come skidding and sliding and tumbling into poor Elizabeth Hathaway and her afflicted cousin, seated in the back corner of the audience. Close on the heels of the dogs, a gang of rough, unruly looking men with guns. The dogs bayed mercilessly at Elizabeth Hathaway and her afflicted cousin, the two of them cowering in on each other, holding each other tight, until at last a young man at the rear of the gang sounded a long blast of the bugle, at which point the dogs fell quiet and exclamations erupted from the shocked audience.

"Dear God!"

"They aren't colored!"

"Don't look like Yankees, either!"

"Look like Lehighs!"

"What in God's name is the meaning of this?" Commodore Crumfield demanded. "This is a private club!" A little unnerved by the weaponry, he did not approach the gang.

"There's no need for alarm!" a short, determined-looking man said as he emerged from the gang and approached Elizabeth Hathaway. "We've come for one man—that's all!"

"Bubby McGaw!" Elizabeth said. "What on earth are you doing?"

"What needs to be done," the short man said, and he took Elizabeth's afflicted cousin roughly by the arm and pulled him away from her.

"My Colonel!" Elizabeth cried. "My Colonel Parker! He's taking my Colonel Parker!"

"This man is no colonel!" Bubby said, and he ripped the costume beard from Abel Horfner's face. "This man is the perverted artist who shamed your town!"

The assembly murmured. Elizabeth trembled.

"Is this true, sir?" Commodore Crumfield demanded of the costumed man. "Are you the perverted artist?"

There was no use fighting it now. "Yes, it's true!" Abel said. "I'm Abel Horfner! The perverted artist with the gigantic schlong!"

At this, several of the audience members fainted. Commodore Crumfield struggled to maintain order. "What do you propose to do with this—this sick man?" he asked.

"Gon' tie him to the tallywhacker, sir!" one of the huntsmen said.

"Gon' make him pay for what he done!" said another.

"Gettin' what's comin' to him!" said a third.

Commodore Crumfield waved his hand in frustration. "Fine! Fine!" he said. "Just get him out of here! All of you! Out of here! And take the three ingrates in the kitchen with you!"

"You got it!" Bubby McGaw said. He entered the kitchen and shivered with delight at the sight before him. Parker Hathaway and friends, bound and gagged. "Well, lookey here," Bubby said, licking his lips. "The koo-koo club."

Still stunned, the club members watched as Bubby McGaw led the four prisoners away. Was that Parker Hathaway, Elizabeth's son? And the other young man, did he not look like a Lawson? Who was that woman, anyway? When the motley bunch was gone, the pack of dogs and hunters close at their heels, Elizabeth Hathaway stood alone, calling weakly after them, "Colonel Parker, my Colonel . . ."

At the head of the room, the Commodore and his vice-presidents conferred, and the Commodore, with a wave of his hands, returned the assembly to order. "Ladies and gentlemen," he said, "it saddens me to do this. Elizabeth?"

Elizabeth turned and stared blankly at Commodore Crumfield. "Harold?" she said.

"In light of these events, Elizabeth, the vice-presidents and I, as the guardians of club honor, feel obliged to revoke your standing membership."

Murray DuChamp approached her and took her by the arm. She tried to shake him loose but couldn't. "But, Harold—" she said.

"Now, now, dear," said Commodore Crumfield.

"I'm a Hathaway, Harold!" Elizabeth pleaded. "Hat's cousin!"

Commodore Crumfield consulted Hat Lawson, then said, "By marriage."

"Lawson, too!" said Elizabeth. "I'm Lawson blood!"

Again Commodore Crumfield consulted his vice-presidents. "This is why we're going easy on you, dear," he reported. "You will not be expelled from the neighborhood. You will be allowed your ancestral home. But if you choose to stay on board, on the fairer side of the peninsula, it will have to be as a nonmember. That is, at your own risk. We cannot promise you protection, or for that matter any other club service that may become necessary in these difficult times. If anyone in attendance finds fault with this sentence, let him speak now."

No one spoke. All looked scornfully at Elizabeth.

DuChamp gave the assembly another moment, then led Elizabeth away. "But, Harold!" she cried over her shoulder. "I'm one of you!"

It was no use. She would find no sympathy here. In shame she crossed the ballroom floor with Murray DuChamp. He nudged her out the door and closed it behind her without so much as a farewell. Humiliated, traumatized, she walked back into the day and on toward home with heavy feet and a blistered spirit. But she would not be beaten. Her father would hear about this. Lawson Parker. Great-grandson of Hamilton Parker, founding member of the club. He would hear all about this.

Her father! She had not checked on him this morning. She had not even tucked him into bed last night. It was true he liked to take care of himself, but also true that he could not always be counted on to take care of himself. Crossing to Bay Street, she looked up at the porch. He was up there, in his usual roost, but still up there from last night or up there again today, she could not be sure.

"Father!" Elizabeth called. "Father!"

Her father did not respond. Asleep, perhaps. He was always falling asleep up there. She hurried inside and climbed the stairs. On the porch, she found her father was smiling an impossibly wide, mischievous smile (this from a man who had scarcely cracked a grin in decades), and she saw, could not help but see, that his loose khaki pants were obscenely taut against the zipper line, as if a small tent pole had been erected there. But if the man looked lively in his face and in his privates, he looked very much undone otherwise. His body was pale and crumpled. Elizabeth shook him. He was rigid as a rolled up rug. Elizabeth shook him again, in frustration this time.

"Damn it, Father," she said. "Picked a fine time to die on me. Mighty fine."

·IX·

OR THE THIRD TIME in a single hour, Elizabeth felt horribly betrayed. First by her colonel, then by her club, and now by her own father. She was, she now understood, completely alone.

But not, as it turned out, for long. Next door, at the Bay House B&B, Bo and Tater Bamber watched the woman tending to the crumpled man. They had been keeping an eye on the body for well near an hour, ever since a riotous racket in the street—dogs, horses, men armed with guns—had inadvertently alerted them to it. Looking out the window, Bo had discovered the mob gathered in front of the neighboring house, and, looking at the house, he had discovered what appeared to be a man sleeping on the upstairs porch. If the unusual sight had captured his attention (he and Tater had thought, after all, that the rundown house was abandoned), it had not captured the attention of the motley gang, at least not for very long. The mob, led on by the hound dogs, had moved on in a matter of minutes. The man had not moved at all. That was an hour ago, and now a woman was shaking the man. He was not responding. He was, it appeared, and despite the woman's rather casual reaction, dead.

"Look at this, babe," Bo said. "He's got company."

Tater joined her husband at the window. "Mm-hm. Is he—?"

"I think he's—dead."

Tater blew a chewing-gum bubble and snapped it. "That would explain the just sitting there all this time."

"It would." Bo considered. "I might see if I can be a help to her. Huh?"

Tater smacked. "A help to her."

"Yeah," Bo said, backing away from the window. "She doesn't look that young. She maybe could use some help. Still got a half-hour before the speech." His speech before the members of the Tri-County Mini-Storage Convention.

"You be careful, hon," said Tater. "Place seems creepy. Especially with a dead man up top. Creepy."

"I'll be careful, Tay-tay," Bo said, and he gave her a quick squeeze on the behind. "Don't you worry."

He would be careful. And strategic. And diplomatic. Truth be told, Bo had his own reasons for offering help next door. In his line of work, death was not so much a tragedy as an opportunity. The dead didn't leave just people behind; they left crap behind. And crap had to have a place. Crap had to go somewhere. The dead went to heaven or hell; their crap went to mini-storage.

"Ma'am?" he called to the woman from the street. "Ma'am?"

She didn't answer or respond in any way. Likely in shock. Bo walked up to the front door and eased it open. "Hello?" he called.

No answer. He moved inside and up the stairs. Very little could have prepared him for what he would find on the second floor of the house. A lifetime in the mini-storage business could not have prepared him for what he would find on the second floor of the house. He had meant to make his way rightwards, for the porch, but glancing left he found himself most decidedly distracted. There at the end of the hall was a room that looked to be full of—no, bursting with—well, *crap*. The temptation was too much. He would have to investigate. "Hello?" he called once more, then, receiving no reply, he made for the room like a shark for chum.

It was true. The room was packed tight. Crap, piled and jammed everywhere. All manner of crap, from the useless to the indispensable, the worthless to the priceless. Mismatched wooden water skis cast among three-piece leather luggage sets, solid brass andirons set in plastic milk crates, two-dollar vinyl beach chairs stacked beside a mahogany wardrobe. Bo's mouth went all cottony. His heart bumped at his throat. This was the crap of his dreams. The crap that had made him. Unable to resist, he cracked the door to the adjacent room. Even more crap. This room, too, packed tight, mostly with antiques, valuable things: sideboards and chaise lounges, silver sets and steamer trunks. He tried a third door and found another random grouping—books, photo albums, a pair of deck boots, stereo speakers, lampshades, a hunting jacket.

Awestruck, Bo stumbled backwards down the hall. The woman could fill five twenty-by-twenties with what she was holding. Only $146 a month, each—$134 with a year's contract. Times five, at least. And who could say what all she might have stuck up in the attic, in the back of the house, in the yard. Had this woman not heard? Did she not know? Had the modern miracle of mini-storage really eluded her? And was it possible that she wasn't alone? Was it not possible that the entire peninsula had whole unit loads' worth of crap hidden away in their homes? Was it not possible that they had all been holding out on him?

He would have to find out.

On the porch Bo found the woman gripping the deceased man by the wrist. (He couldn't help but notice that the corpse was grinning. What was more, it looked to have a bit of a hard-on. The very last thing the man had seen must have given him a whopper of a thrill—just before it killed him.) With her free hand the woman was holding what looked to be a .45-caliber semiautomatic pistol. The pistol's slide was recoiled and the barrel tip exposed, meaning the clip was spent, the gun no threat.

"Ma'am?" he said.

She scarcely started at the sound of his voice, simply turned and pointed the impotent pistol at him. She looked him over, up and down. "Who the hell are you?" she said.

Bo raised his hands in surrender. "I'm Bo Bamber, ma'am," Bo said. "Daddy Bo, some call me."

If the name meant anything to her, she didn't show it. "Uh-huh," she said. "And what do you want?"

Her tone was bitter, accusatory, but Bo stood firm. "Couldn't help but notice you might have a situation on your hands."

"Oh? And which situation might that be? Would that situation be my homosexist son, my unkindly yacht club, or my dead father here? Or maybe it's my town, which in case you haven't noticed, is bobbing along through the middle of the ocean."

Bo looked out at the water, affected a look of concern. "Oh, I noticed. Where you think we're headed?"

"I don't really give a damn," the woman said. She looked off and lowered the pistol.

"Hope it's some place nice," said Bo. "Maybe Hawaii. Someplace like that."

The woman studied him, then looked off again. "Where are you from, anyway?"

"Alcolu," Bo said. "Me and the wife are staying at the B and B there."

The woman chuckled snidely. "Alcolu," she said. "Of course. What are you doing here?"

"I thought maybe I could help you," said Bo. "With your father, there. Unfortunate times like this, a lady might use a little help."

She shook her head—disgusted, it seemed. "What are you doing here in Charleston? Hm?"

"Oh. Business. We're here on business."

"Business," she hissed, not at him so much as at the day. "Business and Jesus rolling down from upstate. It's always business or Jesus."

"Ma'am? I just wondered if I could be of help."

She turned to him. "Son," she said, "unless you can turn this town around and get us back to where we came from, you can't help me with my father. His plot is in the Hathaway family ground at Cedarwood Plantation, on the Santee River. Until he can be buried there, he's staying here. Because he will not be buried at St. Philip's. Never."

"What's wrong with St. Philip's?"

"Plenty," she said.

"So you just going to leave him up here on the porch?"

The question seemed to catch her off guard. "I—" she started. "I have my plan. There's a pine box in there somewhere. I'll put him in there. So you needn't worry."

"Well, I'd be glad to help you dig the box out," Bo offered. "If you like."

The woman gave this a thought. Coming to see just how limited her options really were, she at last agreed to the proposition. "Well," she said, waving the pistol at him. "All right, then. But no funny business."

"Of course not," said Bo, and with the useless pistol aimed at his back he entered the house.

She pointed him back to the second room he'd spied in on. "The ghost room," she said. "Family stuff. I believe it's under those quilts in the corner."

Wide-eyed, his mouth all dry again, Bo worked his way over, under, and between the dusty antiques. "Sure got a lot of stuff here," he said, baiting.

"I'm not in the business of throwing things away," she said. "Never have been."

"Well," Bo said. "There's other ways of storing things, you know. You ever heard of mini-storage?"

"Mini-storage?"

Unbelievable. Somebody wasn't doing their job. Somehow the word wasn't getting out to people like this, people who might prove extraordinarily lucrative. "Mini-storage," Bo said. "Sure. A secure place where you can store stuff like this. Free up some room."

"My mother didn't raise me to just throw things away."

Finally Bo reached the corner. Before pulling the quilts away, he said, "The nice thing about mini-storage is you're not throwing it away. You're just putting it away, until you might use it."

"Well," the woman said. He couldn't tell if he was hooking her or not. "You see it?" she said.

He would have to be patient with her. He pulled the pile of quilts away. Sure enough, there sat a pine box coffin. Finely crafted, in good shape. "Got it," Bo said. "How in the world did you come by this?"

"It was a joke, sort of. My great-uncle Cleland made it for his daddy after his daddy forbade Cleland to marry a Jewish gal he was courting. Said Cleland would marry the gal over his dead body. So Cleland built the coffin, put it under the Christmas tree that year, and ran off and married the Jewish gal. I don't know how it ended up here. We always just put things in it."

"Some story," said Bo, and he pulled off the lid. Inside he found a pile of old swords, bayonets, a few pairs of spurs. He asked what she wanted him to do with the stuff; she said to just leave it any old place. He set the objects on the floor beside the pine box, then tested the weight of the box. Not too heavy, but maneuvering it through the other furniture did prove tricky.

"Mini-storage is perfectly safe, too," he said as he worked his way across the room with the box. "Your better facilities have security cameras and resident guards. It's not even as expensive as you might think."

"I pay someone for this? I pay someone to have my things? That's loony-bin talk."

"Plenty of people are doing it these days," said Bo. "You'd be surprised."

"I wouldn't be surprised at all," she snapped. "Plenty of people are doing a lot of things these days. Plenty of people are eating seaweed. If plenty of people are doing it, that doesn't mean a damn thing to me. If plenty of people are doing it, I'd just as soon not."

For now, Bo had lost her—and she, him.

"Where we gonna put it?" Bo asked. "Him, I mean."

"Here in Liza's room," the woman said. She led him two doors down, into the first reasonably furnished room he'd seen in the house. An enormous rice bed made its centerpiece. At her instruction, he placed the box on the bed, and the two of them moved to the porch to fetch the deceased.

"Be gentle with him," the woman said as Bo lifted her father up off the chair. "Oh, Father."

The corpse was not terribly heavy, but it was a corpse, rubbery and pallid and just a gruesome affair all in all. Worse, the woman hadn't expressed any interest in mini-storage. Still, it was not in Bo's nature to give up so easily. Dragging the dead man down the hall and into the bedroom, he said, "You know, I was thinking. They've got refrigerated units. Refrigerated mini-storage? It might not be a bad idea to store the old boy in one of those, until this business with the town clears up."

The woman scowled at him. "You are loony tune," she said. "I told you, he's not going anywhere but to Cedarwood. Until then he's staying here, with the rest of the ghosts. Now come on, put him up in there."

Bo did as he was told. It was not easy, lifting the corpse up onto the bed and into the pine box, but eventually he succeeded.

"Oh, Father," said the woman, brushing the dead man's hair into place.

"I'm only saying, he may get to—well, he may start to smell, after a while. If you—"

"I thank you, sir, for your assistance," the woman interrupted. "Now if you'll please leave me to mourn the dead in peace."

"Oh," Bo said. "Of course. Yes, ma'am. Maybe I'll check up on you a little later?"

"Maybe you will," she said absently.

"Okay, then," said Bo, thinking, as he turned and left, that she was perhaps the most ungrateful, hardheaded bitch he'd met in a very long while. Thinking, too, at the same time, that he was not through with her. Not by a long shot.

Back at the B&B, Bo could scarcely contain himself. While he prepped in the bathroom for his speech, he told Tater of the old lady's stash.

"A whole houseful," he said. "You would not believe it, Tay-tay."

"What's wrong with her?" Tater asked.

"Plenty," said Bo.

"Who would keep all that?"

Bo straightened his ball cap in the mirror and winked at himself. "Keeping it's fine, honey," he said. "We want her to keep it. It's where she keeps it. You understand?"

"I understand. We could be keeping it for her. Daddy Bo could be keeping it for her."

"For her and for whatever other nutjob old bats around here are keeping things close."

"And when they die . . ."

"I always knew you were a smart one," Bo called.

"She got any family?" Tater asked.

"Didn't see any," Bo said. He stepped out of the bathroom. "There was the old man, but he won't be a problem anymore."

"No?" Tater said.

"Nope. Deader than hell."

Tater approached Bo with an indulgent grin and pulled him close. "Oh, Bobo," she said. "Sometimes I think we're just the luckiest two in the world! It's like—like somebody's looking down on us!"

"We're more than lucky, Tay-tay," Bo said seriously. "We're good. Damn good."

They kissed, then Bo pinched Tater on the behind, pulled back, and said, "I look all right?"

"Good enough to eat up," Tater said.

"We'll eat later, darlin'," said Bo. "I got a speech to give."

He did indeed. And it wasn't the speech he had planned to give, either. Bo might even leave his notecards at home; he wouldn't need them. Instead of congratulating these local so-called businessmen for a job well done in the tri-county area, instead of patting them on the back for unprecedented local growth in the mini-storage sector, he would give them a real piece of his mind. He would ask them how in the world people like the woman next door had slipped through the cracks. As immense an opportunity as the old woman presented to him personally, the thought of all those wasted years, all those years of all that crap just sitting there, in a *house*, infuriated him. Because if there was one thing he believed in more than personal gain—and there was only one thing—it was mini-storage.

To let the town know he meant business, he revved Mama Bess once Tater had climbed in, then threw her into gear and roared onto Battery Street. The trailer leaned dangerously, the tires (and Tater) squealed, and they tore down Battery with fury—only to find themselves, one block down, stopped dead in their tracks by a horse carriage.

Not unusual, really—horse carriages were forever clogging up the streets of Charleston—except that this particular carriage was accompanied by an escort of armed men and hound dogs. It was the same group that had made the commotion outside the B&B earlier, only now they seemed more orderly, more collected, the dogs and men flanking the carriage and marching in step like a regular platoon. A small collection of men sat in the front seat of the carriage, too far away for Bo to make them out. He guessed they were not tourists because they did not rubberneck but, rather, stared straight ahead. Who could say; given the escort, the men might have been local royalty. This might have been some royal procession they were witnessing. Something important.

Royal or not, though, the procession was in Bo's way. Curbing his first instinct to honk angrily, he checked the side-view to see if he might back out and turn around. But already a train of cars, most of them big like Bess, had collected behind him, a train of hardy, hungry machines held at bay by a worthless pack animal.

"Trapped!" Tater cried. "You're going to be late, hon."

"No, I'm not," said Bo, and appointing himself conductor of the train, electing himself representative, he bore down on Mama Bess's horn—a long, insistent blast. Nobody in the carriage so much as turned around, but quite a few members of the escort did. Having gotten their attention and encouraged by a horn sounding a few cars back, Bo gave another blast.

At which point the men lifted their shotguns and trained them on Mama Bess.

Bo raised his hands; Tater ducked. The cars behind let out a chorus of horn blasts. Bo couldn't say if they'd been incited by the display of weaponry or were simply oblivious to it, but one thing was certain: he was in a bit of a pickle. The armed men were approaching, and Mama Bess's sisters were honking away. He waved his hands to assert his innocence, but still the armed men approached. As if he were to blame for it all. As if he were still honking. He wasn't. He had surrendered. But the train hadn't. They kept honking furiously. Fed up, one of the armed men fired a shot into the air. Thanks to the crazed honking, Bo saw the blast—the recoil, the puff of smoke—more than he heard it, but Tater heard it clearly enough.

"Go, Bo!" she shouted. "Go!"

"Go?" he said. "Where?"

"Just go!" Tater shrieked. "She's a Hummer! She's Mama Bess! Just go!"

"Through them?"

"Just go!"

Bo waited a moment longer for some sense of reason to come over the whole bunch, and when it didn't, when the man who'd fired the shot approached Bess and began tapping the window glass with the barrel of his shotgun, Bo went.

He drove slowly but steadily, like a bloated orca bumping its way through baitfish. Confounded, the armed men fell away, the sea of them awkwardly, confusedly parting before the Hummer. Some banged on it with the butts of their guns before jumping back, but most seemed awestruck, amazed that the driver would even consider such a bold act. Their awe empowered Bo; it was amazing what Mama Bess could do. He picked up speed, and when at last he came alongside the carriage he revved the engine, spun his wheels, and roared off, giving a long victory blast of the horn as he went. Embarrassed, confused, and above all furious, the armed men opened fire. Bo swerved back and forth down Battery Street, successfully evading the volley of lead. In the side-view he could see that he'd made a worthy conductor after all: car by car the sisters of Bess were plowing their way through the armed escort, churning up a wake of total chaos. Men were scattering and falling, puffs of gunsmoke splashing randomly, and the horse was rearing up against its yoke, by all appearances preparing to go completely ballistic.

"Hoooooo-weeeeeee!" Tater squealed. "You did it, Bo!"

"Damn right I did!" he said. "Damn right!"

Tater leaned forward and planted a kiss on the console of the H2. "You and our big girl!"

"She's a big bad bitch, ain't she!" Bo said.

"Awww," Tater said sweetly. "She's no bitch. She's our girl." She leaned forward and kissed the console again.

"Easy with those kisses, hon," Bo said. "Don't want to have to get jealous!"

Tater grinned, slid across the seat, and nuzzled close. "Of course not," she said, and she ran her tongue along the edge of his ear.

"See that, girl?" Bo said to the instrument panel. "This my girl. Mine."

Tater giggled. "Mmmm . . . I love it when you talk like that, Bobo."

"I know you do, Tay-tay," he said. "I know you do."

What a rush. He might have turned around and done the whole thing over again. But he couldn't. Not just now. He had a speech to give.

KIRK ASHLEY'S CARRIAGE HORSES had all been trained to tolerate the occasional engine backfire or road crew jackhammer, but they had not been trained to tolerate Armageddon, and so it was that when the procession exploded—engines roaring, men hollering, guns blasting—the horse exploded with it. First she reared and flailed, struggling to free herself from the yoke. Unable to shake it, she charged down the street, the carriage and its passengers clamoring behind. Try as he might, Kirk could not stop her. The more determinedly Kirk dug into the reins and the more furiously he shouted, the more vigorously the mare drove forward. She was trying to outrun the chaos, but she was harnessed to it. When they approached Battery Front Park, she at last saw her chance—a field, an open green field—and made for it. But if she could hop the curb easily enough, the carriage wheels could not. They hit the curb with such force that the carriage launched clumsily into the air and capsized, and she with it.

As the carriage tipped, captive and captor alike made last-minute leaps for the street, so as to hit it on their own terms. Suddenly free, and having run these streets for the better part of their youth, Parker and Phillip knew where to go and how to go.

Across Battery Street and down Stoll's Alley, a quick duck under the Williamsons' fence, through the Dixons' garden and around the Porchers' wall, and they were halfway there, halfway home to 2 Bay. It was not until they stopped in the Porchers' side yard that they paused to untie each other, and when they did, they came to the unfortunate realization that Carolina was not with them. It was, really, foolish to assume that she would be.

"Carolina!" said Parker, breathing heavily. "Where's Carolina?"

"She wouldn't know where to go!" Phillip said. "How would she know where to go?"

Parker worked to tame his ascot, which had quite gotten away from him in all the commotion. "I thought—" he said. "Why didn't you wait for her?"

"Why didn't you?"

"I thought you would!"

"She's not *my* girlfriend!"

"Is she mine?" said Parker.

"Don't you wish," Phillip said, almost in disgust.

"Whatever," said Parker. This was not the time for petty bickering. "The point is, we have to go back and get her."

"Are you mental?" Phillip said. "We can't go get her. Or you can. I'm not going anywhere near those Neanderthals."

Parker considered. He could hear the commotion from here. Guns firing, men shouting, a horse whinnying in agony. Perhaps Phillip had a point. Phillip, who up to now had treated every danger as a game, an opportunity to flaunt his new lifestyle. The night in the brig had changed him. And he was right. This was not the time for heroics. If she had escaped, what were the chances they'd find her? And if she hadn't, what were the chances they'd get within a hundred yards of her without getting shot? Then where would any of them be?

"What about that dear old mother of yours, anyway?" Phillip said. "When was the last time you checked on her?"

"All right," said Parker. "But for the record, I don't like abandoning Carolina like this."

"Well, isn't that chivalrous," Phillip jeered, and then he began working his way through the decades-old hole in the Hathaways' fence. Reluctantly, after a moment's more consideration, Parker followed, and in short order the two found themselves in the back yard of 2 Bay.

The side door was locked, and Parker's mother took her time in answering it. When at last she did answer it, she answered it with a pistol—Pawpaw's .45, if Parker wasn't mistaken—aimed directly at Parker's gut. He felt sure she would lower the thing when she saw who it was—who he was, Parker, her only son—but she didn't. Instead she said, rather flatly, "What do *you* want?"

"It's me, Mommy," Parker said. "Parker."

"I know who you are," she said. She looked at him with suspicion. "Used to, anyway."

"Well, I don't know what that means," Parker said. "But maybe you could ease off with the pistol."

"Who's he?" she asked, pointing the pistol at Phillip.

"Phillip Lawson, Mommy," Parker said. "You remember Cousin Phillip."

"Virginia's boy."

"Yes, ma'am," said Phillip.

"Hm," Elizabeth grunted. Still she did not lower the pistol or move from the doorway.

"Please, Mommy," Parker begged. "Won't you let us in? There's been so much trouble."

Her face tightened. "It's all trouble!" she said. "It's been nothing but trouble since they started this damn thing! This damn—Bravado! And these upstate upstarts! This off-brand religion! Nothing but trouble!"

"You don't have to tell me, Mommy," said Parker.

"I do have to tell you!" she barked. "Look at you! With that— ridiculous haircut! That goddammed prissy-pants—thing around your neck. Like some—some—fairy boy! Some—girl!"

Parker stood stunned. He'd never gotten this from anybody, least of all his mother. Nor had he ever seen such viciousness in the woman directed at anyone, least of all at him. He could scarcely respond. He did not know what to say. Except, in time, this, which he said without meaning to say it or knowing he was saying it, the words just falling out, "But we're all we've got, Mommy. We're all we've got."

She would not accept this. Her face drew even tighter, her eyes sharp as two tiny talons. She began to speak, but she could not speak, and her squint collapsed and her face fell completely slack. She seemed now to be at once searching her son and looking directly through him, beyond him, to some faraway horror. Parker said nothing, simply stared directly back into her and watched as the pistol dropped to the floor and she staggered backwards, as though she had been pushed, and turned away.

"It's all fallen apart," she said. "It's all fallen apart."

Parker was unsure how to follow her. He understood that in her mind, he was part of this falling apart. He bent down, picked up the pistol, and walked at a distance behind her into the kitchen. Feebly she lowered herself into a chair at the kitchen table and stared off at nothing.

"This Pawpaw's pistol?" Parker asked, reaching to meet her halfway, on common ground.

"He won't be needing it," his mother said. She would not look at him.

"No?"

"No."

"Why not?"

"He just won't." Still she did not look at him.

"Well, where is he?" Parker asked.

"Liza's room."

"Is he okay?"

"Better than ever."

Wholly frustrated and getting nowhere, Parker left the kitchen for the stairs. He did not expect to get much farther with his grandfather, of course, but at least he might find a sympathetic ear in the old man. (At any rate, a half-deaf one, one that would not bark back.) Coming to Liza's room, though, he could not find his grandfather anywhere. Only Uncle Cleland's old pine box coffin on the bed. His mother had been at it again, moving the old keepsakes around. Perhaps the coffin had been put there as some sick jab at him; knowing now how she felt about him, he couldn't say. Anything was possible now.

He checked his mother's room and the upstairs porch, called into the storage rooms just in case, then returned to the kitchen. Parker's mother sat unmoved, but Phillip had come into the kitchen and was, it appeared, fixing himself a glass of milk.

"What are you doing?" Parker said.

"She asked me to come in and fix her a glass of milk," Phillip said. "I came in, and I'm fixing her a glass of milk."

"Well, isn't that chivalrous," said Parker. Then, to his mother, "What did you do with him? Ship him off to the Bishop Gadsden Home?"

"I didn't ship him anywhere, and I'm not shipping him anywhere until I can ship him to the family plot."

"What in Christ's name are you talking about?"

"He's dead, you dummy!" she said. "Your grandfather's dead!"

"What? Where?"

"I told you! In Liza's room!"

"In the pine box? Uncle Cleland's pine box?"

She wouldn't answer. Which meant, yes, in the pine box.

"How?" Parker said. "How did he die?"

"I don't know! He just died! People just die!"

"So you threw him in a box?"

"What did you want me to do? Throw him off the Battery?"

"Oh, for God's sake," Parker said. "This is too much." It was too much. His grandfather, not just dead, but dead in a box upstairs. His own mother, ashamed of him, for reasons he could not begin to get into with her. His childhood friend, bitter toward him for related reasons. These people were most decidedly, most willfully, fucked, and they could wallow in their own fuckedness until the end of time for all he cared. There was but one thing for Parker Hathaway to do just now, but one thing he could do to redeem the entire fucked lot of them: track down Carolina Gabrel and save her.

"I'm out of here," Parker said. Then, to Phillip, "You coming?"

"Where?"

"I'm going to help a friend."

"Good luck," Phillip said.

"I'm not the one who'll need it," said Parker, and he left.

ONCE PARKER WAS GONE, Phillip passed Elizabeth the glass of milk and sat across from her at the table.

She took the glass and began to trace shapes in the condensation absently. "Why couldn't he be like you, Phillip?" she said.

"Like me?"

"Strong. Manly."

"Oh," Phillip said. "You wouldn't want him to be like me, Mrs. Hathaway. Trust me."

"Sure I would," she said. "Everybody worried about you. And look at you. You turned out fine. All muscle. Bet you even have a nice girl waiting for you somewhere."

"No, ma'am, Mrs. Hathaway. I don't."

"Sure you do. And you can call me Elizabeth. I'm not your mother."

"Yes, ma'am."

She took a sip from the glass, swallowed, looked off. "Nobody worried about him," she said. "He always did the right thing. He was a good boy. Then when his father died, he—changed. Everything changed."

"Maybe he's doing what he thinks is right, now."

Elizabeth shook her head. "That haircut? Those foolish clothes?"

"Well, things have just gone crazy lately. That's all. They're crazy everywhere."

She was not listening. "What did I do wrong, Phillip? I've been so kind in my life. To so many unattractive people. So many."

"I'm sure you have been, Mrs. Hathaway," Phillip said. "I'm sure you have been."

She looked at him with tenderness. "Elizabeth, dear," she said. "You can call me Elizabeth."

·X·

BY MIDAFTERNOON, the ballroom at the Atlantic Club did in fact resemble a ladies' auxiliary—a long row of sewing machines manned (or womanned, rather) by a small but determined corps of older ladies white and black. The machines hammered away as the women stitched bedspreads, sheets, and pillowcases together to give gradual shape to a multicolored, multimonogrammed patchwork of a sail. Children of the Depression, grandchildren of Reconstruction, the older white women did, in fact, know how to sew. Their younger counterparts did not and had sent housekeepers in their place. Thanks to the insularity of the old society, the incidental proximity of the "help" to that society, the unlikely sailmakers all knew each other and were carrying on, side by side, white and black, like long-lost friends—at least, long-lost acquaintances. Even those whose employer-employee relationships had ended sourly behaved with civility toward one another. There was precious little time for grudges now, precious little time for upturned noses on either side. Having been told what the sail was for, what it would do—save them all from certain doom—the housekeepers were happy to help stitch. They had not, of course, been told of the plan to secede.

On the veranda the club's men had gathered to continue tracking the course of the peninsula and to work out the logistics of their impending secession. Reggie Lehigh, it turned out, was only too eager to dredge the city in half in exchange for a lifetime club membership. All they had to do was settle on a break-off point. It was decided, after heated discussion (at one point, elderly Jack LeGrand made for young Lucas Lofton with his cane) over enormous quantities of whiskey, that the line would be drawn at Calhoun Street, so that they might carry St. Philip's Cemetery with them. Those who had argued for (and fought for, in Jack LeGrand's case) a Queen Street split conceded only after the Calhoun Streeters agreed that the entire area would have to be cleared of all undesirables—namely, tourists and Bravadons and Jamboreeans—before they blasted free. Cleared out, the hotel and restaurant district could then serve as a kind of retreat for the club members. Completely cut off from their ancestral mountain retreats and beach houses, they might still summer away, as it were.

This settled, Commodore Crumfield stepped inside to check on the progress of the sail. It was coming along nicely, his charges working with determination and efficiency. At the current rate, their work would be done by early evening. Then the sail could be strung up between the steeples of St. Michael's and St. Philip's, the lower peninsula cleared of all undesirables, and secession declared. The matter of clearing the lower peninsula raised some concern in him, but only briefly. Commodore Crumfield figured that if he and the other board members could bring down a limit of ducks in a brutally frigid marsh, they could round up a few stragglers. He in fact looked forward to the work. It may well be that the cumyahs and absentee owners had brought impossible piles of cash to the local bank—his bank—

but when all was said and done, the place would be better off without them. A rare case, Commodore Crumfield mused, when the good of the community might actually come before the good of his bank. All his life he had, of course, preached the interdependence of the two, the success of the community as dependent on the success of the bank, and vice versa, but in fact he could not have cared less about the success of the community and would never have mentioned the formula at all had it not made for such hugely successful advertising campaigns. Behind closed doors the Commodore had always joined in the vicious criticism of the city's unchecked expansion, but he knew better than anyone that it was this very expansion that had so nicely padded his own portfolio in recent years. No, he had never been much of a philanthropist, never much of a do-gooder, yet here he was, for the first time in his life, putting people, the community, ahead of money. There was something noble in that, he felt. Something exceptional. It was an unfamiliar sensation for him, to be sure. But these were unfamiliar times.

"THESE ARE STRANGE TIMES," Bo Bamber began. The Magnolia Room of the Swamp Fox Hotel was filled to capacity, a sea of mini-men from across the state sitting transfixed and expectant, waiting like apostles for Daddy Bo's wisdom, Daddy Bo's blessing. "And getting stranger. Normally I would kick off a talk like this with a little joke. Something to tickle you all's funny bone, warm you up. One about a Polack mini-storage manager who pays people to take useless crap off their hands and store it. But I'm not in a funny mood this afternoon, boys. Not at all. Tell you the truth, I'm ashamed. Ashamed of you and ashamed of myself.

"Some of you all may know that I've dedicated most of my life to mini-storage. It's true. My wife, Tater, knows it. She can't hardly keep me off my lots. Has to drive my supper out to me sometimes. I'm not afraid to say that if anybody knows mini-storage, it's me. Any you folks want to argue better be ready to see me after the speech. Outside, with your sleeves rolled up. I know mini-storage. But I'm here to tell you that just this morning, not a mile from where I stand, not a stone's throw from me and Tater's hotel, I learned a hard thing to learn. Turns out, I didn't know everything. Thought I did, but I didn't.

"This morning I saw a sight that'd make you jump up and slap your own mama. It was the Indy 500 of mini-storage, boys. The Super Bowl. The Swimsuit Issue. What was it? What in the world could have got my feathers so ruffed? It was a house—a whole house—loaded with perfectly useless crap.

"And I mean loaded. Room after room, closet after closet, every damn nook and cranny but maybe the kitchen, a bathroom and a bedroom. I saw busted old telephones stashed beside shiny silver goblets, bags of rags on top of antique coffee tables, moth-holed hunting jackets thrown together with dusty wedding gowns. Who does this house belong to? Who does all this stuff belong to? Who does all this useless junk just waiting to be stored belong to? Is it—a drugged out college student? A recently divorced middle-aged woman? A confused cancer patient? A rock band with too much equipment and not enough gigs? If you told me yesterday about this place—this virtual paradise—I would have guessed something like that. Same way you just did. Why? Why would we guess that? Because that's what we're trained to think, boys. That's what we've come to expect. College students, divorcees, sick people. And maybe we've gotten lazy, settling for that. For what we know. Maybe we've gotten stuck inside our own moving box. I'm here to tell you, we're gonna have to get outside that box if we want to do all we can do with this business. We're gonna have to get out of that box and into—Charleston!

"Here we are, gathered together in a place famous for its history. A place where people like to look back. Now I know this sounds complicated, maybe like some elitist fancy-pants kind of college professor thinking. When I told my wife, Tater, she said she never knew I went to Harvard. But I, for one, can't help but think that the people who like to look back are the people who like to hold on. That's what this old woman I found this morning taught me, without even meaning to. Maybe it's a crap-ass transistor radio that no longer works, maybe it's a priceless silver set; she ain't gonna throw it away.

"In my opinion, she's the ideal customer. An old Charleston lady all alone in an old Charleston house. Never thrown things away. Never will. Told me her mama didn't raise her to throw things away. You think she's alone? I doubt it, boys. I seriously doubt it. I wouldn't be surprised if we found enough crap down here to fill a container ship. It could be some kind of sickness bred into these people. We all know about them. Snobby and kooky, with no use for simple hard-working people like us. In a way, that woman made me a little mad. Seemed a little too proud, a little too uppity toward me. I don't take that kind of treatment too well. But my mama raised me right. I was polite. Why? Because I know who I am. I'm Daddy Bo Bamber! And I know how to keep crap, by damn!"

At this, the hall exploded with cheers, shouts of support. Encouraged, Bo rode the wave: "People are scared, boys!" he said. "They want security! They want to know their crap is safe! The time to cut deals is now!"

More cheers, and then the gathered mini-men stood and stirred, chomping at the bit to get to work, scarcely able to wait for Bo to give them the word.

"This old town is full of people who don't throw things away! If you don't go get 'em, you don't deserve to call yourself a mini-man! Think outside the box, boys, and get those boxes in!"

Bo watched as his congregation stormed past him like a herd of hungry boars. He was good. Damn good.

THE WORK OF SAILMAKING finished for now, the women of peninsular Charleston retired to their homes for a much-deserved afternoon rest, assured that having successfully completed their end of the bargain, they could now count on the men to successfully complete theirs. In no time at all, they would find themselves secure on the shores of England, where life as they knew it, a life of tennis matches, dinner parties, and debutante balls, would resume without delay or difficulty and with the added flair of exotic surroundings. Mistresses and housekeepers shared cocktails and idle chat, and in time each made her way to a boudoir or den in hopes of finding a tranquil afternoon nap. But such simple hopes were soon dashed, because in short order the lower peninsula found itself besieged by a pestilence the likes of which none there had ever faced before: the mini-storage man.

Inspired by Bo Bamber's speech, the mini-men descended on the lower peninsula like a plague of locusts, veritably buzzing with hunger and excitement. If they had been shamed by Bo's talk, they wasted little time wallowing; each, on the contrary, was eager to redeem himself in this, the reported Indy 500 of mini-storage. Like kids let loose on an Easter egg hunt or '49ers with pans and dreams, they fanned out through the neighborhoods, scurrying through the alleys and cobblestone streets, and began to make their long-practiced pitches.

They failed miserably, of course. Of those residents who had actually heard of mini-storage, none wanted a thing to do with it and ran the persistent salesmen off with Labradors, brooms, and garden hoses. Those who were not at all familiar with mini-storage proved more charitable, but not much. Thinking the men afflicted, or criminal, or both, they handed the men sandwiches, Coca-Colas, sometimes a dollar or two, before politely asking them to be on their way. Thoroughly confused—and thinking the women afflicted—the salesmen, more often than not, did leave.

Some houses were inevitably hit more than once, and here the latter salesmen would find their rings and knocks unanswered. Inside, mistresses and maids watched through peepholes and cracked drapes, the maids recounting stories their elders had told them of the "burial man," who would come by every Saturday to collect funeral prepayments from the old and the sick, frightening them into payment with horror stories of medical experiments and potter's fields. The white mistresses sighed and shook their heads at the unfortunate tales but generally wrote them off to black superstition. No one could really have been that cruel.

By late afternoon, all but the most determined of the mini-men had given up and settled, sit-in style, outside the mecca of mini-storage, the house that had inspired it all: 2 Bay Street. As if they were indeed facing God, blinded and paralyzed in the face of Him, the gathered salesmen remained outside the decayed house for some time before acting. They shuffled about nervously in the street and on the sidewalk, speculating in hushed voices as to what all might lie waiting inside and calculating deals, terms, conditions they might offer the owner. The scene resembled an auction of sorts—an auction without, as yet, an auctioneer. Finally, unable to hold back any longer, his anticipation and hunger for a deal getting the best of him, a lone young maverick decided to make a move. His name was Tony Lander, of Keepsake Mini-Storage in Orangeburg. A relative newcomer to the business, Tony had been studying Bo Bamber's strategies and tactics from afar for the past year and aimed to give the unwitting mentor a run for his money in the next. Some answered the questions in their lives by asking what Jesus would do, but Tony Lander liked to ask, *What would Daddy Bo do?* Tony knew as well as anyone that Bo Bamber had not made his name by sitting back and waiting for someone else to make the first move. What would Daddy Bo do? Daddy Bo would march through that old rickety gate and get to work. Which is what Tony Lander, after pronouncing that he was old enough to know better but young enough not to care, did. He marched through the collapsed gate and up the porch steps and got to work.

There was really no way for Tony to know what he was up against. He had handled the elderly, yes. He'd even handled the armed. But he had never once handled the armed elderly. Which is exactly what he faced after five or six long rings of the doorbell and a half-dozen insistent knocks of the doorknocker: a small older woman cracked the door and greeted him with a pistol. Just behind her stood a beefy, none-too-friendly-looking young man.

Instinctively Tony jumped back, his hands raised. "Whoa!" he laughed. "Ain't here to rob ya!" He tried to have a look past the woman to the interior of the house, but the beefy young man was very much in the way, all but filling the doorjamb.

"What are you here for?" the woman asked.

"Here to make you an offer!" Tony said.

"It's not for sale," said the woman. At this, she gazed behind him, at the hushed and attentive crowd. She gestured toward them with the pistol. "You hear me?" she shouted bitterly. "Not for sale!"

"Whoa, whoa, whoa!" Tony said. "Easy, ma'am. Not here to buy anything. No, no, no. Got me all wrong."

"So you just want to steal it? That it?"

"Do I look like a common thief?" Tony said. "Ma'am? Do I?"

"You look common enough," the woman said.

"Now wait a minute," said Tony. Though he was not the least bit offended—he could not care less what people thought of him—he did his best to appear offended, even hurt. He called up the imagined support of the fellow mini-men behind him. "Here we come, offering you a service, and you got to go and get rude on us. Really. Thought Charleston people were supposed to have more manners than that."

"Not any more," said the woman. "I see where manners have gotten me. Now you get the hell off my goddamn porch before my son here beats you off."

Beat him off? Tony wisely decided to forego mention of the slip. Instead he smiled and winked once at the chunk of a man in the doorjamb. "Aw, really," he said. "Looks like a nice young man. I don't think he would—"

"You thought wrong," the young man interrupted, and to prove it, he approached Tony with fist cocked.

At which point Tony did, albeit begrudgingly, back down and off the porch. He wanted to give it to them both as he retreated— crazy kooks in a piece-of-shit old house—but he resisted the urge. What would Daddy Bo do? He would resist the urge. He would never offend a potential customer. And the woman was, Tony firmly believed, still a potential customer. Daddy Bo would not give up, not even in the face of a pistol and a he-man. He might back down for now, but only for now.

Inside, after bolting the door, Elizabeth smiled giddily at Phillip and placed a hand on his shoulder. "So nice to have a real man in the house again!" she said. "I've been so long without one! You sure showed them what is what!"

"Not me," Phillip said. "You. Parker would be proud." Though flattered, in a way, to have been called her son (anybody's son, really, as his own parents had had very little to do with him since his coming out), he had no interest in displacing his childhood friend.

"Parker," Elizabeth said. Then, shaking her head, "Pff—Parker? Parker couldn't drive a cockroach off the porch." She left Phillip for the bar. "How about a drink, dear. What will you have?"

"Whiskey sour if you've got it, Mrs. Hathaway," Phillip said.

"Of course I've got a whiskey sour! I love a whiskey sour!" He could hear her gathering the fixings. "They still out there?" she asked.

They were. Gathered in the street, staring at the house as if waiting for the answer to some age-old question to issue forth from it, they looked like pilgrims, like supplicants.

"They are, Mrs. Hathaway," Phillip answered. "They are."

"For shame," said Elizabeth, and she asked him to join her in the parlor. "Really. It's the second time today one of those miscreants has come for my things. And I've yet to understand it. I'm not understanding the difference between those kookoos and garbage men."

"I guess they don't throw the things away. They keep them for you."

Elizabeth squinted at Phillip. This still wasn't making sense. "Complete strangers. Keeping my things. Getting paid to. I'm not getting it."

"I think the idea is, it frees up space," Phillip explained. "Like where I live, in LA, there's not so much space left. And let's say a person finds himself between jobs, or apartments, or—relationships, and he's got to clear some space for a while, make room for the new. Then a man might think about mini-storage."

"Well," said Elizabeth. "I don't see much use in making room for the new. Look where the new has left us."

"And you've got a point there, Mrs. Hathaway. You do. But so do they. They don't have to be such creeps about it, but still."

Elizabeth thought on this, then looked searchingly at Phillip. "LA," she said. "What on earth are you doing out there, dear?"

"Well," Phillip said. How should he put it? "It's a change of pace."

"I'll say," Elizabeth said, and she frowned. "It's just a shame. We need boys like you back home. Excuse me—men like you."

"Maybe one day."

Elizabeth chuckled in spite of herself. "Guess you're stuck for now!" she said. "Unless you're a mighty good swimmer! Which I wouldn't doubt."

"Not that good," said Phillip.

"Another whiskey?"

"Yes, ma'am. But allow me," Phillip said, and he stood up, took Elizabeth's glass, and stepped to the bar.

Elizabeth grinned. "What a gentleman," she said. "A gentleman, wasted on LA. It's a shame, a shame. Probably don't even know what they've got in you out there. Don't know how lucky they are."

The unlikely pair spent the better part of the afternoon sipping and chatting, toasting days gone, speculating over those to come. Ever the grateful guest, Phillip indulged his hostess's more opinionated—if not downright backwards—reflections, and kept his own more controversial thoughts to himself. If Mrs. Hathaway was not an innocent (and who was, anyway?), she could not be entirely faulted for wanting to hold on to a way of life that had, for the most part, served her quite well. Would anyone but a kind of saint, or perhaps a kind of masochist, do otherwise? Phillip was not so naive as to think so. Still, if she really longed to have men like Phillip around, she had light-years of catching up to do as far as attitudes went. But this was neither the time nor the place to confront those attitudes. (He wondered, frankly, if Charleston ever would be the time or place to confront those attitudes.) It was the time and place to enjoy an afternoon toddy, or two, or three, with an elder.

They were well into their fifth when Elizabeth, fired up and not a little potted, stood up and drew the blinds to see if the pilgrims were still standing in wait outside. Indeed they were, and what was more, some of them had taken it upon themselves to construct picket signs, which they held over their heads like so many teamsters on strike. FREE THE THINGS, said one. SAVE IN SAFETY, said another. HOLD ON LOOSELY. Others were less subtle, less creative: SUPPORT YOUR REGIONAL MINI-STORAGE MAN; MINI-STORAGE: IT WORKS FOR ALL OF US; WHAT'S GOOD FOR MINI-STORAGE IS GOOD FOR AMERICA.

"Have to admire their determination," Elizabeth said. "I guess."

"They are determined," said Phillip.

"Even so, I've had about enough. Look at them. Like a bunch of union people. Communists. We should—we should throw something at them."

"Throw something at them?"

"What else is there to do?"

"Well." Phillip considered. "What can we throw?"

"I don't know. You were the boy. What did you throw at people you didn't like?"

Which translated, for Phillip, to what had people thrown at him? Before those days, though, when they were all of them still on the same team, the children of Charleston, they had been fairly vicious with tour carriages and wandering pods of tourists. The pachyderms on parade, his father had called them.

"We used to throw water balloons at tourists," said Phillip. He didn't mention that they had, usually, launched the little bombs from the porches of this very house.

Not that Elizabeth would have cared in the least. "Good for you!" she laughed. "Good, good!"

"Got any balloons?"

"Don't think I've got any balloons. May be some up there, but I don't think so."

"Surely there's something up there we could use," Phillip said.

Elizabeth chuckled, but a bit nervously, Phillip thought. "You know me," she said. "Don't really like to get rid of things."

"Sure. But we need to get rid of the creeps, right?"

"Well—yes. Yes, we do."

"All right, then," Phillip said, and he started for the steps.

"Oh—I just don't know," said Elizabeth, but still she followed him. "I've worked pretty hard at saving."

"Let's just take a look at what you've got."

"All right," Elizabeth conceded. "I suppose we could do that."

The coffin in Liza's room was out of the question, of course, but as soon as they reached Parker's old room, Phillip knew they were in for some fun. Amid the wardrobes, sideboards, and steamer trunks lay stashed all manner of junk—broken transistor radios; creek shoes; an enormous, unopened Big Bag O' Red Rubber Bands.

"Don't know that I can do without all this," said Elizabeth, shaking her head. "I've spent a long time saving."

"Well, which do you want more—all this stuff here or those lunatics gone?"

Elizabeth considered.

"I mean really, Mrs. Hathaway," Phillip said. "What are you going to do with a box of broken telephones?"

"Well." She didn't know. She really didn't. For the better part of her life she'd not only held onto her own family's trash and treasure but collected and held onto the trash and treasure of those around her, all in the belief that trashy people made trash and genteel people made do. "I like to make do," she said. "I was raised to make do."

Make do? Phillip knew exactly what she meant but could scarcely resist laughing quietly at the pun. "Sure you were," he said. "I was, too. But what kind of doo are you going to make with three thousand rubber bands? Seems to me that if you really wanted to make do, you'd get rid of all the—well, all the junk. The extras. And I don't mean store it. I mean throw it away. Out. Off the porch, if you want. At the men who want you to pay them to keep it all. Then see what you've got left and make do with that. That, Mrs. Hathaway, would really be making do. Seems to me, anyway. But it's your house. Your stuff."

Did he have a point? This man, this gentleman, this child of Charleston—did he not have a point? To really make do, as her elders had taught, as her elders' elders had taught, and theirs, should she perhaps do without? He did have a point, and when she recognized that he had a point, it was as though, in an instant, her entire way of life shifted. Phillip watched the sea change take her.

The eyes brightened, then her entire face brightened—*Voila! That's it!*—and she moved past him into the cluttered room and began clearing out the junk with the same determination, fury even, with which she had once collected and stashed the same. Phillip joined her, filling box after box with years' worth of collecting: moth-eaten sweaters, dead footballs, hopeless eight-track tapes. And so on.

When they were through, the room resembled less a junkyard scrap heap, more the storage chamber of some museum. Only the heirlooms remained: the swords and muskets, the family Bibles, the colonial furnishings. If the quarters were still tight, in no way livable, they were no longer impassable, no longer impossibly cluttered with crap. The junk, in time, filled four large moving boxes in the hall, boxes the two of them proceeded to slide down the hall to the upstairs porch with the glee of mischievous children. Below, in the street, the mini-men did not see Elizabeth and Phillip moving the boxes onto the porch; their stares remained fixed on the front door, as if at any moment the two inside might emerge with changed hearts, open arms, deals in mind. It was almost too easy, the mini-men almost too vulnerable, too unsuspecting.

"Sitting ducks," Phillip whispered, and he wondered if Elizabeth were really up to this. If he were.

"Damn right they are," said Elizabeth, and with this she pulled an old creek shoe from one of the boxes, studied it briefly—as if still considering, as if yet weighing its value—then lobbed it over the railing. Phillip watched as the shoe arced, tumbling and turning end over end. It appeared to be traveling in slow motion, all but suspended there, a lone pluff-muddied Keds, until at last gravity caught up with it and it dropped with a thud onto the head of a mini-man. The man did not know what had hit him, of course, nor where it had come from, and he stood stunned for a moment before gazing dumbly at the ground for sign of the object that had assailed him.

"Bull's eye," Elizabeth snickered, and before Phillip could join in with a missile of his own, she pulled another shoe from the box, turned it in her hand like a pitcher finding the right grip, and launched it. Another bull's eye, another dumbstruck mini-man, and now Phillip joined her and the two of them set about unloading with abandon.

The mini-men did not know what to do. Pelted by a hail of old shoes, pellets of pet food, knapsacks, film canisters, assorted office supplies, they sought cover behind their picket signs and behind each other. They hurled insults back at the house, at the people in it, at Charleston in general. They were being pelted by the very crap they had come for, it was true, but they did not want the crap in this way at all—for free, without a monthly payment. The irony, sadly or not, was lost on each and every one of them.

For their part, Phillip and Elizabeth were having a ball. Elizabeth had not felt this fabulously mischievous since the night, decades ago, when she had gone skinny dipping with handsome Park Hathaway off the Atlantic Club dock in the middle of the night; Phillip, since he had covertly kicked the foam machine at the Overdrive into high gear and then made out, right there on the dance floor, with a famous and much desired black model from Barcelona. They lobbed the grenades with the joy of Santa's elves throwing candy from a parade float, and they laughed together at the mini-men's cowering and shouting. When the last of the mini-men had finally retreated and Bay Street stood completely empty but for the assortment of discards, Phillip and Elizabeth embraced. Victory, however temporary, however small, was theirs.

·XI·

HE JAMBOREEANS HAD little difficulty recapturing Abel and Carolina in the wake of the carriage wreck and ensuing chaos: falling, Bubby McGaw leapt onto Abel, and Kirk Ashley onto Carolina. For very different reasons, perhaps, Abel and Carolina represented the most valuable of the four prisoners. If Phillip and Parker had escaped, Bubby could live with that. He wanted Horfner. And yes, for a very different reason, Kirk Ashley wanted Carolina. He had no idea what this woman had done wrong (himself, he could forgive a woman like this most anything), but in any case, he was not about to let her get away. He had made a career of charming sexy newcomers with talk of horses, with personalized one-on-one carriage tours of the peninsula, with drives out to Bounty Plantation in the Expedition. He saw himself as a kind of one-man welcome center, at least for the desirable young ladies who arrived by the bevy for weddings and debutante balls, and who, for the most part, could not wait to be shown around.

In Carolina, though, he was quick to discover he had a different kind of animal altogether. Granted, this was not his usual approach (not on a first date, anyway), to fall on top of the woman and hold onto her with a bear's grip. Still, she did not have to elbow him in the balls.

Good thing he was wearing his steel-plated cup. He always wore his steel-plated cup, whether he was playing ball or not, because to Kirk Ashley, a man's testicles were a man's life. Why anyone would walk around with them hanging loose and vulnerable was beyond him.

"Didn't have to do that, darlin'," he said. "Damn."

"Get—off me!" Carolina demanded. She struggled against him, elbowed him in the groin again, squirmed and squiggled, but it was no use. As strong as she was, as tough as she was, Kirk was stronger and much bigger.

"I ain' goin' nowhere till you calm down, honey," Kirk said.

At this, she struggled furiously. "Not—your—honey!" she said.

"Okay!" Kirk said. Then, calmly, "Okay. Easy." He might have been breaking one of his colts. Yes, she was like a wild colt beneath him. He must hold tightly but talk softly. "Easy."

She calmed, breathing hard, then bucked again, then calmed again.

"Easy," Kirk said. "I'm gon' get up now. Okay? Easy."

She said nothing, simply lay there, and slowly Kirk got to his knees, then stood. "See, sweetpea?" he said. "That's a good girl."

At this, she lunged, meaning to get up and run, but before she could get anywhere Kirk grabbed her by the arm and swung her around. "Damn it, girl!" he said. "You got to ease up!"

"Go fuck yourself," she snapped.

Kirk cringed. No woman had spoken to him this way. Ever. Though it may have spoken less of women in general than of Kirk's preferred kind of woman, none had ever found him anything other than God's gift to their sex. So that when, moments later, Bubby McGaw called, "You got her?" Kirk could only muster a shambling, "Yeah—I got her—I guess." He did have her, quite firmly, by the forearm, but he did not have her in the way he was accustomed to having a young woman—submissive and adoring.

"I sure got him!" Bubby McGaw called, and turning, Kirk saw the costumed artist trapped in a headlock at the hands of McGaw. "Now come on, boys!" McGaw commanded the confused sportsmen. "Pull it together!"

Gradually, after firing a few final rounds at the pack of speeding SUVs in the distance, they pulled it together. They cleared chamber jams and reloaded, then gathered around Bubby and Kirk.

"All right!" Bubby said. "Where's Biddencope?"

No response. The mob shuffled and mumbled, but no one could come up with the man.

"To heck with Biddencope," Bubby said. "To Calhoun Square!"

"To Calhoun Square!" the sportsmen refrained, and they began, again, a slow triumphal procession north toward the park, prisoners in tow.

Along the way, Kirk Ashley employed a number of different, and entirely unfamiliar, strategies to try and charm Carolina, to enlighten her to his innate desirability, but shortly into each new tack he was cut off by a biting insult. When he politely informed Carolina that guests in Charleston were expected to behave with as much gentility as their hosts, she told him his gentility wasn't worth the string in a cat's ass. When he told her he'd never heard such ugly talk from such pretty lips, she told him that if he could get his prick out of his ass long enough to shove it in between his own lips, she would surely appreciate it. And when, finally, he told her that if he were her, he would behave a little more kindly toward a man who was in a position to get her out of this mess, she told him, again, to go fuck himself.

So that when they reached the square, site of the impending crucifixion, Kirk Ashley, who might indeed have made an argument for sparing the young woman, was all for stringing the uppity cumyah bitch up, right next to the perverted cumyah artist.

CONCERNED THAT, CAPTURED, Abel Horfner might finger him as the root of all of this, the reason for it, Harry Biddencope used the confusion of the carriage wreck to break away from the mob altogether. WBUB megaphone still in hand, he scurried like a startled rat through back alley and cobbled lane to put as much distance as possible between himself and the volatile Jamboreeans. Along the way he found himself all but trampled by an equally volatile mob of mini-storage salesmen on their way to who knew where. Rounding a corner to escape them, he smacked into a young man he recognized (once the stars had cleared) as one of the former prisoners. Fortunately the young man seemed as shocked to see Harry as Harry was to see him. Not that the young man recognized Harry. Anonymity, a behind-the-scenes approach, had always been Harry's MO, and had, to date, served him quite well.

"Who are you?" the young man asked nervously, obviously uncertain whether to attack or retreat.

"Nobody," said Harry, backing up. "I'm nobody." With each step he took backward, the young man stepped forward.

"Who are you running from?" the young man said.

"Couldn't I ask you the same thing?" said Harry, with a rare flash of wit.

The young man paused.

"Who are you running from?" Harry pressed.

"Nobody," the young man said, and then he took two steps backward, turned, and ran.

For his part, Harry took one step backward, turned, and ran.

And ran and ran, until finally he had outrun his own breath and could run no more. When he stopped, he had no earthly idea where he was, except to say he was no longer on the lower peninsula. He was uptown, in a neighborhood of clapboard shacks, brick ranch houses, and squat duplexes. The occasional dog was no longer a Lab, a setter, or a spaniel but a scrappy mutt or half-bred pit, and the occasional person—in the yard, in the street—was, well, black. Harry had never visited this side of town, never had reason to. In fact, even if he had had reason— even if the gospel or R&B markets were worth the invested time—he wouldn't have, for fear of being mugged, knifed, or shot. But had he taken a moment now to notice, he would have found the upper peninsula in fact relatively tranquil: if news of the disasters a half-mile south, not to mention news of the separation of the entire peninsula, had made it this far north, that news had scarcely affected the area's daily life. As for his personal safety, had he taken the time to reasonably assess the situation, he would have recognized that the local residents were not assaulting him at all but rather, for the most part, ignoring him completely, as if he were no more than a scrap of trash—a torn plastic grocery bag, say—blowing down the street.

But Biddencope did not take the time to reasonably assess the situation. Instead, he panicked, and once he had caught his breath he began to run again, through the unfamiliar streets. His antics naturally raised some concern in the neighborhood, his panic feeding the suspicion of the residents, which in turn fed his panic. Wild young laughter burst from some quarters, shouts of concern and warning from others. The streets began to fill with the curious, nearly all of them teenaged or younger, and Harry, feeling cornered and outnumbered, found himself hysterically broadcasting, by way of the megaphone, the name of the only black man he knew—Reverend Anthony Lawson, city councilman for the upper peninsula. He was frightened, out of his normal mind, and simply did not know what else to do.

·XII·

T THAT MOMENT, Reverend Anthony Lawson was blocks away, presiding over an interdenominational fellowship picnic at Hampton Park. Although he had first dreamed of an event that would act as a sort of protest, or at least a sort of response, to the festivals of the lower peninsula, the community meeting he called to discuss the matter had proved prohibitively fractious. First Anthony raised the issue of peninsular drift, but it was decided that little could be done about that, and anyway each of the assembled community leaders was eager to call attention to a more imperative matter: his or her protest proposal. Hejugali Lumpru proposed an African Power Rally and called Mazey Weathers's suggestion—a Gullah Expo—a disgusting Uncle Tom sellout. Johnny Harrell wanted to organize a march on the lower peninsula; Lyle Benton argued that they should ignore the lower peninsula altogether and instead focus on their own people with a community-building workshop. Throughout the heated, even vitriolic, discussion, Anthony found himself longing for the transcendent unity of Sunday morning. More and more it seemed that church was the only place without fracture. In church, it didn't matter if you called it Black Power or Geechee Pride, protest or peace—so long as you called it and then sang it loud.

Anthony had found himself distracted by thoughts of the man who had first taught him to sing—thoughts of his father, Colleton Jeremiah Lawson. Who would not be a part of whatever it was they were planning here because he had ignored the boycott and gone to work, for reasons Anthony would perhaps never be able to stomach. He understood that although he and his father shared a deep, thriving faith (his father's faith had cultivated Anthony's own, inspiring gospel choir and, later, seminary), each ascribed very different implications to that faith. He saw his father's faith as a faith of acceptance: the world was the way it was—uncaring, unkind, unjust—and a man's duty was to make his way in it with as much decency and righteousness as he could, staying strong in the knowledge that a better land lay waiting on the other side. Anthony would forever fight to preserve and celebrate his elder's cultural legacy, but this spiritual legacy, this faith of acceptance, he simply could not abide. It was a form of Uncle Tommery, he believed, and it struck a marked contrast to his own faith of action. Because Anthony would not accept that the world was just the way it was. A better land awaited, yes, but in the meantime it was not enough to just be decent to people and hope for the best. Others were not necessarily so decent. Inspired by his faith, in service to it, he meant to improve the way the world was. He meant to take action. He only hoped it was possible to at once preserve his cultural inheritance and overhaul his spiritual one; he prayed that the glory of the gospel was not anointed in the blood of acceptance.

"Reverend?"

Mazey Weathers, calling him back to the matter at hand.

"I'm sorry," Anthony said. "What?"

"Hejugali was saying we need something that will empower the youth. I'm of the opinion that the last thing our youth need is power."

"Yes, something for the youth," Anthony said absently. After a brief, bewildered pause, the discussion group revved up again without him.

The youth. How far was it, really, from the submissiveness of the elders to the cynicism of the youth? Were the two not just varieties of defeat? With no faith to unify and guide them, only anger and bitterness at the helm, the youth tended to adopt an especially self-destructive posture. And that is all it amounted to, Anthony believed. Posturing. Intimidation. Bling-bling. Bang-bang.

"Sir?" Lyle Benton said. "What do you think?"

"Hmm?" said Anthony.

"What will we do?"

Anthony considered. Again he ached for Sunday morning. At last he said, "Can't we all just come together?"

"Exactly," Hejugali Lumpru said. "For a rally."

Mazey Weathers hissed. "We need a cultural festival, and we need it soon."

"No, no, no—a workshop," Lyle Benton said.

"A march, by God!" spat Johnny Harrell. "If we—"

"People, please," Anthony said. "I want the community to come together. Okay? I don't want it to blow apart. I want us to come together."

"Well, of course."

"Obviously."

"Sure."

"Good," Anthony said. "Then we'll have a picnic. In Hampton Park. Interdenominational. All invited. We don't have to name it anything. We don't need an agenda. Let's just get together for good food and good company and take it from there."

The idea, expressed so sensibly and so peaceably by Reverend Lawson, fell over the meeting like cool rain in August. There was no arguing the point. In its simplicity, the proposal was brilliant.

On the whole, the picnic proved a great success. Hundreds came, and they came righteously, ready for fellowship. Kenny Long brought his pig cooker and two hogs; Elijah Roper, ten pounds of fresh shrimp; Terrance Lockwood, three coolers of blue crab. Eugene Laidlaw's fresh-picked tomatoes, cucumbers, and pole beans brightly festooned one table; Lucille Haymore's okra gumbo, Ruthie Long's cornbread, and Miss Martha Rett's potato salad, another. Professor John Simmons's jazz trio, the Crosstown Three, took the bandstand in the morning, with Hejugali's youth poetry group, Dem Def, showcasing their work between sets. Later, gospel choirs from Calvary A.M.E. and Bethel Goodwill shared the stage and called Reverend Lawson up to join them in song.

What was it all about, Anthony mused. Between the steamed blue crab and the boiled collards and the pulled pork, the sweetgrass hotplates and spontaneous spirituals, the affair might have been a celebration of the Geechee life. (And you didn't need a Gullah Expo to hear Gullah, Anthony supposed. You only had to sit back and listen to the old people talk.) Between the free blood-pressure checks and flu shots administered by Drs. Jack Gamble and Nicole Dixon, the passionate talk about the school system and recent city ordinances (which sprang up around attorneys Lyle Benton and Tim Miller), it might have been a community workshop. The point is, Anthony thought as he surveyed the inspired gathering, it doesn't have to be called anything. If he absolutely had to call it something, if he were pressed to name it, he'd call it living.

If ever during the course of the day his pride wavered, that was only because however many had come to the fellowship picnic, not everyone had. Some of the young people had behaved like young people. Too cool for school, they had instead opted to hang at home, on the basketball court, or on the corner. And most of those residents who had ignored the boycott (they needed the work, however menial; they needed the wage, however meager), continued to ignore it and so missed the picnic. Among these latter, Anthony could count his own father, and though he had done well to put that sobering fact out of his mind for the better part of the day, he could not forever. When he joined the choir on the bandstand for "This World is Not My Home," one of his father's favorites, Anthony wept not for glory but in pain.

"You think so much, child," the man had said. "Grayin' yo' head, thinking so."

And Anthony: "I guess a child's not supposed to think."

"Uh?"

"I said—never you mind."

"Got yo' work. I got mine."

"You're not making mine any easier," Anthony had said, sharply.

"No," his father said. "And you ain' makin' mine no easier. Uh?"

Anthony didn't know what to say to that. "Well," he said.

"Well," his father said. "S'pose that means we's even."

"Pshh. I'm not serving drinks to a club that won't have me as a member."

"Ain' much interested in memberin' up with them nohow," his father had said on his way out the door. "You?"

No, he wasn't. But he didn't think a seventy-four-year-old man should have to serve them their drinks, either. He might take comfort in the fact that his father did not actually have to work at the Atlantic Club; that this was not the eighteenth century; that the man was only staying busy to keep from bogging down in the memory of Anthony's late mother. Anthony might draw some solace here, but in fact these realities only complicated the issue because they meant his father had chosen the path. Preferred it. The *Atlantic Club*. Anthony could not fathom that, and to keep from drowning in an attempt to, he would have to view his father not as deeply flawed but as curiously able—the man's daily grind as a mark of strength rather than a flag of surrender. (Truly, Anthony himself would not—could not—serve drinks at the Atlantic Club. Not for a thousand dollars an hour.) Anthony had no choice but to see things this way if he were to stay strong himself and do his own work, the work he had been put on this earth to do. Descending the steps of the bandstand, he rubbed the salt from his cheeks and salvaged his composure.

Good thing, too, because in short order he would need it. The young man, Betty Jenkins's boy, did not exactly sprint across the park, but his step had an urgency to it. He was looking for Reverend Lawson, it turned out, because a bat-crazy white man was tripping out down on Grove Street, hailing him with a bullhorn. Hailing Reverend Lawson.

THE BOY'S REPORT WAS HARDLY as perplexing as what Anthony actually found when he responded to it. At the corner of Grove and Rutledge—Harry Biddencope? Harry Biddencope? Who had never given Anthony the time of day? Rushing toward him and embracing him? Trembling like a frightened child?

"Anthony!" Biddencope said. "Anthony! I was so scared!"

"Of what?" Anthony said.

After a moment, Biddencope's embrace fell slack. He stepped back and looked about at the small crowd gathered in the street. The question seemed to have shocked something out of him, or perhaps into him.

"Scared of what?" Anthony repeated.

"Of—of my people, Anthony," said Biddencope. "They're—after me."

"After you? For what?"

Biddencope didn't answer the question, not directly. "Have you seen Calhoun Square lately?" he said.

Anthony said he had not.

"Well, you ought to," said Biddencope. "Need to, really. A real Monster Fuck Jam. Big black dick and everything."

Surely Anthony had not heard him right. "Do what, now?"

"Yes, sir. Brought in a world-famous sculptor, and he brought in a gigantic black ding-dong. You need to see it, Anthony. Really."

"I guess so," Anthony said.

Here Biddencope seemed struck by a sudden flash of inspiration. The unease fell from his face completely and was replaced by an expression Anthony knew well—the grin of the wheeler-dealer. "In fact, we all ought to!" said Biddencope. "Your people here, they'd get a real kick out of it. If you want to say something, now's the time, Anthony! And Calhoun Square's the place! Everybody's saying something down there!"

"Well."

"We could get a big march going. March on down there. How about it?"

Anthony considered. It was all very interesting, very tempting. Still, could he trust Harry Biddencope? He had never much cared for the man, it was true. When Biddencope first joined the mayor's office, Anthony had hoped to find an ally in him. Biddencope was a cumyah, he was a new face, and as such he might bring new direction to what had become a fairly complacent and predictable office. But in fact, Anthony had discovered, the opposite was true. Under Biddencope's influence, the mayor shelved a number of redevelopment and economic incentive programs he had promised the upper peninsula before Biddencope's arrival on the scene, citing the strategy of his new advisor: so long as prosperity was encouraged, if not enabled, in the outer districts of Mount Pleasant, West Ashley, and North Charleston, prosperity in the neglected upper peninsula would naturally follow. The key, Biddencope argued, was not to give handouts to current residents but to provide development incentives for new arrivals, who would bring not only big money to the city but vitality. It was an old trick, one which Anthony knew well, and with which he had grown increasingly frustrated over the years. He could not stand to see the mayor—who, if he had not exactly been a friend, certainly had not been an enemy—come under its influence, especially at a time when progress seemed so attainable with the economy, local and national, booming as never before. "In time, Anthony," the mayor had become fond of saying, "in time. But for now, priorities." With that, he'd throw Anthony a bone—a new swing set in Hampton Park, replacement bases for the baseball diamond—and be done with it, leaving Anthony ever more embittered but, as always, helpless to do anything to improve the situation.

Indeed, Anthony had run up against the very same wall in regard to the current festival week itself. If the city planned to hold three different major events in the same week, what was one more? He had envisioned a celebration of black history, art, and culture on a scale that would draw national, even international, attention to the rich cultural heritage of his constituents, and in so doing inject a shot of much-needed pride into the upper arm of the peninsula. He had lost a great deal of sleep dreaming of the various performances and exhibits they might host, the press they might receive, and yes, the pride they might inspire. A golden opportunity, he thought. Win-win.

But the mayor was not interested and again cited the counsel of his newest advisor, who argued that a fourth event would be one too many. Resources would be tight as it was, and given the "potentially volatile nature" of the event Anthony was proposing, they would have to think of doing it some other time, when all resources could be dedicated to it. Perhaps in February of the next year.

"In time, Anthony, in time. But for now, priorities."

Anthony had left the meeting enraged, mostly at the always conveniently absent advisor, whose lap dog the mayor had become—who had, somehow, become the peninsula's rudder. He did all that he had in his power to do, which was to call for a boycott of the week's events. But the boycott in fact had very little impact at all: those who had work on the lower peninsula needed the work and went to work, and those who didn't were not all that likely to be attending a mini-storage convention, a sportsman's jamboree, or a hoity-toity white-bread arts festival in the first place. He would not have been surprised to learn that the boycott had been laughed at, if not welcomed, by certain circles on the other side of town, who had scarcely wanted Anthony's constituents around in the first place, except in the capacity of laborers.

And now, who stood before him but the very man he might hold single-handedly responsible for all the backtracking, all the bullshitting, all the regressing, of recent years, begging him to join in a march—no, organize a march—on Calhoun Square. The man had never made any attempt to engage Anthony before or even talk to him. He had treated Anthony, always, as an irritation to be dealt with, nothing more. If the two knew each other at all, it was through mutually repugnant reputation.

Yet here the man was, behaving as though they were old friends, buddies, bloods.

"Come on, Ant!" Biddencope said, smiling. "You've got to see it! Your people—they would love it! What say, Ant!"

"Anthony," Anthony calmly but sternly replied.

"Anthony! My man! Trust me!"

Anthony knew that was the last thing he could do. Instead, he would have liked nothing better than to clock the man in the pearly whites right then and there.

Still, he resisted the urge. There would be time for that later. Because if this were a trap Biddencope was setting, then Anthony would be fully justified in taking the man down. Biddencope wanted Anthony to bring a few folks along, but Anthony would go him one better—or rather, hundreds better. He would call up the entire picnic, and yes, they would march on the square. No trap would be big enough for all of them, and if matters turned ugly, they would win out through sheer numbers and cause.

"All right, Mr. Biddencope," Anthony said. "I'll get some people together."

"You will?" Biddencope looked stunned by his own success, as well he should have been.

"I will," said Anthony, and he turned to walk away. Biddencope followed, but Anthony stopped him. "No," he said. "You'll wait here."

Biddencope's grin fell slack. "What's that?" he said.

"You'll wait here," Anthony repeated.

Biddencope shrugged and gazed up and down the street a bit worriedly. "All right," he said. "I'll wait here."

Biddencope waited and worried, worried and waited, and in time he found himself joined in the street by more supporters than he had anticipated or hoped for. Or, indeed, knew what to do with. Dozens more. Hundreds. They crowded around him, studied him. He grew fearful and brought the megaphone to his lips. "Ant!" he called. "My man! Ant! We're ready! Ant?"

Anthony gave Biddencope a few more minutes to sweat—and Biddencope did, for certain—then made his way up to him. When he did, the gathered crowd turned en masse, fell silent, and at Anthony's instruction followed the pair south toward Calhoun Square.

·XIII·

RRIVING ON THE SCENE by way of a concealed back alley and making sure to keep himself behind cover for now, Parker felt his heart sink at the sight before him. He was, it seemed, too late. Horfner, about whom he could not have cared less, was already strapped to one side of his own sculpture, just below the head of the enormous cock, while Carolina, about whom Parker could not have cared more, was being hoisted up the other side by way of a rope that had been run over the groove at the tip of the phallus. (The urethra, as it were. Horfner's own attention to detail, his own fidelity to realism, seemed to have, in the end, worked against him.) Parker watched as Kirk Ashley himself, with the aid of an appropriated demo deer stand, worked to strap Carolina to the sculpture with a bundle of leather reins. She did not readily submit to the treatment. Parker was proud to see her hiss and kick at Kirk, but her struggles finally proved useless. In another moment, she was lashed fast to the phallus, her back to Horfner's. She would have made a striking figurehead on the bowsprit of some Spanish galleon, Parker could not help but note. But this was not the bow of some Spanish galleon, and she was not made of wood. She was Carolina Gabrel, the woman of his destiny, very much in trouble.

Which she remained, until at last Parker found an opportunity to make his move. Short of breaking through the mob of sportsmen, shimmying up the sculpture, and breaking her free, there seemed very little he could do. But in time, yes, an opportunity did present itself, thanks to his ridiculous brother-in-law's ridiculous need to explain exactly what was going on—in life, in the day—in his own ridiculous terms. Parker watched as Bubby McGaw took the platform that had been built for Horfner and began to preach to the assembled sportsmen. Parker could not hear what Bubby was saying, but by his angry gesturing at the strung-up prisoners behind him and the feverish, self-important gleam in his eyes, Parker could guess easily enough. And it was by way of this—McGaw's obsession with himself, with his own righteousness—that Parker found his chance. Because in the midst of it all, Kirk Ashley, Parker's childhood friend, had withdrawn to enjoy a cigar privately behind the platform. If Kirk was not exactly Parker's ally, he might at least have a sympathetic ear. In any case, Parker knew Kirk Ashley couldn't give a royal damn about religious explanations. The time to act was now.

Parker dashed across Calhoun, then approached Kirk as casually as he could so as not to draw the attention of his brother-in-law. Kirk regarded him with the same suspicious eye with which he had regarded Parker for years, but, as always, he tempered the glare with signature good-old-boy charm.

"Park, my boy. Just in time," he said, and drew heartily on the cigar. "Interest you in a Cuban?"

No time for formalities. "What the hell is this, Kirk?"

"Just your basic lynch mob, that's all," Kirk said, grinning through a veil of smoke.

"What's she doing up there?" Parker said.

Kirk looked up at Carolina, chuckled bitterly. A hard look steeled his face. "Uppity bitch wanted up. I gave her up."

Parker controlled himself. "She's innocent, Kirk."

Kirk's face tightened again. "She's a stuck-up whore, is what she is," he said. "And now—well, now I guess she's pretty well stuck up!"

He made this last remark in a direction and at a volume that Carolina could hear. From her ungainly perch she cut her eyes at him. Parker looked quickly down, away, in case the scene had called up the attention of others, particularly Bubby McGaw.

It hadn't. McGaw was possessed. Nothing short of Armageddon could have distracted him from himself. Maybe not even Armageddon.

"I think you've made your point, is all," Parker said. "Now maybe you could let her go. For me."

Kirk squinted hard at Parker, then spat. "You?" he said. "What do you care?"

"She's a friend," Parker said.

"She's a foul-mouthed cumyah slut, is what she is," Kirk said. He spat again. "What you want with a friend like that?"

"Well, I don't— "

"I mean, what happened to you, Hathaway?" Kirk said. "You used to be—we used to be bubs, you know?"

"Sure. Which is why—"

"And then—what happened? Went all kooky. With the hair, and the kilts, and—all that faggy stuff. People wonder, you know? I'm telling you this as a friend, Hathaway. As one of my boys. People wonder. That's all."

This again. He should not have expected any more from Kirk Ashley. But there was simply no time for this again. Behind him, McGaw seemed to be losing momentum and would like as not wrap things up before that became apparent to his audience. Parker would have to pull out the stops, speak the whole truth.

"Damn it, Kirk," he said. "I think I'm in love with that girl."

"Do what?" Kirk said, incredulous. He looked from Parker, to Carolina, to Parker again. "You?"

Parker would play by Kirk's rules, speak his language. "She's a hottie, don't you think?" he said.

"Sure, but—you?"

"Think I might have a chance," Parker said.

"Really." Again Kirk spat. "You and her."

"Yeah, bub. Let her down. For me. Not for her, not for you—for me. Your boy."

"For you," Kirk said. He drew from the cigar, seemed to consider.

Parker thought he had him. In one stroke, he had redeemed himself in front of a suspicious former friend and rescued, he thought, a new one. "Let her down, Kirk," he said. "For me."

"For you," Kirk said. "Her."

"Yeah."

"Fuck no," he said.

Whatever Parker had done, he had done it completely wrong. Read the situation wrong, played the situation wrong. And now, now Bubby McGaw was most certainly finishing up. Parker panicked.

"You won't?" he said. "Honestly?"

"Honestly," Kirk said. He would no longer look at Parker or Carolina. "I'd advise you to get on, son. Before preacher boy here sees you. That much I can do."

"I'm not getting on," Parker said.

"Suit yourself."

"You're not going to let her down, you can go on and string me up with her," Parker said. It was an extreme approach, a huge gamble, but one way or the other, it would at least bring him closer to Carolina. Even if he lost, he would, in a sense, win.

He lost.

"You like her that much," Kirk said.

"I like her that much."

At this Kirk took Parker roughly by the arm and said, "All right, then. Up you go."

Parker was horrified at the breach of loyalty. Weren't all native Charlestonians, when it finally came down to it—despite hairstyles, political persuasions, general approaches to the twenty-first century—in this together? Apparently not. Still, he was satisfied that, yes, he was on his way to Carolina, and he faced the strapping into the harness and the subsequent hoisting up not with resignation but with a kind of pride. He was going to the gallows, or at least the stocks, for Carolina.

Naturally, Bubby McGaw was thrilled to find a new target, fresh fuel, rising before his eyes. Rising limply above the crowd, a veritable showroom dummy, Parker listened as his brother-in-law let loose:

"Another example of the Lord working in mysterious ways! We lost this heathen, but the Lord found him! He won't let perverts off the hook for long! Just as He will find us—you, me, us—when that day of reckoning—finally—comes, so He has found His enemies—the enemies of the good, the righteous, the redeemed—and brought them to justice! Who says there is no justice in the world? Here, my brothers, I give you justice!"

Parker was pleased to see that the rhetoric did not give rise to the explosion of support Bubby had certainly hoped for. The sportsmen regarded Parker's unfortunate situation as but another curiosity in a day rife with curiosities, and Parker came to rest between Carolina and Horfner, satisfied that if he had not won total victory himself, neither had Bubby McGaw.

"What in the world are you doing here?" Carolina hollered over her shoulder.

"I came for you!" Parker said.

"For me?"

"To rescue you!"

"How do you plan to do that?"

Fortuitously enough for Parker, Kirk reached the top of the deer stand at that moment and, with a bundle of reins, began to strap Parker to the sculpture. Fortuitously, because Parker had no idea how he planned to rescue Carolina, not now. To explain any former plan would be, of course, to admit failure—never an ideal way to commence a courtship.

As he strapped Parker to the stone, Kirk sang a crude nursery rhyme of his own creation: "Parker and Carolina, tied to a cock. Parker getting hard as a rock. First comes love, then comes marriage, then comes a half-breed in the baby carriage!"

Parker hardly knew how to respond to this, but Carolina had little difficulty. "Again I implore you," she said, "to go fuck yourself."

Kirk laughed a big, biting laugh and kept laughing on his way down the deer stand.

"What are you doing here?" Carolina asked Parker.

"I told you!" he said. "I came to rescue you!"

"How?"

"I don't know! This isn't exactly how I planned it!"

Carolina thought for a moment. "And anyway," she asked, "why?"

Why? Why, indeed. Now seemed as good a time as ever for his pronouncement: they might not live to see the morning, and even if they did, there was no telling under what conditions. "Because I'm in love with you!" Parker hollered over his shoulder.

"What?" Carolina cried back.

"Because I'm in love with you!"

"In love with me?"

"In love with you!"

"How?"

How? "Your mind!" Parker said. "Your spirit! Your way!"

"But—how? How could you be?"

"How could I not be? How could anyone not be?"

She paused—thinking about him? Mustering the confidence to tell him she loved him, too? Deciding how she felt? No.

"Because you're gay," she cried.

"Gay! Me?" What the hell? First his mother, now the love of his life.

"Yes!"

"No! Not me! Phillip!"

Another pause. "Phillip?"

"Phillip!"

"Phillip's not gay! He's—cute!"

What? The two were mutually exclusive? Which meant that Parker, because he was, supposedly, gay, was not cute? "I'm not cute?" he said.

"You're *gay!*"

"I'm *not* gay!" Parker said.

"It's okay!"

"What?"

"I don't have a problem with it!"

"But I'm *not!*" said Parker. "Jesus!"

"Don't bring him into it!" Carolina said.

The courtship had become an absurd failure, and if there had been time or means to rectify it, to start all over, Parker was not at all sure how he would. In fact there wasn't time, as a fresh crew of hecklers was at that moment approaching the scene. A crew Parker recognized well: Commodore Harold Crumfield, Hat Lawson, Murray DuChamp. His people. Or rather, what had been his people, once, back in the good old days a week or so ago. What in the hell were they doing here, anyway?

The crew of bluebloods was looking for recruits. Because if they had arranged manufacture of the sail easily enough (woman's work, maid's work), there was now the matter of raising it, a feat that would require the strength (and the folly) of much younger men. They were not inclined to let the visiting Jamboreeans in on the whole plan, the impending cleansing and ultimate secession of the lower peninsula, but armed with the Commodore's bankerly diplomacy and DuChamp's lawyerly persuasion, they felt sure they could recruit the men and then be rid of them with time to spare. Time was of the essence, for certain. Reggie Lehigh's team had already begun pulverizing and flushing the earth from beneath Calhoun Street, which they had found to be little more than marsh mud. (Incredible, really, that a city of such stature had for so many centuries stood on so little.) Word was, the work would be done by midevening. So yes, time was critical, and there was little of it to waste gloating over the successful imprisonment of the enemies of the peninsula.

Still, Murray DuChamp—drunker than usual, high on the apparent victory of the old over the new—could scarcely resist, and while the Commodore and Hat went about recruiting

Jamboreeans, he taunted the three prisoners. For once, the right had won out over the wrong, the old over the new, and he was not about to let the victory go unheralded. So caught up did he become in his victory dance that he did not even notice the departure, with sportsmen in tow, of his fellow board members. When at last he did catch on, finding himself all alone beside the sculpture but for a few stragglers, certainly alone in terms of people he recognized, his people, he kept his cool. He still had half a bottle of Scotch, the enemy combatants were securely bound, and his people would manage the raising of the sail without him. He would stand watch over the park, as it were.

In fact, DuChamp's people were managing fine without him, particularly without his insistence that they aim the peninsula toward France, which had become tiresome. Crumfield and Hat were not wholly naive to the allure of Paris, Brittany, Provence, but when it came down to it, they both felt England a far superior choice in terms of permanent residence. Their names would be recognized in Britain, their pedigrees appreciated, and what the island lacked in cuisine and climate it more than made up for in upland bird hunting, old-school golfing, and high-class socializing—in civility. Hat's father had always said that the jungle begins at Calais, and if ever they wanted to hop across the Channel for a taste of the more exotic, they would certainly be able to. France, they agreed, made a fine place to visit, but no self-respecting gentleman would live there.

It was Captain Sam's hope that rigging the sail between St. Michael's and St. Philip's would allow the peninsula to make use of the Westerly trades, which winds would drive them into the North Atlantic current and ultimately to England, in much the same way explorers and traders had once been driven home from the New World. It could be argued by the optimistic that a tack toward England had been preordained, sanctioned from above, a notion not at all surprising to the board members, whose families had, they felt, been divinely sanctioned for centuries, ever since they had first left England. Providence had smiled on their departure those many centuries ago; no reason for her not to smile again now, on their homecoming.

And so, after obstructing oaks, power lines, and lightning rods had been cleared out of the way, the patchwork sail was raised, lashed first to the lower steeple and upper spire of St. Michael's, then to the same of St. Philip's. Only three men were lost in the course of the work, not a bad percentage given its nature. The three casulaties—scarcely known, scarcely mourned—were buried in the playground lot of St. Philip's with what honors could be mustered, the site consecrated by Bubby McGaw as the Tomb of the Unknown Rigger. Little time was wasted on formality or ceremony, because time was, indeed, running out.

"We have it up," Hat reported to Reggie Lehigh via VHF.

"Roger that," Lehigh barked back. "About done down here."

"About done?"

"Yes, sir, buddy. This shit's squirtin' out like applesauce through a baby's butt. Don't know why this place didn't sink a long time ago. Ain't a goddamn thing under it."

Hat reported the progress to the Commodore, who was more shocked than pleased to hear it. He had a gang of unruly sportsmen on his hands. Satisfied with their work, with a job well done, they were ready to celebrate—again. It was true that the Commodore had promised each of them a bottle of Jack when they were through, but in fact he didn't know where he'd come by four dozen some-odd bottles—that he could spare, anyway. He snatched the VHF from Hat.

"Need more time, Reggie!" he said.

"You ain't got more time," Lehigh spat back. "She's starting to split. It's what you wanted, right?"

"Yes! But not yet!"

"Well, tough shit! We ain't playin' with sand castles here!"

That was the last transmission from Lehigh. Either he'd been lost, his VHF had been lost, or he'd simply had enough.

Things were perhaps working too well. The sail had filled immediately and, having to pull the entire peninsula, was guiding her awkwardly, more east than north, toward Lisbon. But there was no reason to think that, once freed of the burden of the upper peninsula, she wouldn't make straight for the southern coast of England. Excellent. And apparently secession was imminent. Excellent again. But still the problem: how on earth to cleanse the lower peninsula in time?

"All right, boys!" Commodore Crumfield said to the stirring mob before him. "Back to the park! Let's go!"

Wishful thinking, very wishful, that it would be so easy.

·XIV·

"WHAT NOW!" HORFNER cried. They were the first words he'd spoken since being lashed to his sculpture, the first real sign of life he'd shown at all, and so the cry brought everyone— Carolina, Parker, DuChamp—to attention.

"What?" Carolina said. "What's he saying?" Facing west, she could hardly hear the man, much less see what he might be referring to. But Parker could hear him and, turning left, gazing east down Calhoun, he could see very well what Horfner was referring to: not more than a few blocks east, toward the harbor—or rather, the Atlantic Ocean—Calhoun Street appeared to be, well, splitting down the middle. Cracking, actually breaking open, as if being torn apart by a cataclysmic quake. From within the split, an eruption of pluff mud, water, detritus, and trash shot violently skywards. What was more, the crack appeared to be lunging forward—westward, toward them—the filthy geyser blasting like the bowels of some mammoth underground beast. A very hungry, very angry mammoth underground beast.

"Dear God," Parker said.

"What?" Carolina screamed. "What is it? I can't see! What?"

Parker could not have begun to explain, but as it turned out he did not have to. DuChamp, watching from the platform, was more than happy to oblige.

"Secession, by damn!" he cried. He raised his bottle to the sky and pulled a long draw before lowering it. "And this time it's going to stick, you sons of bitches! Wee-hoo!" He took another long pull.

"What's happening?" Carolina said.

Parker did not answer her—couldn't, really—but simply watched, incredulous, as the split blasted forward, gathering strength, momentum, and violence with each lunge. The beast was taking quarter blocks at a time now, ever more urgently, ever more violently, while in its wake, the ocean came flooding in, widening the break still further, so that to the east of Meeting what had only moments before been Calhoun Street was a body of water the width of the former Ashley River and widening.

And flooding forward.

"You hear me?" DuChamp cried with glee. "Going to stick this time!" He commenced a drunken jig around the sculpture, drinking as he stepped, and singing up at the prisoners, "Old times there are ne'er forgotten! Look away! Look away! Look away, Dixieland!" So caught up had he become in his celebration that he did not notice, as Parker did, that the rupture had now in fact reached them. Not twenty yards from the foot of the sculpture, Calhoun Street was crumbling before his eyes. Indeed, even when the spew began to rain down upon them—a foul-smelling hail of mud and shit—DuChamp simply incorporated the turn of events into his victory dance, raising his face to the sky and singing, "Let it rain! By God, let it rain!"

Had he been paying more attention to the course of events behind him than to his hostages and himself, DuChamp might have realized that he was fast running out of time. As it was, in short order he found himself further distracted. Pausing for another pull, he saw, far across the square, what appeared to be a mob of, well, nigras, approaching. They looked to be in no particular hurry and to have no particular agenda—that is, no evident malice—but as the mob got closer, and closer, and closer, it came to resemble to DuChamp a wicked storm cloud gathering and marching forward unpredictably, unforgivingly, and above all, dangerously. Still, his terror was short-lived: after all, this was precisely why they were seceding. So as to be done with this. They would be saved, once and for all, from the burden and curse of the unruly and unpredictable black man. He took one last pull, smashed the empty bottle against the base of the sculpture, shouted, "So long you sons of bitches! Good luck with the Negroes!", and turned to cross the street to safety.

Parker could see, almost taste, the paralyzing horror that seized DuChamp when he turned to find that Calhoun Street as they had always known it was no more. The pedestal honoring John C. himself was now crashing into the water, and if DuChamp wanted out, he would have to do the same. He faced a jump that would have put even a much younger, much more sober man to the test. In another moment, he faced not only a jump but a short swim, the street now a creek, and rapidly widening, until, when at last DuChamp found it in himself to take a step forward, albeit a weak and confused step, the street had become a tidal river, splashed here and there with dolphins, flying fish, even a flock of pelicans.

Parker watched as DuChamp turned back, looking across the square to something Parker could not see. The man again stood pallid, horror-stricken, paralyzed. Now he turned and faced west, where he found some hope, however faint. The spuming split had not yet conquered King Street, and if only he could outrun it, reach King in time, he might yet cross to safety.

If only.

He stumbled before he could start, then started, then stumbled again. If the man would only quit looking over his shoulder across the park, Parker thought, he might have gathered the concentration, the wherewithal, to make it. But the man would not stop looking over his shoulder, and he continued to stumble and fall along the malformed bluff of mud and crud until, yes, there was simply no hope of a safe, dry passage to the other side. The fracture was well beyond King Street now, and almost done with Calhoun altogether. Parker watched with more disgust than pity as the man took one last look over one shoulder—at the square—and one last look over the other—at Parker, Carolina and Horfner—and then tumbled down the new bank and splashed clumsily into the rising water. And so Parker watched as, with dolphins jumping and zipping all around him, Murray DuChamp—fully clothed, fully intoxicated, and never much of a swimmer to begin with—became the first casualty by drowning in the latter-day history of the peninsula. The man did not even make it ten yards before he disappeared beneath a swell, and disappeared forever.

It was only then that Parker considered exactly what was happening in the broader scheme of things. Only then that he thought of his mother, hopelessly trapped—or was it safely secured?—on the other side.

"Mommy!" he called.

"What could she do about this?" Carolina said.

"Mommy!" Parker cried again.

"These aren't exactly her people!" Carolina said.

"What?" Parker said. What people?

"I said, these aren't exactly her people!"

"What people? What the blessed hell are you talking about? What people?"

"These people!" said Carolina, and now, at last, Parker could actually see whom she meant—a crowd was gathering around the base of the sculpture. They were mostly black and mostly laughing hysterically, particularly the younger members of the group. They had never seen anything quite like this— three white people tied to a gigantic black cock—and the spectacle of it, the *justice* of it, was enough to keep the better part of the group distracted from the broader, more incredible spectacle at hand, the swelling river that was Calhoun Street. The older members of the crowd turned away from the sculpture with disgust and then gathered along the newly formed north bank to study the water. Some shook their heads, others looked skyward for a sign, an explanation. Parker distinctly heard one older woman say, "Now, what we gwine do 'bout this?" Meanwhile the younger group had begun jeering at Parker, Carolina, and Horfner, if not maliciously, then not kindly.

An amplified voice broke through the confusion. "People! People! Please! This is not what we're here for!" The amplified voice approached, and soon Parker could make out the man with the megaphone, the man whom he had nearly run over on his mad dash across the peninsula.

As it turned out, Horfner recognized the man, too. More precisely, even.

"Biddencope!" he hissed.

"Who?" Parker said.

"Harry Biddencope. The little bastard who brought me here! Who started all this!"

"Harry Biddencope." Parker considered. The name rang a dull bell.

"Works for the mayor, or the city, or some fuck-ass thing."

Harry Biddencope. Of course. How could Parker forget? Roused from sleep early on a Saturday morning some time last year by his mother shrieking in the kitchen, "Who are these people? This scalawag! No! I do not know this man, goddammit!" Rushing downstairs in his pajamas to find her screaming bitterly at page D-1 of the Saturday *Current*, which in recent years had always featured a profile, titled DO YOU KNOW?, of some local personality. The problem was, they were never local anymore—more often than not, a parvenu businessman who had made a name for himself in the hospitality industry, a handful of facts particularly distressing to his mother. "Harry Biddencope!" she had shouted. "Born in Ridgeway, Ohio! Collects speed boats! Works in radio! And for the mayor! The goddamn mayor! No! I don't know Harry Biddencope! And I don't care to, either!" And for the rest of Parker's visit, his mother had used the name *Harry Biddencope* as a kind of curse phrase—like *fucking hell*, say. When she stumbled on a loose floorboard, she'd hissed "Harry Biddencope!" under her breath. When she burned an English muffin the next morning, she'd shaken her head and mouthed the name at the sky, Godwards. And when she dropped one of the china plates after dinner, she had spat "Biddencope!" at Parker with a violence he did not know she was capable of.

And now here he was, Harry Biddencope himself, with a megaphone in his hand and an unruly crowd before him. Beside him walked a man Parker also recognized—Reverend Anthony Lawson, city council representative from the upper peninsula, organizer and energizer of the black cause in Charleston.

"Biddencope," Horfner hissed. "The little shit. He should be tied up here! Crucified!"

"Let's see what he has to say," said Parker. For all the man's faults, all his reputation, he did at least appear to be trying to calm the jeering crowd.

"Oh, he'll have plenty to say. He's always got plenty to say. 'Come on down, Abel. Build whatever you like. It's a win-win for both of us! All of us! We'll get the exposure of having you, and you'll get exposed before thousands!' Well, I'm exposed all right! For fuck's sake, look at me! I'm exposed! To the fucking jeers of thousands! Not to mention the fucking elements!"

"Let's see what he has to say," Parker repeated, as if they had any choice in the matter.

In fact, it mattered very little what Biddencope had to say, because nobody gathered before him was listening. It was true he had lured them with big talk through the megaphone, with his promise of a spectacle the likes of which they had never seen, but along the way he had talked so much about so little that they had all but quit listening to the voice. It was the voice of a television commercial, easy enough to block out entirely.

"People!" he pleaded. "Please! These are not your enemies! Why, there is the man who built this—thing! This big, black—thing! It's a *black thing!* We understand! That man there understands!" At this, he glanced up at Horfner and winked.

"You fucking fool," Horfner said, but quietly.

"And that woman! That beautiful 'Spanic woman! She's not even from here! She's from New York! She understands the black thing, too! She does!"

"Hold on," Parker said over his shoulder to Carolina. "You know him?"

"I've talked to him," Carolina said. "He's the one who suggested the *Times* send someone down to cover this thing."

"What thing? The black thing?"

"This—all of this. 'Three festivals in one week!' he said. 'Unprecedented in this city!' We'd get a story, he'd get more publicity. Some crap like that. I just wanted to write Charleston. I never had. It was a free ride. By the way, do you still have my notepad?"

"I do," said Parker. Bit of a carpetbagger herself, he thought. It was all about the story for her. The story this, the story that. So she was not without fault. That was good to know. If it all collapsed, if nothing worked out—well, Carolina Gabrel was not without fault.

"You got a story, all right," Parker said.

"Huh. Look at that little bastard."

Biddencope was still pleading, and still pleading in vain. The kids laughed and jeered over and through his announcements, even throwing shoes and coins at the prisoners. Finally Reverend Lawson, looking stern and irritated, nabbed the megaphone from Biddencope, who stood astonished at the nerve of the man. Anthony adjusted his clerical collar, cleared his throat, and said, with the commanding and assuring voice of a born leader, "Brothers and sisters. Brothers and sisters!" At this the elders gathered on the bank turned and approached, a congregation called to attention by their pastor. Those younger members of the crowd who continued to hiss and jeer were quickly hushed by their elders, and the square became utterly silent save the sound of swells slapping the banks.

"Brothers and sisters," Anthony began. "I need not remind you that it is more righteous to forgive than to punish. If ever these sad souls were our enemies, the time to welcome them into our arms, as brothers and sisters, is now. We cannot move forward until we cease looking back."

Shouts erupted from the crowd: "Praise God! Hallelujah!" Fortified, encouraged, Anthony boomed, "In the spirit of forgiveness, let us free these men and this woman! Let us bring the prisoners down!"

The elders prodded the youngsters toward the sculpture. The abandoned deer stand was passed forward, and the three were untied and escorted to safety on the ground, at which point Abel Horfner fled the scene. Though he would scarcely admit as much to another soul, he was terrified of dark-skinned people, outside of cocktail parties and gallery openings.

Watching the three go free, Anthony Lawson savored the singular relief, the profound unshackling that was forgiveness. Whatever was happening in the cosmos, whatever it was that had just befallen this wayward peninsula, people were coming together here. Coming together and showing the capacity to forgive. No small task—for anyone, anywhere. He surveyed the square with satisfaction, intensified all the more when he recognized among the gathering Rainy Lofton and three of the dozen or so older ladies who had foregone the boycott in favor of their work as housekeepers on the lower peninsula. He approached Miss Rainy to thank her for joining the cause.

"Ain' jwinin no cause!" she said. "Guttin' ote while the guttin's gud!"

"What do you mean?" said Anthony.

"Dey spluttin' off. White peoples. Gwine dey own wey. Luk dey dat wadduh. Land spluttin' off."

Anthony looked. The peninsula continued to crack in half. "People did this?" he said. "On purpose?"

"Sho' dey did!"

"How do you know?"

"Yo' daddy! You know he in tight with dem peoples. In de club."

His father! A gut punch of alarm (where was the man now?) slammed hard into fury ("in tight"?) and spread smoothly into relief—surely at last the man, knowing the club's plan, at last the man had abandoned them and come home.

"Where is he now?" Anthony asked, scanning the masses hopefully. "Over by the fountain?"

"Nooo, chile! He still dey! At de club! Say he ain' gwine nowhey!"

An inauspicious moment, truly, for Harry Biddencope to walk up and reach for the megaphone. To say, "Ant! Lemme see that thing! I've got a few words!"

Anthony would not release the megaphone. He was not through with it. He had thought he was, only moments ago, but now his blood was popping. He looked at the river that had replaced Calhoun Street, thought hard about diving into it and making for the far shore, for his father.

Then raised the megaphone instead.

"And now!" he roared, his voice trembling with rage. "In the spirit of justice! Let us string this loud-mouthed cracker up!"

If Harry Biddencope did not know whom Anthony meant, he was not long in finding out, because everyone else gathered there knew exactly who the loud-mouthed cracker was. They closed in around Harry and, despite his desperate pleas and struggles, he found himself being hoisted up the side of the black thing.

BACK AT THE ST. PHILIP'S playground, Commodore Crumfield had a situation on his hands. It seems the Jamboreeans were in no rush to get back to Calhoun Square. They had performed quite a feat in the raising of the sail, not to mention in the capture and imprisonment of the three traitors, and they were in a mood to celebrate with the promised liquor. What was more, they had quickly become enamored of this side of the peninsula, as anyone would. When they started grumbling as much and growing belligerent, Commodore Crumfield, flustered, called on Bubby McGaw, whom he did not really know but whose powers of organization and motivation might prove useful at a time like this.

"I need to move these folks," he told Bubby. "Now."

"What's the hurry?" McGaw said.

"Never mind what's the hurry. Can you not move them?"

"Well." McGaw considered. "I'd like to say the spirit of the Lord could move them, sir. But frankly, they aren't moved by that as much as you might think. Or hope."

"What will move them?" Crumfield asked.

"Liquor. They want their liquor," McGaw said, shaking his head. "Pathetic, but true."

Crumfield thought for a moment. "Tell them the liquor's on the other side."

"The other side?" said McGaw. "Heaven?"

"The square, damn it!" Crumfield said. "Tell them the liquor's in the square! And do it now!"

The man spoke with such authority, with such confidence in his own righteousness, Bubby McGaw was hard pressed to refuse him. But nor was he above giving his own hand one last try. He stepped up onto a bench and announced at the top of his voice, "Gentlemen! Your prize awaits you on the other side!"

Naturally the announcement only further confused the situation.

"Cram it, preach!" a sportsman hollered.

"No more sermons!" called another.

"Where's our liquor, goddammit?"

Well, he had tried. But he was preaching to the hopeless—the addicted and corrupt—and at last Bubby swallowed that fact and sent them to what he believed would be their booze-sodden doom. "It's in the square," he said with resignation. "Your liquor awaits you in Calhoun Square."

If the crew was less than thrilled at the prospect of yet another hike across the peninsula and at having to abandon this more luxurious and livable side of that peninsula, the prospect of celebratory liquor was, as before and ever after, as it was in the beginning and ever would be, sufficient motivation to move them—en masse, guns, dogs, and all—squareward.

The Commodore sent Sam Haynely to man the navigation station at the club, and then he and Hat followed the pack, kept them moving, determined to confirm the final cleansing of the peninsula with their own eyes. If Providence were with them, as it had been for so many centuries, the timing would be just right, and they would be free to sail without the burden of undesirables.

They were horrified, then, to discover, not two blocks up Meeting Street, on the horizon, a body of water where Calhoun Street had once been. What with the sun winking off sea swells, seagulls circling, and pelicans gliding, they might have been walking to the beach. Walking up Meeting Street to the beach.

"Hurry!" Commodore Crumfield screamed. "You—we won't make it! The—liquor's getting away!"

And they did hurry. To the best of their generally overweight and fatigued ability, they hurried. The hounds and retrievers bayed and yipped with the excitement. They ran ahead eagerly, hungrily, only to come to a sudden skidding halt at Meeting's muddy end. Some of the dogs were forced over the side and down the mud bank by the momentum of the portly group behind them. They slid waterwards, then feverishly clawed their way back up to find their masters and await instructions.

Across the water, Calhoun Square was floating away. It seemed that all the prisoners but one had escaped from the sculpture. What was more, the square was overrun with dark people. A very close call, the Commodore thought. But if secession had proved successful in its primary aim—to separate from the upper peninsula—it had, for the moment, proved less so in its secondary aim: to provide a thoroughly cleansed lower peninsula. There was no denying that on the one hand, the break had come at precisely the right moment. On the other, the Commodore was still stuck with the nutjob Jamboreeans.

He had to think fast. What was the only thing more important to a public-lander than his dog? His truck, of course. And their trucks, for the most part, were still on the other side, parked in and around Calhoun Square.

"Your trucks!" the Commodore hollered. "They'll steal your trucks! Your Z71s! Your Durangos! Your Rams! The darkies will steal them! Steal them!"

At this, the sportsmen opened fire on the far bank. Gunsmoke puffing, muzzles blazing, they resembled the front line of some ragged Confederate militia. But they were armed mostly with shotguns, not muskets. The pellets of birdshot and buckshot sailed scarcely halfway across the divide before dropping pitifully into the water.

"Hold your fire!" the Commodore commanded, and the sportsmen held their fire. "You won't get them that way! You'll have to charge, by damn! *Charge!*"

For the most part, the assembled sportsmen were considerably less eager to obey this particular command.

Opening fire was one thing; plunging into a swelling sea quite another. Flustered, some sent their dogs in, but the dogs, finding no fallen birds or training dummies, turned around and swam back to the bank, their heads lowered in shame.

"Your trucks!" the Commodore pleaded. "The Negroes will steal your trucks! They'll play—Negro music in them! Jungle music! Ghetto music! In your trucks!"

A last-ditch effort, but to the Commodore's surprise, it worked. Because the Jamboreeans could not have this at all. Losing the truck was one thing, but losing it to jungle music was, apparently, quite another. The Commodore watched—amazed, thrilled—as with no further provocation they began to leap off the bluff and make furiously for the other side. Fully clothed and booted, toting shotguns and ammo boxes, and far from peak condition to begin with, they swam in vain, and became, as the Commodore and Hat looked on, the next victims by drowning in the strange latter-day history of the peninsula. Dogs returned masterless, baseball caps and camouflaged coozies bobbed on the swells and washed ashore.

For their part, the dozen or so sportsmen who had exercised better judgment and remained on the bank now openly wept like children—not for their fallen comrades, but for their trucks, lost forever to dark people and jungle music.

NAVIGATOR SAM HAYNELY might have—no, should have— foreseen that the lower peninsula, once liberated from the weight of the upper, would present an entirely new kind of watercraft. It was made considerably lighter by secession, for one thing, which meant that as an oceangoing vehicle it was considerably less stable and considerably more vulnerable to shifts in wind and current. What had been a kind of oceanliner—massive, solid, unshakeable—now more closely resembled a sportfisher sans engine, pitching and yawing without conviction in the swells like so much flotsam, the sail billowing and slacking in the breeze, which itself could not seem to make up its mind. Without an engine, with only the whims of fate to depend upon, freedom, it seemed, was worthless.

If not downright dangerous. Though he would not yet dare report as much to the Commodore, Sam Haynely monitored his instruments with increasing anxiety. He was accustomed to directing the directable, managing the manageable—the streamlined, the seaworthy, the massively powered. He had never been the sailor his father and grandfather had been, preferring from his youngest days a school of hungry kingfish in glassy seas to a steady afternoon blow. He had no answer when the Commodore asked, via VHF, what they might do about the slacking sail, much less what they might do about the dozen or more public-landers they were now, apparently, stuck with. Crumfield sounded tense, even panicky, and trained as he was in the art of calm, as any man who brings three-hundred-thousand-ton freighters into port must be, Captain Sam urged Crumfield to do just that—remain calm. It was an approach much more easily proposed than practiced, even for a pilot of Sam's experience. According to his instruments, the newly liberated lower peninsula was now tracking—if bobbingly, if clumsily—still, most decidedly, Gibraltarwards, the trend of its motion southeasterly. He was not sure how to explain it, except that now, freed of the upper peninsula, and perhaps the better part of its foundation (that is, its keel) courtesy of the dredging operation, the lower peninsula had not gained maneuverability but lost it and was now spinning in slow circles, the sail not only failing to pull them out of the rotation, but in fact contributing to the same. If this trend continued, they would soon lose any chance of gaining the friendly North Atlantic current and the Westerlies and find themselves instead at the mercy of the Canary current and the Northeasterlies. That is, they would soon be making for the continent of Africa, a continent that would, indeed, be very difficult to avoid. By all indications, they were headed exactly the wrong way.

For now, in the interest of maintaining calm, Captain Sam would keep this news to himself. And Commodore Crumfield did take some solace in Sam's assurances. His was the very voice of calm, the voice you wanted behind the controls of an airplane in turbulence or, more appropriately here, a seacraft adrift. (And they were certainly adrift; he could feel it now more than ever, the very earth beneath his feet rocking and bobbing, the horizon seesawing nauseatingly.) The sportsmen had all but abandoned the commodore without threat or even insult, the loss of their trucks apparently overshadowing their mad desire for the drinks he owed them. Bewildered and saddened, they had disbanded without direction, and where they had gone he neither knew nor cared. For the moment, he had been released of responsibility for them, and he made his way toward the Atlantic Club confident that all could be, as all always had been, resolved from there.

·XV·

I N THE HOUR OF SECESSION, Bo Bamber found himself in an awkward but by no means unfamiliar position. The authority and apparent success of his speech (the gathered mini-men had made for downtown Charleston and its treasure trove of storeables like linebackers for a fumbled football) had so lathered Tater up that she could not wait until they got back to the Bay House B&B. She could not wait until they got back to Mama Bess. She could not even wait until they got to the first floor of the Swamp Fox. No sooner had the glass elevator begun its descent than she jammed the emergency stop button, tore open her blouse, and all but tackled Bo to the floor of the elevator car, pulling him on top of her and, shortly, into her. "Now, Daddy Bo," she huffed. "Now!"

Bo could not refuse her even had he wanted to, which he didn't. She was wetter than marsh mud, her breath hotter than a sandhill in July. He had to focus elsewhere lest he explode too fast—a rare occurrence, but one he knew Tater could not abide. The one thing, perhaps, she could not. She was the most accepting of women otherwise, most ideal, at his complete beck and call, except on the rare occasion when he failed her in this way. If he did, he could be assured of an uncomfortable afternoon at best, she distant and nervy, he submissive and apologetic. The one state of affairs Bo Bamber could not abide.

And so he must focus elsewhere. Baseball no longer worked, owing perhaps to a particularly naughty night they had recently enjoyed with a miniature Louisville Slugger. And so, instead of closing his eyes and thinking about baseball, he simply opened them and looked out the glass window of the elevator, down toward Calhoun Square, where he was certain to find some distraction or other.

Indeed. A bit more of a distraction, perhaps, than he had bargained for.

"Jungle bunnies," he said, stunned at the sight of so many, all in one place.

"Ah!" Tater moaned. She seemed remarkably close to climax, hotter than ever. "My jungle bunny! Hot bunny! Hot jungle! Oh!"

"A river!" Bo said.

"Eeee! Come me a river, Bo!" Tater squealed. "A river! Come me a river!"

She climaxed, clutching, squirming, squealing, and, finally, collapsing limp and exhausted, an indulgent grin smoothing her face. "Baby?" she asked. "Did you?"

No, he hadn't. But there was hardly time for that now. "Damn it, Tater!" he said, pushing her off of him. "Look!"

She did. "What—? Jesus Christ, Bo! What are they—? What—?" She grabbed him by the shoulder, swung him around to face her, and then took the words straight from his mouth:

"Mama Bess!"

He had parked her just in front of the hotel, in the loading zone, meaning to mark his territory, stake his claim, announce to the gathered mini-men that Daddy Bo was here, Daddy Bo was mad, and Daddy Bo meant business. Now his decision had backfired. The position of prominence had become a position of exposure to whatever ugly, savage deeds the jungle bunnies were brewing in the park. Even as the elevator descended, he mashed the lobby button. "Come on!" he said. "Move, dammit!"

"What will happen, Bo?" Tater asked. She was cowering in the corner. "What will they do to her?"

"Trust me, you don't even want to know," Bo said. He imagined Mama Bess stripped naked, or worse, tricked out with ground effects and a rib-crunching bass rig like some ghetto whore. In a word, jig-rigged. When at last the elevator car bumped softly to a stop, he ordered Tater to stay put. "This may get ugly," he said.

"Daddy Bo!" she shrieked, but Daddy Bo was gone.

To his surprise and profound relief, Bo found Bess standing just as he had left her, untouched, waiting patiently there in front of the hotel like a good girl. They had not gotten to her yet, had not seen her despite her size and her position. Or if they had seen her, they had simply marked her, saved her for later. Because the mob, he now saw, was not moving toward the hotel at all but away from it, across the square toward the giant tallywhacker, like pilgrims called to a divine sign.

Bo hurried back through the lobby, fetched Tater, and together they jumped into Bess's lap. Before firing the engine, Bo reached across Tater and pulled his .38 from the glove box. He checked the clip—packed tight, as always—and placed the pistol on the console between them.

"What—where will we go?" Tater asked.

"The hell out of here, that's where," Bo said, and he fired Mama Bess up. She answered with a grumbling purr, the purr of a lioness in heat, and for good measure—for fair warning to anyone who might be entertaining designs on her—Bo revved her, hard. She responded willingly, happily, with a roar.

"All right," Bo said. "Let's do it!"

"Now?" Tater asked.

"What—? Yes now!"

"Doesn't seem like a good time, that's all!" Tater spat. Still she obligingly leaned over and began working at Bo's belt.

"What are you doing?" Bo yelled.

"What you said! It!" she screamed, and she released his tally from its lair.

Flustered and furious, Bo slapped Tater's hands away and slammed Mama Bess into drive. She lunged eagerly, eight cylinders of desire, six liters of passion. Unfortunately, there was nowhere to go. Thirty yards down King, she had to stop abruptly, painfully, midcoitus. Where there once had been a street, there now flowed a river. The fact was, if they had not paused to check the pistol, to rev the engine, or to discuss, in their own peculiar way, semantics, Bo and Tater might have made it. But it was definitely too late now, at least from here. The channel measured twenty yards across and growing. Bo had little doubt that Mama Bess could make it down one bank and up the other, but she was not, he knew, a swimmer. It was difficult, even distressing, for him to accept that his girl had a limit, but yonder that limit lay.

"Daddy Bo!" Tater cried.

"I don't know!"

Looking west, though, Bo did see an opportunity, however distant, however slim. The river had not yet claimed all of Calhoun. It was certainly working hard to. But if he could find a parallel route, perhaps they could outrun the fracture and cross over to the other side—the better side, where lay all the storeables, all the crap, where lived all the *white* people—before the city was split completely in two.

He jammed Mama Bess into reverse. The trailer jackknifed and crashed through the glass door of the hotel lobby, and Bo wheeled Bess around and charged north up King into the heart of the upper peninsula, the rundown neighborhoods and housing projects.

"I'm scared, Daddy Bo!" Tater said.

Bo rested his right hand on the .38 beside him. "Don't be scared, dammit!" he said. "Look for a left turn!"

They found one, but the tiny street went nowhere, only deeper into lower-class housing for three blocks before T-boning at a soccer field. Bo wheeled right, then left again and down the next block, but this one dead-ended after two—and so on, so that in such a way they made a zigzagging path north and west across the upper peninsula, Bo's grip on the pistol tightening at every turn, and every turn finding them deeper in unfamiliar territory, farther from the Bay House B&B. Mama Bess obliged the thrusts from zero to seventy to zero and back again without complaint, as eager to make an escape as anyone. Tater was terrified but kept quiet except to point out streets.

At last they made it to the Crosstown, where neighborhood gave way to bypass. A highway sign directed them toward West Calhoun, and in no time Bess was pushing seventy on the bypass.

"Daddy Bo!" Tater cried. "Will we make it? Daddy Bo!"

Bo did not answer. He was tending to another woman. He was with Mama Bess, who, if she did not need to be adored just now, did require his undivided attention. She was, he knew, their only hope. Below them, running perpendicular to their own course, the sudden river would in a matter of moments gain the ocean, and so split the land—and the bypass—completely in two. Bo did not slow. It was a risk like no risk he had ever taken. If they did not make it, if they were so much as half a second behind the rushing water, they would plunge into the ocean. Still, he did not slow. He would risk his life, and Tater's, and Mama Bess's, rather than strand the three of them on the dark side of the peninsula.

"Let's go, girl," he encouraged Mama Bess. "Come on, baby." They climbed, climbed, Mama Bess doing all that she could.

"Do it, Princess!" Tater cried with considerably more volume and urgency. She kissed the dashboard—French kissed it, her tongue slathering the vinyl. "Do it!"

Bess gained seventy-five, eighty, eighty-five, ninety, all eight cylinders roaring with determination, as though she had no more interest in being trapped on the upper peninsula than her brood did. In the interest of maintaining purpose—once Bo had made a decision, he did not turn on it, he did not renege—Bo had ceased looking down, over the side of the bypass. He had made his decision and, as all his decisions were, it was final. He pressed on.

But pressing on, looking forward, there was simply no way to ignore the fact that the bypass was already splitting apart at its peak, the far side now shifting leftwise as if shaken by a massive quake. Still they charged on. Ninety-five, a hundred, one-oh-five . . .

And charged, and charged, and when at last they made the summit, screaming along at 115, they faced a formidable jump. Twenty yards, easy. Two first-downs.

"Daddy Bo!" Tater screamed. Then, "Daddy Booooooooo!"

No hesitation, none: they launched and floated through the air, time itself seeming to hesitate now as the front wheels spun for something solid to grab hold of, something to do about this. There was nothing to do about this, nothing but float and hope against gravity. Tater and Bo both leaned forward instinctively and hugged the dash, eyes closed, their last view a horrifying one—the far side of the bypass all crumbling concrete and wrenched rebar. They could not bear to look, and after what may have been the longest moment of their lives they were slammed backwards from the dash, their eyes blasted wide open by deployed airbags, as Bess landed on the far side, her front tires now screaming for purchase against the broken pavement and Tater crying as she tried to beat back her airbag, "Daddy Bo! We—made it! We made it! Mama Bess did it!"

She had done it, they had made it, and they might have made it for good, incontrovertibly, if it were not for the trailer full of repo'ed crap, which, as soon as Bo backed off on the gas—to handle his airbag, to gauge their position—dragged them down. They tumbled end over end, twisting and turning through what was surely the second-longest moment of their respective lives.

One abbreviated triple backflip later, the entire rig crashed into the water akimbo, upside down. But what might have been, in an earlier, less safety-conscious age, a most fatal wreck, in fact proved fortuitous: the windshield shattered to pieces on contact, and the twin airbags (Mama Bess's mammaries, as it were) broke free and floated to the surface, bearing a dumbstruck Bo and trembling Tater, who now clung to the bags for their lives. The safety feature had indeed saved those lives, in however roundabout and unusual a fashion. Truly, no crash test could have foreseen such a bizarre turn of events.

Unfortunately, there was little the remaining airbags could do for Mama Bess herself. No matter that there were four of them, no matter that they had all deployed on first contact with the far span of the bypass. The weight of the trailer was simply too great, and just as it had sought the water's surface from the broken span and dragged the rest along for the ride, it now sought the bottom of the ocean and dragged Bess along. Together Bo and Tater watched helplessly as their girl, upended, headlights peering to the sky, slowly sank out of sight and so became a martyr. Their martyr.

"She saved us," said Tater, weeping. "She died to save us."

"She was a good girl to the end," Bo said. He had to swallow his own teary breaths, the first of his adult life. "The best of girls."

At this, a last bubble—massive, the size of a weather balloon—blubbed to the surface like a fart in a bathtub, expelled a cloud of steam, and was gone.

"May she," Bo choked, "may she rest in peace."

Tater now wept desperately. But her despair only strengthened Bo. He would have to take control of the situation. They would have to move on, and he would have to be the one to move them. Searching, he calculated that they were equidistant from each of their options, fifty yards or so, half a football field either way. Which meant, really, half a football field from their one option: the lower peninsula. He explained to Tater that it would be best if she released her own airbag and joined up with him on his. Working together, they could surely make the lower peninsula by dark. But Tater, still weeping, still despairing, would not let go of her bag, her one memento of Mama Bess, their girl. She would not let go, and so at last Bo abandoned his and joined Tater at hers, and then began to swim them to shore.

·XVI·

ON THE TOP PORCH AT 2 Bay Street, Elizabeth Hathaway observed that the horizon had begun to seesaw. It was nothing she had not seen before. A seat on the top porch customarily brought with it a toddy or four, and so, yes, the horizon had often seemed to seesaw from here. Still, the motion looked far more extreme than usual. Elizabeth first attributed this to having drunk far more than usual.

"Oh, my," she said to Phillip, who was sitting and sipping in the rocker beside hers. "I believe I've outdone myself, dear."

"It was a good fight," Phillip said. "And it looks like we've won."

"Yes—but, oh my. Our little celebration. It's got me—I feel like we're—like the whole world is—rocking." She stood up to take control of herself, only to fall abruptly back down into her chair, a tumble she again attributed to the excesses of their victory celebration.

"It is rocking," said Phillip. "We're at sea, after all."

"Yes, but—"

"It seems more severe now. The rocking."

"Yes."

"We may be in a rough patch. In the ocean."

"Yes," Elizabeth said. "Well." She resumed her sipping, comforted by Phillip's quiet strength, his knowledge, his surety.

The two sat and sipped together for the better part of the afternoon, content and bemused as an elderly aristocratic couple on the deck of an old cruising schooner, until toward nightfall their musings were interrupted by the scrape of the home's rickety iron gate across brick.

Elizabeth sat up. "Who?" she asked. "Are they back?"

Phillip stood and rounded the porch, but by the time he reached the street side, the uninvited guest or guests had passed through the gate and up the steps. He could hear footsteps crossing the downstairs porch, then a hand working the doorknob.

"Excuse me?" he called. A pause in the working of the doorknob. "Excuse me!"

Now the steps crossed back down the porch, and two portly men—armed, camouflaged, ball-capped—appeared below. They gazed up and down the street stupidly.

"Hello?" Phillip called, and they looked up, a pair of round, grizzled, dumbstruck faces. Phillip recognized them from earlier events he would rather forget, but if they recognized him, they did not appear to care.

"Can I help you?" Phillip asked.

"Looking for a house," one of the men said.

"A house," Phillip said.

"Somebody lives here?" asked the other man.

"Yes," Phillip said. "Somebody lives here."

"Goddamn."

"And they mean to keep on living here. If you don't mind."

"Well excuuuuuse us," the first man said, and then the two conferred privately. Phillip could make out only the occasional curse word, but then the two were leaving. They left without shutting the gate behind them.

"They're back?" Elizabeth asked when Phillip returned to her.

"No," Phillip said. "Somebody else."

"Somebody else? What did they want?"

"A house."

"A house? What kind of house? For what?"

"Didn't say," Phillip said.

"Goodness gracious," Elizabeth said. "Who raised these people? Lord! Will you fix me another, dear? I think we need another."

"Of course," said Phillip, and he stood up.

"Looking for a house. Never in my life," Elizabeth said. She handed Phillip her tumbler, then before he reached the door she stopped him with a startling question. "Do you know how to use a pistol, Phillip?" she said. "Hm?"

THE TWO MEN WERE LOOKING for a house, and they weren't alone. When the reality of the situation had settled upon them—their trucks were gone, and no amount of weeping, cursing, or darkie-hating would bring them back—the Jamboreeans set about exploring their new home on the lower peninsula en masse, with an eye peeled toward available housing. They were in a state of general exhaustion, and though they considered themselves outdoorsmen, they were not about to sleep outdoors, on the ground like so many Appalachian Trail hippies. For every three buffed and polished mansions stood a paint-flaked, crooked-porch fixer-upper which could not possibly house the kind of people they knew to live down here. Surely these houses were between owners. That is, available.

What they were quick to discover, as the homeless mini-men had discovered before them, is that the rundown homes were more often than not the occupied ones. Run off from the rotting porches, they had a look at the more polished offerings, to find the better half of them, amazingly, uninhabited. Available. Most of the empty houses were exquisitely furnished, like so many ten-thousand-square-foot hotel suites, with well-stocked bars showcasing bottles upon bottles of top-shelf liquor that had not even been opened. The homes were spotless, as if cleaned up and prepared just for them, the thirsty, exhausted sportsmen. The hounds and retrievers, too, ran through the homes in amazement, finding pewter water bowls, canned gourmet dog food, feather dog beds. There was no explaining it, nor any real need to. By early evening, each of the men had staked his own claim, moved into his own manor, and begun having his way with the top-shelf drinks. The only problem was deciding who would host the neighborhood get-togethers that invariably sprang up, as each was eager to entertain and so impress his neighbors in the splendorous luxury of his new digs. The abundant porches, they found, offered an easy solution to the problem: each man could stay at home, on his own porch, and simply broadcast his cheer to the porches opposite and adjacent. An improved kind of block party, if you will, the entire block raising Cain, each participant having room to burp, fart, and scratch himself. Before long, entire blocks of the lower peninsula were resounding with guffaws and *goddamn*s and *hell yes*es. So that, in the matter of an hour or so, the culture of the lower peninsula had been completely transformed.

Again.

What neither the sportsmen nor the mini-men before could have known, even had they cared to, is that they were the beneficiaries of not-so-distant prepartum Charleston history: the renovated, mod-conned, slicked-up estates belonged, for the most part, to newer, absentee owners, and so were now, as they were most of the year, available.

And avail of them the Jamboreeans and mini-men did, with the relish and abandon of million-dollar lottery winners, and to the horror of those few natives who remained, who had not witnessed anything quite like this since—well, who had *never* witnessed anything quite like this, and had neither the know-how nor the means to do anything at all about it.

EVENING ON THE ATLANTIC CLUB veranda found a regrouping of the board, with one notable change. DuChamp had long since gone missing, and in his place, in his actual rocking chair, now sat young Kirk Ashley, who was in fact too young by decades to be a club officer, much less a board member, but whose assistance now, in this troubled hour, the others would be hard-pressed to refuse. It may well be that the Ashley clan had been snubbed ever since the sale of the Livin' Past to a foreign interest, but young Kirk had more than proved his value in the capture of the traitors and so had been granted an honorary, if temporary, seat on the board. DuChamp's seat.

"Uppity cumyah bitch," he laughed. "Should have seen her face, boys. Should have seen it."

"Right," Commodore Crumfield said. Despite the round of champagne he had insisted upon, to celebrate secession and the successful raising of the sail, he was not exactly in a celebratory mood. For one thing, they were stuck with the mini-men and lingering Jamboreeans, and for another, something about the intensity with which Captain Sam was studying his instruments, something about his constant scribbling and calculating, the faint but definite furrow on his brow, had the Commodore worried. True, Captain Sam had not expressed any reason for concern, but nor had he expressed any reason for celebration. He had said very little at all. Most telling, the Commodore thought, Captain Sam

had not touched his flute of champagne. He had not even glanced at it.

"What you got for me, Captain?" the Commodore asked.

Captain Sam finished a calculation before answering: "No more than I had last time you asked—what? Five minutes ago?" he said.

The answer was uncharacteristically blunt for Sam Haynely, uncharacteristically rude, and it spoke volumes more than an actual answer might have. Captain Sam Haynely, ever cool, was losing his cool. Not a good sign.

"Well," the Commodore said. "Just wondering what we can do here."

"Not a damn thing right now," Captain Sam said. "But give it time. See what time does for us." With this, Sam's voice turned reassuring again, calming. "May have to reset the sail come morning. We'll see."

Crumfield had no clue what this meant or might entail, but the tone of Captain Sam's voice sent him into the clubhouse's emergency bunkroom, AKA the Dog House, with a measure of peace. He was pleased to find Bubby McGaw, who had retired to the bunkroom an hour earlier, already snoring.

"Never was a sailor myself," Kirk Ashley said to Hat Lawson after the Commodore was gone. "Like to be in control, you know? Like to have a good engine. You count on the wind, you might as well ride around on unbroken colts. Wild stallions. Which is a trip, don't get me wrong. But you ain' gon' get where you want to go on a wild stallion."

Ain' ? Gon' ? Since when did Ashleys talk like mudflat people? Like roofers? It was as if the sale of the tour enterprise had brought them down in the world rather than up. Hat was miffed by this. Disturbed by it. No—appalled. Had he been party to it?

This transformation? Prior to the storied sale, there was in fact little higher the Ashleys could have gone. They'd stood as regents of the Saint Bedelia Society, vestrymen of St. Philip's Church, and trustees of the Day School, in line to direct the Atlantic Club itself. After the sale, the Ashleys had been quietly stripped of these positions, one by one, the old guard meaning to make a lesson of anyone who would sell out to foreign interests—or anyone with the nerve to make so much money so quickly. Hat himself had toed the party line. He had voted with the rest. He now wondered, had they all been grievously mistaken in their approach? Bringing down what was arguably the most powerful name—economically, at least—on the peninsula? Had they not perhaps thrown everything off, all the old rules, with this?

"So—England, that the idea?" Kirk Ashley said. "Never been to England. You, Mr. Lawson? You been to England?"

Yes, he _been_ to England. "Many times," said Hat. "Yes."

"Hell," Kirk went on. "I hardly been out of the county. Except for skiing, out west. And a few duck hunts in Canada. England, though. Never been there. They got some lookers?"

"Beg your pardon?" Hat said.

"Women," Kirk said. "Foxy ladies. I'm hoping to find some foxy ladies, Mr. Lawson. Foreign models. Imports."

"Well," said Hat, and he considered. "England's not very far from France. Let's put it that way, shall we?"

"Hah. All right. We shall." Kirk gulped down what was left of his champagne. "France, huh. Gon' be a real world traveler after this. Yes, sir. High class."

With a little luck, Hat was thinking, the young man would cross the Channel to France and stay there.

"How 'bout tours? Carriage tours in England. How 'bout that? Maybe I could get somethin' goin' there. Huh?"

"Believe the tourist trade is all locked up in England, Kirk," Hat said. "But in France, well. Carriage tours of old Paree. Now I can see that." He could. He could see, very clearly, Kirk Ashley trying to maneuver a horse carriage down the Champs-Elysees, amid swarms of furious Frenchmen shouting and cussing and honking, the "lookers" too disgusted with him to waste a breath laughing at him.

"Paree?" Kirk asked.

"Paris, Kirk," Hat said. "The capital of France."

Kirk laughed. "I know about *Paris*, Mr. Lawson," he said. "You said Par*ee*. Strong champagne, huh?"

"Right."

"Paris France Europe. High class. I mean." Kirk reached behind him for the bar bell. "So I just yank this? And the little old nigra comes runnin'?"

Hat tightened. "Right," he said. "Well—not running."

"I figured that," Kirk said, and he tugged the rope with a force that nearly derailed the bell altogether. "Hurrying slowly, as only a nigra can!"

Just as he said it, CJ Lawson came through the door and onto the piazza. He did not approach Kirk but Hat. "Sir?" he said.

"More champagne!" Kirk cried.

Still CJ stood waiting on Hat. "Sir?" he said again. After a moment, and with a measure of hesitation, Hat nodded, and CJ left for the bar.

"What's his deal?" Kirk asked. "Never heard of the Ashleys?"

Hat shrugged. Chances were, CJ Lawson had heard of the Ashleys, which would fully explain his behavior. The old man had been loyal to—party to—the various causes of his employers all his life, causes whose *raisons d'etre* he could not be expected to understand or, if he did, give a damn about, but in whose execution, in whose implications, he had obediently—and skillfully—participated. No, they did not make them like CJ Lawson anymore. His breed, Hat knew, was dying off as quickly as Hat's own.

"What you reckon he's doing in there?" Kirk laughed. "Taking a nap?"

Reckon. Hat refused to honor the question with an answer.

"I tell you. We don't even use 'em anymore. The darkies. Not out at Bounty. No, sir. Know what we use?"

"What?" Hat asked.

"Mexicans," Kirk said. "You want a boy who'll work, you get a Mexican. A Mexican'll shovel wet horse shit all day. He'll shovel fast, too. I'm talking Speedy Gonzalez. No breaks, no goddamn sitting around leaning on shovels, no complaints. You show him what to do, and he won't stop doing it till you tell him to stop. And you know, it's funny. Guess who pointed this out to the old man? Guess who, of all people."

"Who?"

"The Arabs. I mean, here we are thinking all these years that we got to use the darkies. Don't know why. Maybe 'cause they here, you know? Always been here, always used 'em. But that ain' no reason to do a thing, is it? Just 'cause it's always been done? Just 'cause it's like that? Well, yonder come the Arabs to buy the company and first thing they do is replace all the jigs with beaners. And the old man couldn't believe it. He never trusted the beaners anymore than the jigs. But then he saw how they worked, how they didn't stop working until you told them to stop, and he changed his mind. Then he changed his work force."

"I see," Hat said. The demographic shift was not news to him, and he was happy to be beyond the age when such a shift might matter to him. It had taken him long enough to fathom the African soul—he had little interest in taking on the Latin soul now.

"Where is that old—" Kirk started, but he was interrupted by CJ coming through the door and onto the veranda, bearing a chilled magnum of Bollinger on a silver tray. "There he is!" Kirk said. "We's just talkin about you!"

CJ ignored Kirk completely, stepped past him to Hat, and proffered the bottle to him.

"Hey," Kirk said. "I'll do the honors."

Neither Hat nor CJ Lawson so much as glanced at Kirk.

"Hey!" Kirk said. "Talkin' to you, boy!"

Hat took the bottle and thanked CJ, and then CJ hobbled past Kirk Ashley.

"Hey!" Kirk said again. "You deaf, old man?!"

But CJ was already through the door. Kirk sat dumbstruck for a moment, then, after Hat had uncorked the bottle, let it fly: "That old nigger deaf?"

"No," Hat said. "Not so far as I know."

"Well, what's his problem? Huh?" Kirk asked. "You saw that, right?"

"Saw what?"

"The old jig walked right past me. I mean, what the fuck? It's exactly what I'm talkin' about. They ain' just lazy now; they're goddam uppity. Like I wasn't even here. Like I—"

"Could you"—this was Sam Haynely, who could not hold back any longer—"for one second, just shut your goddamn mouth?" Hat and Kirk both glared at Captain Sam, stunned. The man was not known for his foul temper or foul language. He had spoken scarcely a word since Kirk arrived on the scene, had simply sat focused on his instruments. But now he let loose, completely. "Really," he said. "Would it be such a terribly difficult thing for you to do, boy? To just shut it for a while? Or maybe you Ashleys think you own the air now, too? That it? You won a goddamn lottery, and now you got the right to broadcast your shit—and that's what it is, boy, it's shit—now you got the right to broadcast your shit whether anyone's listening or not, whether anyone cares or not, whether anyone is about to throw your own uppity ass off the dock or not? Because that's about what you'd be good for, as far as I can tell. A goddamn anchor. Then you'd be useful. Wouldn't have to listen to you then. You hear me?"

Kirk heard him. Hat drank to keep from laughing hysterically. Even if Captain Sam's outburst did not bode well for whatever Sam was determining from his instruments, for their current course, Hat would not have traded anything, not even a secure fate, for this public humiliation of Kirk Ashley.

"All right then," Captain Sam said, and he sat back down at the navigation station and turned to his readings. "Maybe you'll shut that mouth for a while."

In fact you could not have shut Kirk Ashley's mouth with a vise clamp just now. He sat slack-jawed and dumbstruck as a common cow. But he definitely was not talking. No, he was not saying a thing.

COME MORNING, THERE WAS no way for Captain Sam to hide, spin, or otherwise evade the truth: the newfound peni-state was making a direct, albeit bobbing and yawing and spinning, run for the coast of Morocco, courtesy of the Canary current and the Northeasterlies. If the construction and raising of the sail had been a remarkable achievement, the sail was proving of little use now, in fact steering them in precisely the wrong direction. If they did not take drastic measures soon, they would make landfall on the Dark Continent before day's end.

"We're going to have to reset it, Harold," he told the Commodore over coffee.

"Reset it," Crumfield said.

"The sail. We don't, we're going to have some real trouble. Soon."

"What kind of trouble?"

"African trouble."

"Christ almighty. Thought we were done with African trouble. Huh? We ever going to be done with African trouble? Huh?"

"Not if we don't make a course correction. And soon."

"All right," the Commodore said. "Goddammit, all right." In fury he hurled his coffee cup oceanwards, only to see it tumble pathetically in the wind and break against the club's seawall. He stepped inside and for the second time in a week sounded the emergency air raid siren.

Hearing the call, most of the club members were only too happy to come running to the relative safety, the relative civilization, of the clubhouse. In the course of the night, their neighborhoods had been overrun and essentially taken hostage by all manner of noisy, disrespectful upstate trash and their howling hounds. The new arrivals had raised merciless hell until dawn from the porches, cupolas, and gardens of the most luxurious mansions, causing a general reevaluation of the lower peninsula's stance on absentee ownership. At least the absentee owners had the courtesy to remain, for the most part, absent. It seemed secession had not lived up to its promise. Liberated from the black problem, freed of the absent-owner condition, they were now stuck with the worst of their own. With trash. It was a most unacceptable turn of events, and when they had gathered in the ballroom, they told Commodore Crumfield as much.

Commodore Crumfield was disgusted but by no means surprised to hear it. But at the moment, he explained, there were bigger issues at hand than the changing face of the neighborhood. Fearing general chaos, he did not go so far as to mention the looming possibility of Africa but simply pointed out that at this point their destination was by no means certain—that, in fact, they were currently veering away from jolly old England.

"France?" Lofton Wheeler asked. "Are we going to France?"

"Not exactly," Crumfield said.

The crowd stirred. Most, it seemed, would have settled for France if they absolutely had to. Most had indulged in the especial delights of French culture since grade school. But Spanish culture, no. And definitely not Portuguese. In Europe, France was the limit, as far south as a civilized human being might call home.

Before the stirring could grow, the Commodore called attention and explained that there was a simple solution to the problem. All that was needed, he said, was a course correction to the north. A simple resetting of the sail. Gazing out at the shriveled faces and broken bodies of the majority of the club's membership, he knew that, if left to them, there would be nothing simple about it. But here he found an opportunity to redeem the fiasco that had been the premature secession. It was the law of civilization, the rule of history, that the less civilized did the dirty work. The brutish, the young, the primitive. Conveniently enough, the peni-state now held an abundance of the brutish and primitive. They were the very men who had raised the sail in the first place; they had been recruited easily enough to do that work, and they would be recruited easily enough to do this work. If the elder members would sit tight in the safety of the clubhouse, free to enjoy an open bar and a lunch buffet, he and the younger members would set about recruiting the new neighbors to the task.

Appeased by the promise of an open bar and free brunch, a day of cards and billiards while the rude invaders were put to the necessary work, the elder members sent the Commodore and his diminutive posse off with their blessings. On the way out, the Commodore and Bubby McGaw stepped into the Dog House to rouse Kirk Ashley, who was so hungover the air raid siren had scarcely stirred him. The Commodore did not care for Kirk, but he had a feeling he might need him. Anyway, the boy had no right to the Dog House, or any other club privilege, in the first place.

As it turned out, the work of recruiting was not so easy as the Commodore might have guessed or, indeed had promised. In fact, the posse failed to rope a single one of the new residents. And not just because the men were horribly hungover, not just because they were armed and ornery—but because the mini-men and Jamboreeans had become so enamored of their new homes, their new place in lower peninsula society, that nothing short of a rain of cluster bombs could have moved them from those homes, that place. Not even the threat of Africa. They could defend themselves, they argued, and, as if to prove as much, they did defend themselves—with shotgun, hound dog, and beer bottle—from the Commodore and his gang. By midday, Commodore Crumfield had not a single recruit and was forced to consider the unconsiderable—they would have to set about the work themselves. Or face Africa.

"The most important thing," he explained when they reached St. Michael's, "will be to not let go. We cannot let go once we have it untied. We let go, and we'll have—I don't know what we'll have. But it won't be a sail. We'll have Africa. That's what we'll have. And we can't have that. Can we?"

No, they couldn't. The very thought of it was enough to send Bubby McGaw and Kirk Ashley up the steeple staircase—Bubby to the veranda that girdled the lower steeple, Kirk all the way up to the top of the spire. Each felt destined to do this, chosen, blessed, and thus unstoppable, if for very different reasons—Bubby chosen by the Lord, blessed by the Lord, empowered by the Lord; Kirk Ashley chosen, blessed, empowered by virtue of being Kirk Ashley, heir to more money and land and power than, well, God.

So up they went, certain of what they had to do, and certain that they would succeed in doing it. At the level of the veranda, where they would have to part, Bubby asked Kirk to lower his head and join hands for a brief prayer, which Kirk did until, peeking, he saw that Bubby had lowered his head, at which point Kirk simply gazed around at the massive gears and ropes and pulleys of the bell tower and let Bubby say his thing.

"Lord, we are gathered in your house at this moment of our greatest need. We ask for your blessing and strength as we set about your work. We ask your help in steering this holy city away from the savage heathens, the infidels, the devils."

Here Bubby paused, and Kirk added his own small prayer. "And away from the darkies," he said.

Bubby shifted, unused to the intrusion of a layperson while he was offering prayer. But this was no time for formalities. "Amen," he said, and then he hugged Kirk awkwardly, wished him luck, and sent him on his way up the steeple staircase. "May the Lord be with you," he said.

"All right," Kirk said and began his climb up the narrow winding stairwell to the porthole at the top of the spire.

The sail luffing, Kirk and Bubby both found the task of unlashing it from the veranda and spire easy enough, and each made a few wraps around his waist with the slack end of the rope in order to secure it, to *not let go*. The problem was what to do next. The problem particularly struck Kirk, at the top of the spire. The rope was secure, yes, and so was he—inside the spire. There was no way for him to pull the sail down the steps, the way he'd come.

"What now?" he hollered down to Bubby.

"Don't let go!" Bubby hollered back.

"I know! But what now?"

"Bring it down! The jungle bunnies!"

He could have used a few at the moment, that was for sure. This was exactly what money was for, and power. You paid someone else to figure this out, and then someone else to do it. But that could not be done, not now. This was up to him. He would have to, somehow, take his end of the sail down on the outside. Fortunately there was ample slack in the rope to loop it around the thin top of the spire and so give him a leveraging point that would enable him to lean back and ease down the steeple like a rock climber descending, the sail at his back. After several unsuccessful attempts—practice throws, he considered them—he had the slack end of the rope around the spire. Okay. He tightened the slack and carefully squeezed out of the porthole, locking his feet against the sill.

"Now, bring her down!" Bubby called. "Don't let go! The darkies!"

And slowly, carefully, making sure not to stare too long at the town far, far below, Kirk began to step down the spire, feeding slack to the rope as the spire widened. It was working. Goddamn it all, it was working. Soon, he was halfway there.

Which is as far as he got. He had just come to the end of the rope, the spire ever widening as he descended, requiring more rope, more, and he was wondering what to do about this—

perhaps he could jump, or slide, he might make it to the veranda, thirty feet wouldn't kill him—he was just figuring this out when the sail billowed and the rope around his waist tightened as if to cut him in two.

"You got it!" Bubby called. "Don't let go! The darkies! You got it!"

In fact, Kirk didn't have it. Were he a sailor, he might have realized that as he descended he had, in effect, been sheeting the sail in, thereby enabling it to make better, more sail-like use of what wind was available. Now, like a well-tuned spinnaker, it was beginning to billow mightily.

"Don't let go!"

But Kirk had to let go, at least of the rig looped around the steeple. Or else be cut in half by the force of the sail pulling against it, tightening the wrap around his waist. Already he couldn't breathe. Already his internal organs were being crimped.

"Don't let go!" Bubby pleaded.

Kirk let go. He released the slack end, grabbing fast and tight to the wrap around his waist.

And then he was flying.

Bubby McGaw, too. Flying. Bubby, too, had put a wrap around his waist, to ensure that he wouldn't let go, and now the unlikely spinnaker ripped them both from the steeple and whipped them through the air like some massive, furious bull. Still they would not let go. As if there were yet some hope, some chance, they rode the tornadic turns of the sail back and forth and up and down until finally, to the horror of those watching from below, *it* let *them* go.

First Kirk, whom it flung over the law offices and banks of Broad Street and then into the Atlantic Ocean. Next, on the back swing of the same luff, the sail threw Bubby, who went hurtling over the rooftops of the lower peninsula to finally crash into the reflecting pool at the Bay House B&B.

"A flag," one of Commodore Crumfield's deputies noted.

"What?" the Commodore said. "Goddammit! What?"

"You asked what we'd have if they let go. Well, there's your answer. We've got a flag."

And that is precisely what they had. Freed of its bindings, and of the two who would have bound her again, waving proudly from the spire of old St. Philip's, a flag indeed.

·XVII·

"THAT DOES IT," SAID Elizabeth Hathaway. She and Phillip watched as a very wet, very confused Bubby McGaw flipped and flopped and generally struggled to collect himself, to find his bearings, in the waters of the neighboring reflecting pool. He had dropped in out of nowhere—true to form, Elizabeth thought—and hit the water next door with a monstrous splash.

"How—?" Phillip started.

"It hardly matters, does it?" Elizabeth said. "I won't live with this. I can't. Let's go."

"Go?" Phillip said. "Go where?"

"I don't know," Elizabeth said. "Away from here."

She'd had enough. Awakened earlier by the air raid siren, she presumed that the alarm had been sounded in response to the latest catastrophe to befall the lower peninsula: the occupation of the same by mini-men and Jamboreeans. She and Phillip had nervously observed the occupying forces through the night and were now forced to face them in the light of day. It had not been a bad dream; there were indeed hounds tearing up the local gardens, there was indeed line dance music blaring up and down the block, there were indeed men in camouflage tank tops passed out on neighboring porches. Yes, the occupation was real, and

Elizabeth did not doubt that the club's membership had been called to do something about it. But she was done with the club. Even had they come begging her back, asking her help—which of course they had not—she would not have obliged them. Instead she had begun forming her own, private plan. Now, with her son-in-law coming to what was left of his senses next door, her plan crystallized. It was an extreme plan, but it seemed the only option left.

"We'll have to jump ship," she told Phillip.

"Ma'am?" said Phillip.

"This won't do, Phillip. I won't live with these people."

"I understand that, but—"

"The absentees were bad enough. But this. I won't live next to tacky. I won't live with trash."

Phillip opted not to point out that she had in fact been living with a fair amount of trash, piled high in the various rooms of her house, for the better part of her life. He heard her. But still—jumping ship? Seemed over the top, even for Elizabeth Hathaway.

"Well," he said. "Do we have a boat? Or even—a raft? I would imagine it's a long swim to—to wherever. To anywhere."

Elizabeth considered for a moment. "I guess that old coffin will float," she said. "Should, anyway. Don't you think? Mm?"

It is hard to say whether Elizabeth would have taken such an extraordinary measure alone, without Phillip Lawson at her side. To be sure, she was nowhere near physically capable. It took no less a muscled specimen than Phillip to hoist the coffin onto his back and walk it down the stairs and then down the street to High Battery, ocean's edge. But even had she been able to get the old pine box this far, it's doubtful Elizabeth would have been able to handle the emotional challenge of it all. Like as not, she would have remained and complained, as she had done for the better part of her life. But with Phillip beside her, who had taught her how to let go of things, how to live again, by damn, she felt there was little she could not do. That is, that the two of them, working together, could not do. Not the least of which was leaving the town that she had clung to for so many years. She would not be held hostage in her own town any longer. She could not beat the occupying forces, no, but she would not join them. She would leave them. They could have the place.

For his part, Phillip held out hope, up until the final moments, that when he launched the coffin over the side it would sink to the bottom of the ocean like so much dead weight, as it were, leaving the two of them to devise another, more reasonable course of action. But the thing did not sink. Rather, after hitting the water with a hollow splash and briefly submerging, it bobbed to the surface and floated patiently in the swells, as if waiting for them.

Elizabeth greeted the sight with glee. "Hah hah!" she cried. "The old boy'll save us yet!" And before Phillip could stop her, before he could say or do anything at all, she was over the rail and falling, falling to the water, her linen dress billowing upwards as she went.

She was in no shape to swim, not even the ten yards or so she would need to gain the makeshift raft. If her dress had not trapped balloons of air on the way down (it now surrounded her, billowy and bloated as a wineskin, effectively bouying her), she might have sunk already, and no sooner had Phillip realized this than she had. She called his name, weakly, wetly, but urgently, and he would have to go in after her. He had no choice. It was that or leave the woman to drown and then deal with Bubby McGaw, who was now approaching from behind, calling "Hey! Hey!" Phillip did not turn to face the man at all. Instead, he jumped.

Jumped, took the fragile, frightened elder under his arm and swam her sidestroke to the bobbing coffin. The two then threw their arms over the pine box, clutching as tightly as two survivors of a sinking ship to flotsam.

"We made it!" Elizabeth squealed. "We made it!"

Made what? Phillip wondered. There was no chance of climbing the seawall, reboarding the peninsula. The Battery had been built to keep seafaring invaders out, after all. And there was not a speck of land in sight, only ocean and seesawing horizon.

"And just in time, too!" Elizabeth said. "Look!"

At the Battery railing, Bubby McGaw stood hollering and waving his arms stupidly. They could not hear what he was saying for the water blurbling against their ears, but it was clear he was wondering what the hell they were doing and why the hell he had not been invited to do whatever it was with them.

"Hah!" Elizabeth said. "Jackass! He can have it! All of it! Help me up, would you, dear?"

Carefully Phillip eased her up onto the coffin. She came to sit spraddle-legged, like a surfer waiting in the lineup for a choice wave. "Here," she said. "Room for two." Phillip pulled himself up at the other end, straddled the coffin, his back to Elizabeth's. He felt the tiny but determined pressure of her back against his. "There, now," she said. "That's not bad, is it?"

No, it really wasn't, so long as he could ignore the bump and thud of Lawson Parker's corpse against the coffin planks beneath him, bumped about dully and deadly by the ups and downs of the swells.

"What—?" asked Elizabeth. "What is that fool doing now?"

Phillip turned. Yonder came Bubby McGaw, swimming hard toward them, still hollering, his words choked and blundered under the water splashing his face. Soon he would reach them.

"Beat him off," Elizabeth said. "We'll have to beat him off. He is not coming with us."

Coming with them where? Phillip could hardly see clobbering a man under these circumstances. Even a man like Bubby McGaw, who deserved a good clobbering if anyone did.

Approaching, Bubby chose Elizabeth's side of the raft.

"Mom," he gasped—breathless, exhausted.

"Don't you *Mom* me, you fool!" Elizabeth said, and she kicked at him.

"Ow! What the devil?" Bubby had to back off. She had a good kick for an older woman. He had to tread water with what was left of his energy and, then, play what was left of his deck. "He's a homo, you know! You're riding around on a raft with a gay man!"

"Don't make me laugh," Elizabeth said. "He's more man than you'll ever be!"

"Oh, really? Why don't you ask him! Go ahead, ask him!"

"I don't have to ask him," Elizabeth said. It couldn't be true. Could it? It couldn't.

Bubby felt her confidence waver and approached again. "Really, Mom," he said. "You and me, we're family. He's—he's not family. But you and me—" Bubby was running out of energy, out of time.

Elizabeth was not. Fired up, furious with all the questions, all the doubts, she kicked her son-in-law solidly in the jaw. "We are not family!" she said. "I've got none of your blood! And you've got none of mine! And you never will! You hear me?"

It was hopeless on this side. Bubby had to accept that. Which, for the moment, left him only one option, an option he might willingly have drowned to avoid. But the body won't do it; it won't willingly drown. He let himself bob to the other end of the coffin. To Phillip Lawson.

"Hey," Bubby said humbly, pitifully, to Phillip's shins.

Phillip looked down at Bubby. "Hey," he said.

And then Phillip laughed. Oh, did he laugh.

EVEN AS SOME ESCAPED the wayward lower peninsula, others continued to arrive. With considerable effort on Bo's part, the Bambers did, in time, make the shore, which itself presented another struggle through pluff mud and assorted filth. When at last they came to solid ground they were exhausted, grubby, and disoriented, Tater still sniffling up tears and still clinging to her airbag. Heroically Bo led them onward, around the Battery and toward the Bay House B&B.

Along their way they were hailed from the porches of the harborside manors by assorted sportsmen and mini-storage salesmen, who had, it appeared, taken up residence. If the mini-men recognized Bo in his sodden state, they did not show the respect due a master from his protégés. On the contrary, they jeered and taunted, as if their simple positions on the grand porches, verandas, and widow's walks, as if by no more virtue than their being there in those mansions, they had somehow earned superior, even godly, status.

"Losers!" the men taunted. They had to shout over the vicious barking of territorial hounds.

"If it's called tourist season, why can't we shoot 'em?"

"Go back where you came from!"

"Yankee go home!"

"Yankee? It's horrible, Bo!" Tater said. "Just horrible! Who do they think they are?"

"Ignore them," Bo said firmly, and by way of example, as difficult as he was finding it, he ignored them and led Tater onward.

In time they came to the B&B, only to run up against further rejection.

"I'm sorry, sir," Mr. Brimkey explained. "But we're under new management."

He looked as scared as Bo was furious. "What new management?" Bo said. "What in—"

At this, a camouflaged, armed man entered the foyer.

"Who the hell are you?" Bo said.

"Purvis Willard," the man said. He shucked a shell into the shotgun's chamber as if to punctuate. "And I live here. 'Less you're here to clean the rooms, I guess you'll be going."

"Where's Beto?" Bo said, as much to Mr. Brimkey as to this Purvis Willard.

"Who?" Purvis Willard said.

"Beto. The Mexican boy."

"He don't work here no more."

Bo looked at Mr. Brimkey for some explanation, but Brimkey had none, only an expression of fear, uncertainty.

"Now you listen here," Bo said to Purvis Willard.

Purvis Willard trained the shotgun on Bo's gut. "I don't think so," he said. "Mr. Brimkey, show these bums to the door."

Bums. Bo and Tater found themselves on the street again, like a couple of—well, like a couple of bums. Bo looked uneasily at the ramshackle house next door: 2 Bay, home of the treasure chest of crap and the impossible old woman. He was desperate. Surely the old woman would help them. No, there was no surely about it, but at the moment he could see no other option. He led Tater through the teetering gate and up the porch steps.

There was no answer at the door. He gave the old woman plenty of time, but she would not answer. Trying the knob, he found the door unlocked. He stepped carefully into the hall. He called—and called, and called. No response. No sound anywhere. It was as if the house, and everything in it, had been abandoned. Left behind.

But why? And left to whom? They were questions Bo did not care to linger over. In the spirit of the day, Bo took the opportunity presented to him, interpreted the turn of events in a manner most suitable to him. However rundown, however cluttered, 2 Bay had been most thoughtfully left to them. The Bambers.

"It ain't Tara," he said to Tater. "But it'll do."

·XVIII·

FTER SECESSION, DRIVEN now by the North Atlantic current and the Westerly trades that had once ferried merchants and explorers home from the New World, the upper peninsula had begun drifting slowly toward the Old, Harry Biddencope strapped to the sculpture at the bow like some perverse figurehead. While Reverend Anthony Lawson could not know exactly where his community was headed, it had been most decidedly, at last, liberated from the lower peninsula and all its attendant frustrations. In short order he appointed himself mayor of the community and, lackeys in tow, established himself in the Governor's Suite at the Swamp Fox Hotel.

Anthony's first order of business was to appoint Parker Hathaway and Carolina Gabrel as caretakers of—that is, bringers of food and water to—Harry Biddencope. For while Anthony had no intention of releasing the man anytime soon, he did not mean to kill him or even to do him irreparable harm. He meant only to teach the man a lesson. Anthony's second order of business was to establish a committee to look into a solution for the dangerous restlessness of the community's youth, which was nothing new and which in fact had been exacerbated by the recent developments. If many of the young people had wanted out when the community was still attached to the mainland, back in the days when a young man or young woman might have actually gotten out, they wanted out even more so now that there seemed no way out at all. Indeed, an acute epidemic of cabin fever had spread rapidly through the youth, and something would have to be done to cure it lest the entire community implode with their brewing rage.

The committee immediately went to work brainstorming. Lyle Benton suggested a soccer tournament; Johnny Harrell, a youth church group; Hejugali Lumpru, a boxing league. Mazey Weathers pointed out that sports leagues and youth groups had been tried in the past, with dubious success. What was needed, she argued, was an entirely new approach to the problem.

"Why not put the burden on them?" she said. "The young people?"

Her fellow committee members looked at Mazey apprehensively.

Still, she continued: "Tell them that if they want out, they'll have to do something about it themselves. Don't do it for them. We can't keep doing it all for them. At some point, they have to take responsibility."

The argument was met with universal hostility. The committee accused Mazey of washing her hands of the whole affair, of not really caring, even of talking like a Libertarian. She took great offense to the accusations, but while she was expressing that offense, Lyle Benton stepped in and developed her suggestion.

"We could encourage them in a certain direction," he said. "Give them some idea how to go about getting what they want, how to get out of the situation they find themselves in."

Here the commotion over Mazey's argument subsided.

"What do they want?" Anthony said. "What do they really want, deep down?"

"Want a way out," Johnny Harrell said. "With all due respect, Reverend, I think we've established that."

"All right, yes," Anthony said. "A way out. But what would give them a way out? We're in the middle of the ocean, if you haven't noticed."

"Could build a big boat," Lyle Benton joked.

All of the commissioners laughed at this—all but Reverend Anthony Lawson. "Hang on," he said, and he considered for a moment. "Maybe it's not such a fool idea. I think we'll all agree that more outrageous things have happened lately. Why not encourage them to build a big boat? Not for us, but for themselves?"

Mazey Weathers nodded at the suggestion, but the others argued that it would never work, for the obvious reason that a big boat doesn't just get built because people want it to. Somebody has to know what he's doing. In response, Anthony pointed out that among the middle-aged members of the population, carpenters, metalworkers, and mechanics were in no short supply and surely could be persuaded to experiment with their skills and to take on apprentices, in the name of saving the community from self-destruction. Neither was lumber, metalwork, or machinery in short supply: the many condemned homes on the West Side were available for dismantling and stripping. For use. And was Ray Mercer's junkyard not brimming with jalopies? Surely something could be done with those engine parts. Granted, there was no telling whether the boat-building project itself would actually work, whether a boat would actually be produced, but in the meantime such a project would keep the youth focused and busy and teach them valuable skills besides.

Loony, perhaps, but the committee agreed that in the absence of any better ideas, the plan was certainly worth a try. When the meeting was adjourned, they set about recruiting craftsmen and posting flyers:

WANT OUT?

GET ON THE BOAT!

MORNING, CALHOUN SQUARE

FROM THEIR POSITION AT the edge of the square, Parker and Carolina (and Harry Biddencope, as much as was possible) watched the project take shape, or attempt to take shape, anyway. That first morning, it was difficult to say exactly what was going on. Like as not, few of those gathered in the square could even say. But Carolina was not long in finding out, and once she had, not long in helping pull the project together. Though she had not the faintest idea how to go about building a boat, she did know how to recruit, organize, and delegate, so that what began and might have ended as a loosely gathered flock of vaguely interested teens all but mocking the efforts of their seniors to instruct them, became, under the influence of Carolina, a sort of boatworks. Her zeal was irresistible to even the most cynical of kids, her optimism contagious. Belief—in yourself, in your work—was half the battle, she explained. Maybe three-quarters of the battle. If they believed in themselves, there was little, really, they could not do. No doubt they had heard such talk before, but this girl lived it. Her own story, which she recounted by way of example, held them spellbound. She'd come up in the projects of the Bronx, she said, and the Bronx made upper Charleston look like Beverly Hills. She never knew her father and was raised by a mother who spoke no English and worked as a maid at the Southampton Yacht Club, cleaning up the shit of the rich. And if they thought the shit of the rich smelled any better than their own, they had another think coming. Did they see her, Carolina Gabrel, cleaning up the shit of the rich? Did they not hear her speaking English? Success, she told them, may be handed to some, but it hadn't been handed to her, and it wouldn't be handed to them. If she'd sat around and waited for it to be handed to her, she'd be speaking Spanish and cleaning up the shit of the rich. Instead, she believed in herself and worked her way up and out. Sure, she could have sat around and complained about the unfairness of the world, she could have sucked down beer and popped pills to kill the pain, she could have sat back and made fun of anybody who tried to make their own way—but what if she had? Where would she be now?

Her audience replied in unison, "Cleaning up the shit of the rich!"

They listened to her as they had listened to few others in their lives. The young men, stunned by the impossible combination of hot looks and supreme righteousness, wanted to do her bidding, and the young women, impressed by Carolina's determination (and by her ability to stun the young men), wanted to emulate her. This woman lived her own advice, and that seemed to mean much more than a simple schoolroom platitude ever could. It certainly proved more inspiring: by the end of the day, the loosely gathered horde had been divided into three specific teams—woodwork, metalwork, and mechanical—and each team had begun to scour the upper peninsula for materials, depositing them in designated sections of the square. In appreciation for Carolina's efforts, Anthony Lawson renamed the square Plaza Gabrel, and his commission watched as the project gathered momentum

daily. There was still no telling what would come of it besides a
sense of purpose and self-worth. But what more, really, had they
ever wanted for their children?

Between rallies, Carolina returned to Parker's side to report the
progress of things boatwise and to comfort him in his bereavement
for his lost mother and lost town. To let go of the past, he would
first have to memorialize them, which approach came naturally to
him. He began by recounting the story of a childhood in
antepartum Charleston, tales of learning to waltz and to fox trot in
dancing school while the kids from the suburbs taught themselves
the bump and grind; of scaling the downtown steeples in the wake
of Hurricane Hugo, the construction scaffolds impossible for
young revelers to resist; of discovering the delights of the opposite
sex in cemeteries after dark, clumsily necking and groping there
beside the restless ghosts; of lobbing water balloons at hapless tour
carriages; of planning, with most every other Charleston boy, to
one day become a harbor pilot and get paid to run the most badass
boats at the dock. He spoke of the days before Hurricane Hugo,
before the general resortification of the town, back when the
porches and yards were used—by elders, by children, by dogs. Back
when the town was lived in. Of sipping and musing with the old
people, driving through the countryside on Sunday afternoons
with the same.

Carolina was fascinated by these small histories and anecdotes
and by Parker's intense attachment to them, but she knew, also,
that there was another side to the story, and that if ever Parker were
to move forward, he would have to confront it. In time, she
delicately inquired about the Charleston establishment, how it had
gone about protecting itself, preserving itself, all these centuries—
if indeed it had. And so Parker told her the story of the ultra-
exclusive, centuries-old St. Bedelia Society, where membership

could only be passed down through the father, and the tale of its upstart cousin, the Assembly, which Parker's own great-grandmother had established in order that exclusivity might also descend through the distaff. He listed the myriad upstart societies that had been formed in the years since, each new group, as a matter of course, a little less exclusive than the one before it, but a little more exclusive than the next one to spring up, and heartily proud of that. He explained that the extant clubs invariably greeted the newly formed with a strangely pleasurable disdain—pleasurable because their own, established society was granted that much more cachet by the arrival of an upstart and given one more group to look down upon, to feel superior to. A regrettable characteristic of the Charleston establishment, Parker confessed, this having to feel superior to others. A regrettable characteristic of people in general, Carolina pointed out.

Above them, Harry Biddencope had little to say about all this. Naturally, he only wanted to be set free. His early calls begged for forgiveness, appealed to their decency as fellow human beings. This approach failing, he got nasty. And the nastier he got, the closer Parker and Carolina became.

"So you're with them," Biddencope snapped bitterly. "The blacks. That's just great. Lift up the black man and tie up the white man. Because all the blacks are good and all the whites are bad."

"Nobody said that," Carolina said.

"But it's what you think," Biddencope said. "It's what people like you think."

"Actually, it's not," Carolina said. "Not even close. No thinking person could think that way. Or the other way."

"There you go again," Biddencope said. "Intellectual talk. Elitist talk."

Carolina squinted up at Biddencope. "Elitist?" she said. "Where did you get that? Your butt?"

By way of defusing the confrontation, Parker said, "We're not in charge here, Mr. Biddencope."

"But even if we were, we wouldn't do things any differently," Carolina said, and she winked at Parker.

"Like it's all my fault," said Biddencope. "Everything that happened, it's all my fault."

Carolina considered for a moment. "In a way," she said, "it is."

"Oh yeah? How's that?"

"Bringing all those people to town. All at the same time. Bad idea."

"It's called business, bitch. It's how the world works."

"*Works* being the operative word, here," Carolina said.

"Do what?"

"I wasn't there very long, but it seems to me that the intact city, or part of it, the part I liked about it, the defensible part, didn't have anything to do with the world *working* at all. It had to do with *living*. Living well. Almost a Continental approach to things, if you'll pardon the word."

"Whatever," Harry Biddencope said. "Everybody's got bills to pay."

"And you're paying yours now," Carolina said. "As I see it."

"What the fuck ever."

Parker was pleasantly surprised by Carolina's take on his lost native city. Of all she had been through there, all she'd seen, she still had found a way to defend a part of it. Having been there only a short time, and a fairly atypical short time at that, she got it. And by virtue of that, even hardly knowing him, she knew him. He didn't mention any of this, or his earlier declaration of love, or her earlier mistake regarding his sexual orientation. Neither did she. But in her conversation, and in the way she looked admiringly at Parker while she skewered Biddencope, she was letting Parker know that she did not hold him responsible for the wrongs of his people, which after all were not unique in the history of the world, and that she respected him for trying to preserve, in his own way, the virtues of the same.

In their time together, throughout their conversations, Parker kept waiting for the other shoe to drop—for Carolina to ask for her notepad and begin scribbling away, to commence converting his people, his town, his life into just another report. But she never did ask for the thing. She seemed thrilled simply to hear the tale and grateful to him for telling it.

Not, however, so grateful that she would spend the rest of her life with him, or even go to bed with him. For the latter purpose she had enlisted a young man by the name of Lonnie Simmons, whose initiative and determination with the boat-building project (to say nothing of his exquisite abs) she had found irresistible. When she first divulged the little fling, as she called it, Parker felt betrayed. He, Parker Lawson Hathaway, had been abandoned, cast off, replaced by a—a—he sensed the worst of the old instincts rising in him—it wasn't right, there should be a law, rules. . . . But he was old enough by now to understand the roots of that instinct, the reasons for it: fear, anger, and, ugliest of all, envy. Understanding this, he squashed the instinct and instead asked, rather boyishly, what a man like him might do to win a woman like her, in case he came across another Carolina Gabrel in his life.

Never one to belabor a point, Carolina told him. "Well," she said. "For starters, you might consider a wardrobe makeover."

"Sorry?" said Parker.

"The—ascot? Is that what it's called? And the pocket watch? I don't know."

She was flirting, right? This was a joke. Right?

"You?" Parker asked. "Wardrobe?"

"What do you mean?" asked Carolina.

No joke. The woman was dead serious.

"Wardrobe?" asked Parker. "Wardrobe matters? To you?"

"Well—sure it does," she said. "Yours just isn't very stylish, that's all. These days."

She might have been Kirk Ashley. Or his mother, Elizabeth, at her worst.

"You asked," Carolina said. "Now you know."

"Now I know," said Parker.

Now he did know. Wardrobe. Of all the ridiculous things for this brilliant young woman to concern herself with. He handed Carolina Gabrel her notepad, then straightened his ascot, adjusted his watch fob, and walked away.

·XIX·

HEN THE ATLANTIC CLUB first spotted land—a faint but unmistakable rise, like a mole, on the eastern horizon—Captain Sam Haynely was not at all sure what to call it. He had no charts for the smaller concerns of the Eastern Atlantic, and the revolving motion of the peni-state had long since haywired his instruments. Still, he was fairly certain that they could not have made Africa. Not yet. Even so, he advised Commodore Crumfield to sequester CJ in the Dog House. They might need a bargaining chip.

Unfortunately, word of the sighting itself traveled much faster than word of the theories surrounding it, and in no time at all the new residents were collecting their arms and ammunition, heeling their hounds, and lining up on the Battery infantry-style. Not the most advisable way to introduce oneself to a foreign port, the board members knew, but at this point there was very little they could do to control their new neighbors—or anything else, for that matter. And even if there were, it was too late.

Because they had been spotted, too. When the patrol boat first approached—slowly, warily—Harold Crumfield, Hat Lawson, and Sam Haynely hurried to the end of the club pier to wave their arms at the craft, if not in surrender, in a call for attention, in a spirit of diplomacy, as if to say that the men lined up on the seawall in no way spoke for the peni-state. Themselves, they were willing—eager, even—to explain, to negotiate, to come to some understanding here. But if the patrol boat captain saw the flailing elders, he likely thought them mad, or in any case less deserving of his attention than the veritable army gathered along the seawall, toward which he now proceeded, still slowly, still cautiously, to the sinking hearts of the board.

There's no telling which of the sportsmen fired the first shot at the patrol boat. Had he lived to tell about it, had his opening shot marked the beginning of some glorious rout rather than the beginning of a crushing defeat, he undoubtedly would have bragged his way into the history books. As it was, the opening shot quickly (and predictably) became an opening volley, with the entire front line blasting away. In response, the patrol boat, which stood in no real danger from a line of shotguns and pistols but certainly had been given a clear sign of the strange vessel's position, sprayed the Battery with a blistering round from the 40-mm gun mounted on its bow.

When the battle commenced, the board members fled for the clubhouse and herded the membership into the back barroom to wait it out. The fight was no sooner started than ended. There was not a man left standing on the Battery. Those who weren't massacred in the first return volley leapt onto Battery Street and fled for their lives. Still the membership waited—some cussing, some crying, some drawing side arms. Commodore Crumfield gave the situation a good ten minutes, then, with his pistol drawn, stepped outside the door to have a look.

He watched as the patrol boat edged up to the pier and docked. In another moment, five men stepped off of the boat and began walking up the pier toward the club. Five heavily armed men.

Commodore Crumfield stepped back into the bar. "Lay down your arms, gentlemen," he said. "They've got bigger ones."

The armed did as they'd been told, and Commodore Crumfield stepped outside with his hands raised, in hopes of staying alive. When the soldiers approached, they trained their machine guns on him and then, as he led them into the back barroom, on the membership as a whole, which for the most part still sat huddled together on the floor.

"*¿Qué es esto?*" the captain of the small platoon demanded. "*¿Qué hacen ustedes? ¿Quién son ustedes?*"

There was not a Spanish speaker among the club's membership, nor even an English speaker who recognized Spanish speaking. But there were a number of rusty French speakers, and, terrified, they barraged the captain with the question most natural to a terrified rusty French-speaking traveler: "*Parlez-vous anglais? Parlez-vous anglais! Parlez-vous anglais?*"

"*Oui, mais oui; biensûr, biensûr,*" the captain replied. "*Mais en francais vous me demandez est-ce que je parle l'anglais. Je crois que c'est tres intéresante. Non, bizarre. Tres bizarre!*"

Which response created no small confusion. If the captain indeed spoke English, he had answered in French—a fairly sophisticated French, at that, one that threw the rusty-French-speaking members of the club off completely. Still they did their textbook best: "*Comment t'appelle tu!*" "*Et vous!*" "*Abientôt!*" "*Comment allez-vous!*" "*Bonjour!*"

The captain was obviously miffed by their attempts. So was Commodore Crumfield, who stepped forward to handle this as a Commodore should. "Do—you—speak—English?" he said to the captain.

"Yes, yes, of course, of course," the captain said. "*¿Y usted?*"

"What?"

"And you? Do? You? Speak? English?"

The soldiers laughed at this. Commodore Crumfield did not.

"Goddamn right I do," he said. "Who the hell do you think you are?"

"This is what I would like to know from you," the captain said. He walked slowly about the room, surveying the bright silver sailing trophies and antique model schooners; the mounted mallard, red-tailed fox, and marlin; the elegant gaming tables and well-stocked bar.

Noting the captain's obvious admiration for the club's accouterments, Hat Lawson stepped forward and said, "Those people, those people with the guns, they do not represent us."

"Those people," the captain said flatly, "they do not represent anything anymore."

Again the soldiers laughed, but their captain quickly shushed them. He stepped behind the bar to the wine rack, removed a bottle, nodded approvingly at the vintage. "So then, tell me, who are you," he said, to no one in particular.

"We're the Atlantic Club," Commodore Crumfield said proudly. "Oldest yacht club on the continent."

"Yes?" the captain said. He inspected another bottle, squinted with mild distaste. "And this would be what continent?"

A very good question.

"Well," Commodore Crumfield said. "We're the oldest yacht club around." It was all he could muster.

"Yes?" the captain said. "And how old is that?"

In unison the entire club membership responded, "One hundred and eighty-three years."

The captain looked at them all, smirked smugly. "One hundred and eighty-three years. This is nothing."

The membership seemed shocked to hear it.

"I am of the Basque Country," the captain said. "In the town of my home we have farmhouses older than this."

Here Hat Lawson spoke up. "We're—Charleston," he said. "Charleston, South Caro—Charleston. We're Charleston. Part of it, anyway."

"What is this? Charleston?" the captain asked. "What is this Charleston? What?"

"This is Charleston," Hat said. "We are."

The captain nibbled on the inside of his cheek, glanced about the barroom a last time. "You should place a Rioja in your collection of wine," he said to the men and women before him. "A 1991 Rioja. You will not be sorry."

What this had to do with who they were and what they were doing here, none seated there could say. They could only watch as the captain gave a series of curt orders to his men, then gestured toward Hat Lawson. "You," the captain said. "You come with me. We must speak with the people of my government."

"Yes, sir," Hat said. He walked toward the captain, but then paused just before he reached him. "May I bring a *charge d'affaires*, sir?" he asked. "With drinks?"

"Of course," the captain said. "Diplomacy without drink is like a sail without wind."

Hat nodded, then left up the stairwell. In another moment he returned with CJ. Between them they were bearing a bottle of Maker's Mark, two tumblers, and a silver ice bucket.

Watching Hat and CJ join the captain at the door, Commodore Crumfield fumed. He could not understand why Hat had been chosen and not him. Hat was only a vice-president. Hat wasn't the Commodore. And CJ! What the hell was a shard-jay duh-fair, anyway? Who were these people? As the captain reached for the door, Crumfield said, "Mind my asking who you work for, buddy?"

The captain paused. "The government of Spain," he said. "You are in the Canary Islands, my friend. You are in Spanish territory." With this, he and Hat and CJ were gone.

At the moment, the peninsula might well have been a Canary Island, floating as it was just off the northeastern tip of the chain. In fact, when Madrid first got word of the events, several government officials suggested anchoring the peninsula, calling it one of the Canaries, and developing it as a kind of upscale island resort and free trade zone. La Isla Sin Pasaporte, it might be called, or simply Charlestonia. But after speaking with Hat Lawson for little more than an hour, the Spanish government instead dispatched a fleet of tugs to tow the island far, far away. It was never disclosed exactly what had been said during the abbreviated negotiations (stunned by the outcome, by the absolute impudence of the Spaniards, Hat Lawson never spoke again), but whatever it was convinced the Spanish that the accidental emigrants, despite their excellent taste in decor and defensible taste in wine—despite their undeniable gift for living well—were completely demented and best escorted away. And so the lower peninsula was towed several hundred miles to the west and released—left to float, by way of the trades, into the doldrums of the Horse Latitudes, where her residents would pose little danger to anyone but themselves.

·EPILOGUE·

HE ENGLISH SAILOR WHO first spotted the wayward upper peninsula was in no way certain how to report the discovery to his home port of Plymouth—in particular, how to report the figurehead at its bow, at least without sounding mad or, worse, crude. The authorities would simply have to see for themselves. Which they did while the strange vessel yet lay some fifty miles to the southwest of Plymouth. The British government first dispatched a helicopter to authenticate the claim and then a cruiser full of ambassadors to do something about it.

While Reverend Anthony Lawson was not equipped to fight the Royal Navy, nor was he prepared to resubmit his community to the rule of another power. Truly, they had all had enough of that. But to his surprise and profound relief, Anthony found the British government much more reasonable than he had ever found city council in former Charleston. The officials boarded peaceably, and after marveling at the tale of the island's Atlantic crossing, settled into negotiations.

It so happened that the economy of Plymouth was in need of a boost of some sort, and the development of a new tourist destination, especially one that so remarkably retained a tropical climate, might be just the thing. For those looking for a getaway, the island might be promoted as another Barbados—but closer and more affordable. For those searching out history, it might be touted as the logical next stop on an itinerary that commenced in Plymouth, the home port of Sir Francis Drake and the Pilgrim Fathers. A slice of the New World floating here beside the Old, the island might showcase what had, after however many bizarre turns of fate, become of the early explorers' efforts.

Anthony argued that his community was not all that interested in becoming a curiosity or a museum piece. He pointed out that his people had lives here—rapidly improving lives, at that. The British submitted that, historical precedent notwithstanding, they had no intention of interfering with the lives of the island's natives. On the contrary, they would offer citizenship and all attendant social services to the same and redevelop the island's needier neighborhoods with an eye toward obliging native first, visitor second. Anthony conferred with his advisors, who found the plan for the most part agreeable, so long as the British accepted four conditions: Johnny Harrell wanted all development contractors to employ native workers; Mazey Weathers wanted the proposed development to include the building of a respectable K-12 school; Lyle Benton wanted the island to retain sovereignty in the governance of all things local; and Hejugali Lumpru wanted to build a world-class athletics facility.

A tall order, perhaps, but one which might offer England's long-suffering reputation as a ruthless imperial power a chance at redemption. To resist the temptation to grab this island—an island which had literally come to them, and had, it could be argued, once belonged to them—to resist the temptation to take it by force and colonize it, and to instead grant its citizens sovereignty and privilege, that would be most, well, most civilized. More important, the material benefits of developing a new tourist destination outweighed the price of the island's demands, and after conferring for little over an hour, the British officials expressed as much.

The Isle of Good Faith, as the upper peninsula came to be called, was anchored where it floated, and then redevelopment began in earnest. The first phase of renewal involved the removal of the obscene sculpture at the island's eastern tip, which was perhaps the only turn of events that could possibly have drawn Abel Horfner out of his hiding place in the rec hall at Hampton Park. When he heard the shouts in the streets reporting that the big black cock was to be dropped into the ocean, he made fast for the square, took up the ropes that had bound Harry Biddencope only hours earlier, and tied himself to the base of his sculpture, at which point the demolition crew had to halt its work. The authorities were furious to have been stymied so early in the game, and the ensuing fracas was so heated that it made the front page of not only the London *Times*, but *Le Monde*, where Abel's story caught the eye of an aging patroness of the arts who immediately called for Horfner—and his sculpture—to be shipped to her estate in the Loire Valley. Here Horfner, after the requisite period of aimless despair, began to work again. His new sculptures were characterized by a compelling fusion of nautical forms and sexual themes and found a market in points as varied as Bilbao, Cape Town, and San Francisco.

HARRY BIDDENCOPE DID NOT hang around. No sooner had he been released than he began negotiating a ride to the mainland on a work barge. He lingered in the pubs of Plymouth long enough to confirm, for the pub crowd, the worst stereotypes regarding Americans abroad, then secured passage on a freighter bound for Miami, where there was yet room for a man on the move.

AFTER SAYING HIS farewells to Carolina, Parker Hathaway made for London, which he found most accommodating for a dandy of the old school. In London he was not presumed gay or not gay but eccentric, and admired more than avoided. In time he opened a small antique and curio shop on a lively block in the borough of Camden Town. He called the shop Elizabeth, which invariably confused his customers, but which confusion Parker was only too delighted to clear up. He regaled his listeners with tales from the New Old-New World, tales of bubbas and debutantes, pig picks and sermons, jamborees and yacht clubs, hound dogs and Hummers. And finally, most lovingly, he moved them with the tale of one woman's struggle to hold on to all things passed, the tale of a woman at once held tragically captive and made triumphant by her own refusal to let go. With the tale, such as he knew it, of his mother, Elizabeth.

ALL HER LIFE CAROLINA GABREL had hungrily immersed herself in the histories of others and resisted her own. She could trace this resistance back to a precise moment at age twelve, when she had asked her mother to tell her the story of *familia* Gabrel—where it was they had come from, what it was they had been known for. She had wanted more than simply "Colombia," more than a father killed in a mining accident, which facts she already knew, which facts were as much as she had ever been given. She had wanted a town, a people, places and faces to which she might moor her restless wonder. But asking her mother, she encountered the usual stone wall vis-à-vis all things passed. There was no reading her mother's face to understand why—whether the past was too painful to her, or too private to her, or completely insignificant to her. Her mother had said simply "Andalucía," in fact going further back, much further, than Carolina had meant her to go (or even at the time knew she was going), but providing no more detail than this, no more history. Simply "Andalucía." And stubbornly refusing any further inquiry, belittling Carolina for her curiosity and sending her to her homework. From that moment on, Carolina had disregarded any impulse to find out her roots, her ghosts, associating the simple impulse in herself with frustration and heartbreak, with the impossible divide that would always lie between herself and her mother. It was an approach that had served Carolina well in love and in work: always moving forward, never looking back, her curiosity and her desire insatiable, she left her lovers exhausted but aching for another day with her, her readers enlightened and waiting for another installment from her. But through it all, a tiny knot had burrowed and nested deep in her heart, waiting there to be rubbed loose and set free. Waiting, perhaps, for Andalucía.

Now, as her train passed through the Sierra Morenas into Andalucía, Carolina found the butterflies and jitters that normally marked her arrival in a new land notably missing. Instead, she found the land and its people strangely familiar to her, as if she were, indeed, coming home after a long time away. But the sensation itself—of familiarity, of comfort, of coming home—was entirely foreign to her and baffled her mind even as her heart discovered peace. Amid the bright swirl of Sevilla and the festive bustle of Cadíz, Carolina felt oddly level—and oddly unhinged— by that feeling. She traveled the region for a month, in order to fully explore the strange new goings-on in herself. Each day she mailed a postcard to her mother, from the bright beaches of Costa de La Luz, the mountains of Granada, the lush valleys of Río Guadalquivir. She wrote of one day bringing her mother here, to this spirited land by the sea. There was no telling how her mother would receive the sudden flurry of correspondence, but still Carolina wrote to her daily, as if to convince herself of the region's allure. (In all her stay, it was all she wrote, these postcards to her mother.) And there was no denying that allure. Andalucía was as splendorous as its name, as intriguing and inspiring a place as Carolina had ever been. It was a land anyone would have been proud to claim, to call home. Truly, Carolina might have stayed forever here in the land of her ghosts, might even have made a family with Francisco Escobedes, the scion of a Sanlúcar sherry bodega who proposed after only a week with her. But staying—anywhere—was not a natural state for Carolina and could not be forced. There would be time enough for stillness and comfort in death. For now, there were too many histories in the world, of the world, left to tell. Seductive as this land might be, she could not call home a place that allowed her to forget that. That allowed her only postcards. Now that she understood this, she could move forward again.

PHILLIP LAWSON, ELIZABETH HATHAWAY, and Bubby McGaw (and Lawson Parker, after a fashion) drifted aimlessly at sea for two days before they were finally spotted and rescued. The first day adrift little was said at all, save Bubby's occasional request for Phillip to let him up onto the coffin, which requests Phillip pointedly refused. If he did not have it in him to shove the man away from the raft altogether, or even to berate him for his odious politics, he was not about to grant him any favors. For her part, Elizabeth kept entirely to herself, disgusted with Bubby, or Phillip, or both, Phillip couldn't say.

On the second day, Elizabeth did begin to talk, but not to the living. Undoubtedly suffering from dehydration and exposure, undoubtedly disoriented, she held earnest conversations with her dead father about events she could not have actually experienced.

In a way, it seemed as though she were not actually speaking to her father, but allowing her father—or, occasionally, her father's house—to speak through her.

"The bridge across the Ashley," she said. "I know. An absolute disgrace. What was so horrible about taking a launch? What was so horrible? . . . Yes, we had chickens then. Right there in the yard. Five hens and a bantam rooster. . . . That was clever! A tombstone for the silver! HERE LIES H.S.T. Hidden Secret Treasure! Fooled the hell out of those Yankee scalawags. . . . There wasn't anything. Nobody had anything. But we made do, by damn! We made do! Hats! From palmetto fronds . . ."

"She's gone crazy," Bubby said when it became apparent that his mother-in-law's behavior was not just some momentary lapse on her part or some fleeting hallucination on his. "Not that she had very far to go."

"Shut the fuck up, Bubby," Phillip said.

But Bubby didn't shut up. Perhaps to compete with Elizabeth, or perhaps because he himself had succumbed to exposure, before long he began to sing—Sunday school songs, of the worst variety, and with a most nauseating voice. His repertoire included "Michael Row the Boat Ashore," "Kumbayah," "Onward Christian Soldiers," and "Jesus Loves Me, This I Know." If Bubby had known the verses to each song, that might have made the singing halfway bearable. But Bubby didn't know the verses, only the refrains. He shuffled and repeated them, shuffled and repeated, sometimes even confusing them:

"Onward Christian soldiers, row the boat ashore . . ."

"Michael row the kumbayah . . ."

"Jesus loves me, this I know, for the soldiers told me so . . ."

His performance had the sound of a late-night advertisement for an album of church songs gone horribly wrong, sung by an inebriated but still thirsty frog. Through it all, Elizabeth continued yammering about the bridge and the chickens, the buried silver and the palm frond hats, so that when at last they were picked up (off the coast of Liberia, by a tramp freighter on its way from Sumatra to deliver a cargo of "NO STRESS" T-shirts and coozies to Salvador, Brazil), Phillip was relieved to find that none of the crew spoke any more than the most rudimentary English. For the time being, he did not care to comprehend what anybody had to say about anything. So long as the men got him to dry land.

Which the sailors did. In time, the freighter made port in Salvador, and Phillip, once he was at least fairly assured as to Elizabeth's well being (she'd been escorted off the freighter with the coffin, then received, with Bubby, by a Bahian priestess), caught a bus to the beach, where he learned the hard way that not every Brazilian donning a banana hammock is available or even interested, and that some Brazilians donning banana hammocks can tend to violence. But he learned the easy way that emergency room service in Brazil—even if it's true that the ambulances look like white hearses, and may have their stretcher-doors tied shut with bungee chord—is sufficient on the whole. And in time, in a great deal of bizarre time, Phillip found his way to Rio, where he became a concert promoter and event coordinator, hosting fabulous seaside soirees that drew entertainers and guests from around the globe. With Phillip at the helm, the night never died there.

NEITHER ELIZABETH NOR BUBBY ever fully recovered from their dementia. Arguably both had suffered milder forms of it all their lives. But in the small Bahian village of Cachoeira, the touched, especially those who sang and those who communicated with the dead, were held in special regard, even considered blessed, and so

Bubby's and Elizabeth's respective afflictions in fact served them quite well in their new home. The town, in effect, adopted the two: the old woman from the sea, who conversed with the dead, and her afflicted son, who could not stop singing. The two of them were housed, together with the coffin, in a riverside *pousada*. They were attended to by the Sisters of the Good Death and visited frequently by pilgrims from near and far. With nourishment, and thanks to the incomparable inspiration of the Bahian countryside, Bubby's voice improved, as did his repertoire, until he came to charm locals and visitors alike with sweetly sung medleys that integrated Galician sea chanteys, Bahian folk songs, and the occasional Sunday school hymn.

For their part, Elizabeth and her late father were given the singular honor of launching that year's Festa de Boa Morte—the first time in history the distinction had been given to white people. It was bestowed after the Sisters, setting out to embalm Lawson Parker, found the man fully erect and wholly grinning. On a regal carriage drawn through cobblestone streets by a brightly festooned mare, with her father's coffin beside her, Elizabeth sat high, like a saintly queen, and so set into motion the grand indulgence that was the Festival of the Good Death.

CJ LAWSON'S POSITION as Hat Lawson's *charge d'affaires* was to be the last of his life. Left behind in the confusion of Hat's abrupt debarkation, he asked to remain on the patrol boat even as the peni-state was untied and turned over to the tugboats. When asked why, he told the Spanish sailors that, really, he would rather go home. Which response created no small bewilderment. The man seemed to want two different things at once: he wanted to go home, but he didn't want the crew to take him there. Finally, the Spanish wrote the confusion off to mental illness and resolved to deliver CJ to a hospital on the mainland.

As the patrol boat steamed toward Spain, CJ found his way to the bunkroom and settled in for a well-deserved nap. He did not wake up before they reached Cadíz, or after.

IT IS IMPOSSIBLE TO SAY what CJ would have made of his former home's fate. Perhaps he was fortunate to be spared it. Anthony Lawson's noble intentions notwithstanding, the Isle of Good Faith could not control the demands or resist the temptations of economy any better than those before. These were people, after all. And so it was: the Geechee Land theme park, the Gumbo Junction shopping mall, the Codfish Row restaurant district. A casino called Porgy's Palace, an upscale housing development known as Sweetgrass Estates. Over time the island became wildly successful, hugely prosperous—and it showed.

What CJ Lawson might have made of all this, we cannot say. We can suppose, however, that he would have appreciated the tribute that would one day be paid to him, in the form of the boat in Plaza Gabrel. When at last the craft was completed, no one had any maritime use for it. Some wanted to jettison the thing altogether, arguing that it represented a past best forgotten. Surely a more economically prudent option could be found for the space: an ideal site for another mall, say, or a convention center. But as it so happened, the referendum that was called weighed heavily in favor of leaving the boat precisely where it stood, as a sort of artistic and historic centerpiece. Splendid, enormous, arklike, the craft was painted all the colors of land and sea by the children of Weathers Elementary, and in a festive ceremony that recalled fellowship picnics of old, Reverend Mayor Anthony Lawson christened the piece, this boat on dry land, the *Colleton Jeremiah*.

THE END

·ACKNOWLEDGMENTS·

For faith:
Mom and Dad, Nan Morrison, Bret Lott, and Marian Young.

For fuel:
Benjamin Pryor—the Dioptic Bedrock, John Elderkin, David
Jones, Imad Rahman, Padgett Powell, Callie Witham,
and Andrew Geer.

For sturdy porches:
Nathalie Bernal, Sheila Waksman, Luciano Nascimento,
Carolina Tripoli, Laura Fresneda, Shirley Gibson,
Cale and Katie Jaffe, Richard and Hayden Geer,
and Rett Quattlebaum.